"I'd be very interested in hearing what you have to say about my future."

Jess looked up in surprise as Adam entered her tent. He'd opened his wallet, and she caught sight of his Breeder's Club card. What was a Thoroughbred breeder doing in this area of the carnival? What did he expect from her? Since her vanity was a little stung by his obvious disbelief in her credentials, she decided to play her part to the hilt.

"Very well. That will be $5.50." She took the money from him, bounced the coins in her hand a few times, then brought each one between her teeth as though to test its authenticity. "Always give the customer a good show," Madam Zola had said, so Jess pulled her blouse away from her breasts and slipped the bills and both quarters into the neck of the loose garment. But the moment she did it she experienced a sudden fear that the coins would slide right through her clothes onto the worn carpet. They didn't, thank goodness, and she couldn't help a little sigh of relief.

Instead of being impressed, her customer seemed to find further amusement in her efforts. He crossed his arms over his chest and smiled.

"A fascinating demonstration," he remarked in a soft, low voice. "I'm only sorry I don't need change."

ABOUT THE AUTHOR

Ann Evans has dedicated this, her second Superromance novel, to the memory of her father. The author spent her early childhood in Ocala, Florida—horse country! One of her fondest recollections is of her father picking her up during her school lunch hour. They'd drive to a Thoroughbred stable nearby, park under the trees and watch the mares and foals in the pastures. As Ann describes it, "While we ate the picnic my mother had packed for us, my father would tell every horse story he knew—from Pegasus to Man o' War. He was a wonderful storyteller who thought horses were the most beautiful animals on earth. I agree.

"Some of the scenes from *The Man for Her* evolved from these early memories of mine. I hope that a little of the love my father instilled in me for these wonderful creatures shines through in Jess and Adam's story."

Books by Ann Evans

HARLEQUIN SUPERROMANCE
701—HOT & BOTHERED

THE MAN FOR HER
Ann Evans

Harlequin Books

TORONTO • NEW YORK • LONDON
AMSTERDAM • PARIS • SYDNEY • HAMBURG
STOCKHOLM • ATHENS • TOKYO • MILAN
MADRID • WARSAW • BUDAPEST • AUCKLAND

ISBN 0-373-70752-5

THE MAN FOR HER

Printed in U.S.A.

For Robert Sollars Bair
With love and appreciation for all those lunch
hours we spent beside the pastures.
I was listening, Dad, and I still miss you.

CHAPTER ONE

"THIS WILL NEVER WORK," Jesslyn Russell said for the third time. "I look ridiculous."

"You look mysterious," Zola corrected.

Turning in front of the trailer's full-length mirror, Jess regarded her reflection once more. The belt of fake gold coins hung low on her waist like a slave trader's manacles. The colorful blouse dipped dangerously at her breasts, and the sleeves kept sliding down to cover her hands.

Mysterious? Not a chance.

Foolish? Definitely.

Jess shook her head. "The only thing mysterious about this scheme is why anyone in their right mind would think I can pull it off. This is not going to work. Look at me!"

Seated at the Formica kitchen table, Zola lifted her chin a full two inches in the air. She wasn't a young woman, but with her aristocratic bearing, high cheekbones and black hair that had yet to show the slightest sign of gray, she was still an imposing figure. If Jess hadn't known better, she would have sworn Zola actually *was* the haughty, mysterious fortune-teller she professed to be. "You insult my clothes?"

"Not your clothes. Just me *in* them. You're five-ten. I'm five-three. I look like I've been playing ladies dress-up in my mother's closet."

She turned again. The gypsy skirt swirled and eddied

prettily around her legs, but the waistband was much too big and settled ridiculously low on her hips.

"We can pin it." Zola forestalled Jess's next objection.

"What about my hair?" Jess asked, lifting a handful of curls from either side of her head, then letting them fall. The long tousle of red settled every which way. "No one's going to believe a red-haired, gray-eyed carnival fortune-teller with freckles."

Her father, who had watched the discussion between the two women from a safe distance, came to stand behind her. Placing his hands on her shoulders, Murdock Russell, known to everyone as "Doc," met his daughter's eyes in the mirror. "Pony-girl, Zoe won't be able to visit her sister in the hospital if someone doesn't take her place. You'll make a wonderful fortune-teller. Remember how you used to complain that you never had adventure in your life?"

Jess tilted her head back until her cheek rested against her father's. "I was sixteen when I said that, not twenty-six. I'm too old for adventures."

Zola was rooting through the china cabinet that doubled as extra bureau space for the carnival fortune-teller's enormous collection of costume jewelry, doodads and horoscope charts. She pulled open a drawer and a riot of colorful scarves foamed over the sides. Plucking one out, she waved it at Jess. "Wind this around your head. Like so." She demonstrated with a series of wild arm movements.

Jess complied, and she had to admit, the turquoise-and-green scarf wrapped turban-style over her hair helped to give her a more authentic look. A few minutes later, Zola completed the image by adding bangle bracelets, one large hoop earring and three gold-coin necklaces.

I look like an overdecorated Christmas tree.

"I don't know about this," she said with another dubious shake of her head. A stray red curl popped from beneath the turban, and she poked it back viciously.

"Who's going to complain?" her father pointed out. "Ocala's just a short stop in the carnival circuit. By the time someone figures out you're not Zola, we'll have moved on to the next town."

"All right. You win. But as soon as you get back tomorrow, my fortune-telling days are over." She looked at her father. "Who's going to run the ponies for me?"

"No one will mind if you shut down for a day or so," Doc said in his subtle Scottish burr. "People in Ocala don't pay a buck to plunk their kids on a pony when most of them have their own—with better bloodlines than those overgrown German shepherds you take care of."

"Don't insult the ponies," Jess protested. "They may not be mine, but they're as important to me as your pigs are to you."

"'Twasn't an insult, lassie," Doc soothed quickly. "I know you take good care of all the animals."

Mollified, Jess jerked the sleeves of her blouse up her arms. She cast one last, disgusted glance in the mirror. She'd been a gypsy fortune-teller less than ten minutes, and already she could predict the future. "This," she muttered, "is going to be a disaster."

THE GUY WAS TROUBLE—she could see it in his eyes.

Jess didn't like the mistrust in his gaze, the way his bushy eyebrows puckered together, as though someone had taken an invisible stitch in the middle of his broad forehead. He wasn't buying any of her fortunes, optimistic as she tried to make them. In another few minutes he'd have two and two together and realize her ability to foretell the future ended with her firm belief the sun would rise tomorrow. After that, it was all bluff and show, and evidently not very good bluff and show, because, just like Jess's two previous customers, this guy was on the verge of demanding a refund.

"What about my business?" the burly man across the table asked her. "Am I gonna turn a profit this year?"

Jess chewed the inside of her cheek. This could be tricky. Stay away from specifics, Zola had warned. Surreptitiously Jess gave her customer the once-over. Bib overalls, CAT hat tilted back on his shaggy hair. Dirt under the fingernails. In this small, rural, Florida community, if you weren't in the Thoroughbred business, you were a farmer. She didn't have to be much of a soothsayer to guess that this fellow belonged in the latter category.

The man swayed closer toward her across the table, and the faint odor of beer teased her nostrils. Although it was still early in the day, this man had obviously already found the carnival beer tent. Maybe he was inebriated enough that he wouldn't remember how inaccurate a fortune-teller she was.

"Well...?" he prodded.

Look, buddy, what do you want from me? I'm doing the best I can here. It had gotten hotter in the tent, hadn't it?

She swallowed hard and jumped in with both feet. "Oh, absolutely. You should have no problem finding a market for your...uh...product."

Dancing caterpillar eyebrows mated again. "You mean the bulls?"

Jess hid a sigh of relief. At least she must be on the right track. "Of course the bulls. Everyone will want one." Gingerly she flicked a finger over the man's palm, as though inspiration were written on the callused flesh scored by a slightly grubby lifeline. "See your business line here? Very long." With an air of mystery, she added daringly, "I predict that by the end of this year there will be one of your bulls in every pasture in the county and every cow will be impregnated."

There! That ought to make this guy happy.

The man blinked in confusion. After a long moment, his sagging features settled into thunderous rage. "I raise *pit* bulls, not cattle!" He snatched his hand away and stood so suddenly Jess thought his suspenders would pop. "You ain't no gypsy fortune-teller. Where's Madame Zola? She read my palm last year, and every bit of what she said came true."

Jess didn't bother to inform him that Madame Zola was really Mabel McAllister from Schenectady, New York. If there was one drop of gypsy blood in the woman's body, it was there by accident.

Trapped in her network of lies, she took refuge in an attitude of haughty disdain. "*I* am Madame Zola's protégée, and fully capable of giving you an accurate reading. Shall we try again?"

"Ha! You ain't nothin' but a green kid who wouldn't know readings from road apples. I want my money back!"

Jess's gaze became frigid. The take from today's business had been meager at best. Zola would be furious if Jess gave anyone their money back, an idea that went strictly against carnival policy. "No refund," she said firmly.

"Don't mess with me, little girl. I want my money."

More afraid of Zola's wrath than this man's blustering, Jess shook her head mulishly. The heavy hoop earring that dangled from one lobe bounced against her cheek.

The man's features took on a purplish hue. He raged and threatened, but Jess refused to budge. She had grown up around hot-tempered men and was adept at tuning them out or calling their bluff. This man was no different. A little bigger than most, maybe.

Eventually, the farmer seemed to run out of steam. He jabbed a finger in her direction. "You ain't heard the last of this," he swore menacingly, then stomped out of the small, dimly lit tent.

Jess watched him storm across the midway, hoping he was nothing more than a blustering big talker who'd had too much to drink. Five-fifty wasn't that much, and Zola had reassured her that customers unhappy with their fortunes seldom did anything about it. Most people chose to believe what they wanted to believe, and discounted the rest. Once the farmer's anger cooled, maybe he'd feel less inclined to make trouble.

She should never have agreed to this ridiculous masquerade. A headache throbbed to life behind her eyes. The turban was too tight. Her scalp itched. She wished Zola would come back where she belonged, before Jess's customers banded together and strung her up by her fake coin necklaces.

ANGELA CONNOR TOOK one glance at her brother's face and yanked hard on his shirtsleeve. "Adam, stop looking like someone's got their hand in your back pocket."

"I can't help it. You know I hate coming to places like this."

"You hate going anywhere that doesn't involve an engraved invitation," the teenager said. "Can't you just relax and have fun for a change?"

"No. We came here to go to the horse auction." His scowl darkened as they narrowly missed colliding with a teenage boy and girl exchanging a passionate kiss in broad daylight. "Not to mingle with a bunch of sweaty, pubescent teenagers or Mr. and Mrs. Middle America taking their kids out for as much cotton candy as they can stuff into their faces.''

Angela shook her head in disgust. ''Honestly, you've turned into such a snob. You sound more and more like Iwanna every day.''

Connor frowned in his sister's direction. ''I've asked you not to call her that. Her name is Tianna. One day you're going to let that nickname slip, and then where will I be?''

''Less one annoying girlfriend, I hope.''

''She's not my girlfriend, Angel...''

''She already knows I don't like her.''

''You could change that attitude.''

''I don't see why I should,'' Angela replied airily. Then, with a sly, sideways glance at her brother, she added, ''Unless you're planning to make her a permanent member of the family. You're not, are you?''

''That's none of your business, Miss Nosy-pants.''

''She's not the one for you, Adam. Even if her daddy does own the biggest and best horse farm in the state.''

''How about letting me make that decision?''

''Well, I know you don't love her.'' Then with a worried look, she added, ''Do you?''

Adam wasn't about to discuss love with a sixteen-year-old girl who thought every marriage ought to last until your dying day, and every man should want to throw himself off the nearest cliff if he couldn't have the woman he loved. Sometimes he wondered where Angela got such fanciful ideas. Certainly not from him.

He tapped the end of her nose affectionately. ''Ti's been a friend of our family for a long time, Angel. If we ever move beyond that stage, I promise you'll be the first to know.''

She made a face at him, then glanced around the midway wistfully. Her eyes lit with excitement. The look on her face pulled at Adam's heart.

Angela was the only family he had left, the only person who understood what made him tick, and though he was fourteen years her senior and didn't understand half of what she said most of the time, he loved her more than anyone else on earth. Maybe it was because she was the spitting image of their mother, pale and blond and bursting with enthusiasm. He had inherited his father's features: brown eyes, black hair, and a temper to match. Sometimes it was difficult for anyone to believe they were brother and sister.

"Oh, Adam, look!" Angela's hand shot out to point across the midway.

He turned. Across the shuffling throng of fairgoers, he made out the small tent with a dusty banner flapping weakly in the slight breeze.

MADAME ZOLA
YOUR GUIDE TO THE FUTURE

Another smaller sign proclaimed: Fortunes $4.50. Someone had crossed out that amount with a felt-tipped marker, upping the price to $5.50.

Evidently, a trip to the future had recently gotten more expensive.

Angela tugged on his arm, intent on wading across the sea of people. Adam brought her up short. "Uh-uh. Not a chance."

"Oh, come on. It'll be fun."

"We've already had fun."

"We have not. We haven't done half of what I've

wanted to do. I couldn't even get you to spend a lousy quarter on the coin-toss game.''

"Did you see the prizes they were offering? Would you please tell me what use you could possibly have for a plate with Elvis's picture on it?''

"That's not the point.''

"Angela, I'd sooner pound money down a rat hole than have some cackling old hag hold my hand for five minutes. I don't believe in that stuff.''

"Well, I do.'' Angela set her chin stubbornly. "I want to go.''

"All right. You go. Waste the money.'' They stopped in front of the tent, which on closer inspection looked even more flimsy than he'd first thought. "I'll wait out here for you.''

"No, you have to do it, too, Adam.''

"Why?''

"Because I want to hear what the fortune-teller has to say about you. Aren't you curious to see if she knows anything about what's going to happen with the stables? Or whether Midnight Star is really as good as you think he is?'' She cast him a sly sideways glance. "Or about your relationship with Tianna?''

"I can tell you right now, she won't know a thing.''

"Please…Adam.'' Angela pouted prettily.

When had he ever been able to refuse his sister anything?

He glanced around, hoping that one more effort at resistance would wear her down. "If anyone from the country club sees me, I'll be the laughingstock of the locker room.''

"No one's going to see you. Your friends don't come to these things. Remember?'' She nudged him toward the gap in the tent opening. "Now, you go first.''

"Why?"

"Because I'm too nervous. If she really is a spooky old hag, you can warn me."

Adam frowned. "Wait here. Don't move. I'll be out in five minutes. Probably less than that once she figures out I'm not buying it."

"Just don't make her so mad she puts a hex on you," Angela called after him as he swiped aside the tent flap.

BORED AND RESTLESS, Jess stole a peek at the wristwatch pinned inside the waistband of her skirt. One more hour and she could shut down and go to the horse auction. The tent got too hot in the middle of the afternoon to make staying open practical. Besides, customers weren't exactly beating a path to the door. Maybe word had gotten around that she wasn't a very good fortune-teller.

Fine. The idea of not having to rattle off another string of nebulous prophecies to a giggling teenager was very appealing. She chewed her bottom lip. Except everyone who worked in the carnival would know what an inept gypsy fortune-teller she'd made. And Zola and her father would never let her live it down.

The candlelight was supposed to create a mysterious atmosphere, but all it did was make her eyes burn. She blinked against the sting. Her back ached from hovering over palms at the round table covered by a fringed scarf, and the coin necklaces felt as though they'd been weighted with lead. This fortune-telling stuff wasn't as easy as it looked.

She rose to stretch the kinks out of her spine. With idle interest she scooped up the crystal ball that sat in the middle of the table, jiggling it in her hands. What were these things made of, anyhow? Glass? Plastic? She turned it over, expecting to see Made In Taiwan stamped somewhere, but the smooth surface had no markings. She lifted it to the meager candlelight provided by a wrought-iron sconce standing in the corner of the tent. Holding the ball against one eye and squeezing the other shut, Jess tried to peer into the center of the sphere.

She couldn't see a thing.

"I've always wondered how that works."

She jumped at the sound of a male voice, turning so quickly that the crystal ball slipped out of her fingers. It bounced once, then rolled across the carpet to stop at the feet of the customer who'd just entered. He bent to retrieve it, and she caught the gleam of blue-black highlights in the man's hair.

With languid grace, he extended his hand to her, offering the wayward object. "Your ball, Madame," he said, and she heard the slightly sarcastic lilt to his voice.

The tent was small, but closing the distance between them made Jess strangely uncomfortable. His features were shadowed by the dim light, yet she got the distinct impression this man found her a curious surprise. When only a few feet separated them, her uneasiness escalated. He was handsome in a dark, brooding way that reminded her of some of the Gothic novels she used to read. He had a wide, generous mouth, but it didn't look as if he did much smiling.

In that moment she caught the tiny upward curve of his lips as his eyes met hers. For a man who didn't appear to find much humor in life, the fact that he found her amusing was annoying and oddly threatening.

Gathering the tattered remnants of her composure, she lifted her chin. "I didn't hear you come in."

"So I gathered."

She plucked the ball from his fingers. "Thank you."

His eyes, a dark liquid brown, held hers in a look that

made no attempt to hide his interest. Her body indulged in a moment of peculiar internal chemistry before Jess told herself it was just the awkwardness of the situation and turned to reposition the crystal ball on the table.

She let the moment draw out, facing him again only after she felt absolutely certain she was back in control. "May I help you, sir?"

"I'd like to see Madame Zola—your mother, perhaps?"

Mother! Jess nearly choked on irritation. She lifted her spine, trying to yank as much dignity as possible out of her five-foot three-inch frame. "Madame Zola is away. *I* have taken her place."

He looked skeptical. "Does Madame Zola know that?"

Good-looking or not, this man was quickly losing points in Jess's book. Holding her temper, she said, "Would you care for a reading, or not, sir?"

"Actually, I believe I'd be very interested in hearing what you have to say about my future," he said.

"Very well. That will be five-fifty."

He nodded agreement, and Jess waited patiently while he slipped the money out of an expensive-looking wallet. Her eyes fastened on the quick glimpse of a blue and gold breeders' association card. She looked up at him with new interest. Her father had carried one just like it until two years ago. A Thoroughbred breeder having his fortune told? What did he expect her to say?

She realized he still observed her with an odd intensity. Because she found the look in his eyes so disturbing and her vanity still stung a little from his obvious disbelief in her credentials, she decided in that moment to play her part to the hilt.

The man handed her some bills and two quarters, and while he looked on, she bounced the coins in her hand a few times, then brought each one between her teeth as though to test its authenticity. Then she pulled her blouse away from her breasts and slipped the bills and both quarters into the neck of the loose garment. It seemed a very gypsylike thing to do, something Zola would recommend to give the customer a good show, but the moment she did it she experienced a sudden fear the coins would slide right through her clothes to bounce on the worn carpet. They didn't, thank goodness, and she couldn't help a little sigh of relief.

Instead of being impressed, her customer seemed to find further amusement in her efforts. He crossed his arms over his chest and his mouth lifted in a smile. "What a fascinating demonstration," he remarked in a soft, low voice. "I'm only sorry I don't need change."

Her senses went on red alert. This man was unsettling, infuriating. She wished he'd stop looking at her in a way she couldn't fathom.

"Please have a seat," she ordered.

He did, then laid his right arm across the table, palm up. She found her own chair across from him. He leaned forward, and Jess was suddenly aware of how small the distance between them had become. She glimpsed a small area of fine, dark chest hair at the base of his throat. The clean, tangy smell of expensive after-shave wafted to her nostrils. She looked down and realized he had wonderful hands: long fingers, the palm not callused or imbedded with dirt, but smooth and strong.

She realized she was going to have to pick up that palm.

"Is this the wrong one?" the man asked. "Would you prefer my left hand?"

"No," she replied quickly, wishing Zola had been the type of gypsy to read tea leaves instead. More calmly she added, "It takes a moment for the forces of the universe to respond to my telepathic call for guidance."

"I would imagine," her customer agreed.

She slid her fingers under his, clasping them lightly. His hand was warm, but hardly threatening, and Jess scolded herself for being so foolishly hesitant. Her eyes found his, and she had the strangest notion he knew exactly how she felt. At the edge of all that interest in his burnt-wood gaze, she witnessed the tiniest flicker of sympathy.

As always, the fear she was being made fun of stiffened her pride past all good sense. This man might not believe a word she said, but he was going to get a reading he'd remember for the rest of his life.

She gazed into his palm a few moments, employing every one of the tips Zola had given her. Frowning concentration, preoccupied murmurs, pregnant pauses. Anything to create the right atmosphere and effect.

Watching her, Adam tried hard to keep his expression seriously intent. It wasn't easy. Since he had entered the tent, his initial surprise had warmed to a healthy male interest.

Madame Zola's replacement boasted a creamy complexion, delightfully sprinkled with a toss of freckles across the nose and high cheekbones, pouting, petal-pink lips that struggled to look severe but ended up begging to be kissed, and eyes the color of soft summer rain. All this was packaged in a petite, curvaceous body that moved in an endearing, yet insinuatingly sexy way.

She looked no older than Angela, but considering the way arousal curled throughout his insides at the sight of her, Adam hoped he was wrong about that.

Her brows, delicate copper-colored arches over those large gray eyes, drew together in displeasure as she gazed down at his palm. "Oh, no!" she suddenly cried with a gasp of horror. "This isn't good."

On the contrary, little gypsy. I've got a feeling this ought to be very good. He resisted the temptation to laugh and schooled his features into mild concern. This woman wasn't any more gypsy than he was. "Problems?"

"I'm afraid you may not like what I see." Her features looked genuinely unhappy.

"That's a shame. Because I definitely do."

"Do what?"

"Like what I see," he said, his meaning all too clear.

Her frown deepened, and Adam could tell she didn't like his reaction. She wanted distress. She wanted fear. What she got was an overactive male libido that even he didn't expect. He took one look at the rigid set of her mouth and knew he'd gone too far. He was in for big trouble. And yet, even as he acknowledged the thought, he had to resist the temptation to reach out and pull that silly turban off her head just to see what her hair was like, whether it complemented that delicate complexion. He had a feeling it would.

"This is your business line," she explained as her finger hovered over, but didn't touch, his palm. "All these bisecting lines running through it mean failed investments. Financial ruin, I'm afraid."

He sighed. "Ah, well. It's only money."

Her features tightened. "Your lifeline is here."

"And..."

"It's short."

"Really? How unfortunate." He shrugged. "But then, no one lives forever, do they?"

Keep up this attitude, buster, and you'll be lucky to get out of this tent alive. She redoubled her efforts, doling out dark, dire predictions for every line in his palm—social acceptance, personal happiness, family relationships. Each reaction from the man was infuriatingly the same. He responded with an affable nonchalance, undercut by mocking disbelief. Jess's irritation with him, and the way he made her feel, climbed a notch, straight into dull anger. What right did he have to be so damned contemptuous? *And good-looking.*

"What about my heart line?" the man asked suddenly. "After all this gloom and doom, surely I'll be compensated with a brief, but wonderful love life?"

She went very still. Slowly her eyes traveled up to meet his. The hot, provocative look she saw in those dark brown depths threatened her already shaky composure. "I-I'm afraid it's almost nonexistent," she responded weakly.

"Maybe you should look again," he coaxed in a husky murmur.

Suddenly aware that control had shifted, Jess returned her glance to the table. The man's hand now held hers, and she watched in fascination as he stroked his thumb up and down the smooth cup of her palm with the same seductive gentleness she had glimpsed in his eyes. The light, warm touch sent tingles up her arm.

"Have you noticed? My heart line's nearly the same length as yours," he told her.

The tip of her tongue slid forward to swipe across her suddenly parched lips. His fingers moved to curve around her wrist, brushing faintly back and forth across the jump of her pulse. She realized belatedly it had been a mistake to tease and taunt this man.

"You have a lovely hand," he remarked. "Very fine-boned, yet strong. I don't have to be a fortune-teller to see that."

Her heartbeat slowed to a crawl.

"How old are you, little gypsy?" he asked after a long, thoughtful silence.

His words broke the mesmerizing spell. Jess's head snapped up and she jerked her hand out of his grasp. She pressed it close to her body, as though it had barely escaped being singed by fire.

"Old enough to know a come-on when I see one," she stated flatly, then stood so quickly that she had to grasp the back of her chair to keep it from toppling. "I think you'd better leave. I'll give you your money back if you like."

The man stood with unhurried grace. "As enjoyable as that might be to watch—" his eyes settled on her breasts "—I think I've gotten more than my money's worth."

His expression sifted into a mixture of troubled regret and bewilderment. Watching him, Jess suspected the man was almost as stunned by his actions as she was. He removed his wallet and tossed a twenty-dollar bill on the table, his manner suddenly all business. "Your next customer is my sister, Angela. She's sixteen, thinks she wants to be a physical therapist, loves the color purple and anything that smells like lavender. She's not mixed up with any boy, and I don't want her to be, so don't predict a bunch of love foolishness. Give her a future with a couple of kids and a tall, dark, handsome man for a husband. Got the idea?"

Jess gaped at him. As relieved as she was to have this strange encounter over, a stirring of disappointment filtered through her, as well. How could she ever have found this arrogant, overbearing man attractive?

"I think I get the picture," she snapped. "Anything else?"

One corner of his mouth lifted. "Yes. If I were you, I'd stick with the crystal ball. Palms don't seem to be your strong suit."

CHAPTER TWO

"THEY-RE-E OFF!"

Enthusiastic spectators pressed close against the railing, and Jess made a mad grab for her sun hat to keep it from being jostled off her head. She stood near the entrance of Russell's Racing Pigs, listening as her father called the race, his faint Scottish burr barely discernible over the loudspeaker's blaring distortion. The contest would be over in less than thirty seconds, taking longer only if Musetta, Carmen, Yum-Yum and the rest of the girls were feeling particularly uncooperative.

Today, the animals made the turn on the short course in no time, amid cheering encouragement. Moments later, Nedda squealed and grunted across the finish line and retrieved her prize—a single Oreo.

Murdock "Doc" Russell, once a top Thoroughbred trainer, the man who had single-handedly led Ricochet to a Triple Crown win, hefted the pig in his arms, displaying the wiggling, pink bundle to the crowd like a trophy. "The winner, folks!" he yelled. People clapped appreciatively. "Next show at two o'clock. Come back, and bring your friends."

Before her father could spot her, Jess turned, picking her way through the slowly dispersing mob.

The act was decent, honest work, she reminded herself. It had kept food on their table for nearly two years, and the novelty of racing pigs always drew a crowd. But no matter how many times Jess watched the show, it still saddened her.

Doc was a horseman, not a pig keeper. He should be with the Thoroughbreds he loved, back in Lexington where his knowledge was respected and his advice was still sought, even after such a long absence. Her father's expertise as a trainer could be matched by only a handful of men in the country. He *could* return to the racing circuit, and though it might be difficult, it wouldn't be impossible to revive his career.

How many times had she used those arguments with her father? And how many times had he stubbornly refused to consider them? Too many to count. She accused him of wallowing in self-pity. He accused her of attempting to run his life. She tried to convince him it was time to go back. He claimed he was happier without the constant stress.

Besides, he had told her, horses were mean, skittish creatures—beasts that did nothing but bite and kick—and he didn't miss them at all.

She knew his words were a lie. He *did* miss them. He missed everything about the racing world. From clocking early-morning exercise runs in the misty dawn, to final bed-down, where the soft nicker of tired Thoroughbreds wafted across the cool night air. That had been his life; he had loved it.

And every bit of it was gone now. Because of what Doc missed so much more. Beth Russell, his late wife.

Jess loved and missed her mother, too. But she feared Doc's feelings of guilt over his wife's death would take *him* to the grave, as well. He hadn't been able to put the past behind him, and lately he'd found far too many reasons to find forgetfulness in the bottom of a bottle.

After her mother's death almost three years ago, Jess

had seen her familiar, comfortable lifestyle change overnight. In the space of one week, Doc had sold the house
she'd grown up in and everything in it, quit his job and
disappeared. The note she'd received in her final semester
of college had been ridiculously brief and downright
frightening. With instructions not to worry, Doc had informed her he would be in touch. Of course, the moment
she could get away from school, Jess had quit her part-
time job at the veterinary hospital and set out to find her
father.

It had taken her a few months to track him down. His
former co-workers had mentioned a traveling carnival, in-
forming her that Doc had become quite friendly with the
fortune-teller. But it had been Jess's friendship with one
of the Breeder's Association bookkeepers that had finally
paid off. The woman had given her the address of the
bank where her father deposited his monthly pension
check, and Jess had simply camped on the bank's doorstep
until he showed up.

He'd insisted she go home. She'd refused. Veterinary
school could wait. Her father needed her. He hadn't ar-
gued further, probably thinking she'd give up eventually.
But she hadn't. She'd stayed. And now, nearly two years
had slipped by.

He needed to get on with his life.

And she needed to get on with *hers*.

But how? And when? The sad fact was, she was no
closer to answers than she had been when she'd first
tracked down her father at the carnival.

She made her way along the crowded midway, savoring
the smells of food—sausages, roasted ears of corn, cotton
candy. Heated sweetness teased her nose, and she waved
at Henry Bascom, alias Hans, the Belgium waffle king.

Bumping into a knot of teenagers, she apologized and

moved on, refusing to acknowledge the flirtatious invitation she saw in the eyes of one of the boys. It irked her that male attention often came from young men barely out of college. She couldn't help her youthful face.

Her thoughts strayed back to the curious, disturbing confrontation she'd had earlier with the horse breeder. Dark eyes and that equally dark, glossy hair. Broad shoulders. Now *there* was a man with the kind of mature good looks that could tempt a woman to lose her heart.

Until she discovered he was such an arrogant jackass.

So maybe she shouldn't have tried the gypsy fortune-teller routine on him, but pride and stubbornness, two of her most troublesome traits, had spurred her on. He could at least have *pretended* to believe.

Oh, what did it matter now, anyway? She wouldn't see him again. After giving the man's sister a reading anyone would be happy with—one he'd dictated, she remembered resentfully—she'd watched the two of them disappear into the midway crowd, so different that she'd never have guessed they were related. With idle interest, she'd noted that the young girl limped slightly.

With a couple of hours to kill, Jess had changed out of the fortune-telling outfit and into her customary jeans and T-shirt. Feeling less conspicuous, she headed for the auction barn. Set well away from the midway and rides, it provided a cool oasis from the heat of the day.

Entering the cavernous structure, she stopped inside the door to wait for her eyes to adjust to the subdued lighting. She pulled off her sun hat, ran a distracted hand through her hair and let her gaze wander along the white railing surrounding the center ring. Ocala took its Thoroughbred business seriously, and this structure reminded her of some of Lexington's best.

She liked to be level with the bidding floor, not in the

stands where the action seemed less immediate, and the din of excited voices could be lost in the echoing rafters. Spotting the perfect vantage point, Jess wove her way through the crowd.

A pang of homesickness twisted in the pit of her stomach. She missed Lexington. She loved the auctions. The high-strung antics of nervous Thoroughbreds. The boisterous anxiety of horsemen angling for the same prime stock. The hush and murmur of the crowd when the bidding rose above a million dollars. Did Doc miss that excitement as much as she did? Jess thought she knew the answer to that.

He should be here with me. But how can I ever convince him of that?

ADAM SPOTTED HER the moment he entered the barn, though at first he didn't realize who she was. The spotlight had caught her in its roving white glare, turning the tumble of red hair to silken fire. The eyes of every man in the building had probably been drawn to the sight. Then her head swiveled as the next animal entered the ring, and he would have recognized that impudent profile anywhere.

Madame Zola's inept little protégée.

He remembered their earlier encounter with pleasurable regret and more than a good amount of surprise. He never flirted indiscriminately with strange women. Long ago Adam had learned how disastrous those childish amusements could be to a man's reputation in this town. That a petite redhead masquerading as a gypsy fortune-teller could resurrect those unfortunate habits both puzzled and annoyed him.

He watched her flick a springy curl away from her face, a nonchalant yet oddly graceful movement that sent a shimmer of interest down his spine. As a fortune-teller she'd been hopeless, but as a woman she was damned attractive.

Angela tugged on his arm and pointed across the arena. "How about those seats over there?"

There wasn't anything wrong with her suggestion, but as his sister moved in that direction, he caught her elbow. "How about closer to the ring?"

His insistence brought puzzlement to Angela's eyes, but Adam pulled her along, even as he debated the wisdom of forcing another encounter with the redhead. They hadn't exactly parted friends. Oh, hell. He might be asking for trouble, but Adam realized he didn't want to leave without at least one more look.

Twenty feet away from the woman, he pulled up short. "Isn't that the fortune-teller?" he asked Angela in feigned surprise.

His sister frowned. "I don't think so."

"I'm sure it is. Let's say hello."

Over her look of astonishment, and before she could object, Adam propelled her forward. He knew he could count on his sister's natural friendliness to get them through the awkward moments of reacquaintance.

She didn't let him down. They'd no sooner reached the railing when she tapped the woman on the arm. "Hi. Remember us?"

The redhead turned. Her response was a polite smile, touched with a hint of wariness. "Yes, of course."

Her glance traveled to Adam. Oh yes, he could see she remembered him. And not with any particular fondness. Gray eyes that had been smoky in the tent now glinted like cold steel.

Angela made a quick introduction for them both.

"I'm Jess Russell," the fortune-teller replied.

"Do you come to the auctions often?" his sister asked.

"Whenever I can."

"Adam's promised to buy me a horse today so I can learn to ride."

"Really?" Jess commented with the lift of an eyebrow. Those glacial eyes returned to him. Without a trace of sincerity, she added, "What a generous guy your brother must be."

So she hadn't forgiven him his earlier rudeness. A smile tugged at his lips as he considered ways to redeem himself.

When her icy smile failed to ruffle his composure, Jess turned back to Angela.

"I'm scared to death of them," his sister was saying, "but we own a breeding farm here, and everyone we know rides, so I figured it was time to take the plunge."

"Once you overcome your fear, you'll love it," Jess said. "What's the name of your stable?"

"Rising Star Farm," Angela supplied enthusiastically. "Have you heard of it?"

"I'm afraid not."

"Well, you will one day. Adam will see to that." The girl motioned excitedly to the latest animal to enter the ring. "Oh, that's a beauty! I just love white horses, don't you? So romantic."

Before Adam could remind Angela they'd come here specifically to see two gentle quarter horses Alan Parkside had up for bid, Jess Russell spoke up. "Pretty, but too steep in the shoulder. She'll give you a hard ride."

Brother and sister regarded her in mild surprise.

"Do you know a lot about horses?" Angela asked.

"I grew up around them." There was a heartbeat's hesitation. "My father is...was a trainer."

Adam didn't miss the subtle tightening in the woman's posture. His sister's query had touched a nerve. He thought he saw naked sorrow flicker through her eyes for the briefest of moments. Then Angela asked another question, and Jess gave the girl her full attention.

He had to admit she'd captured his interest. Jess Russell's natural, unadorned loveliness was unusual in this day and age. Her hair lay thick, curling across her shoulders like a red cape. She had dimples that played hide-and-seek with her smile. He listened as she laughed at some comment Angela made, and discovered that he enjoyed the surprisingly husky sound.

It had been years since he'd been this intrigued by a woman. Jess Russell stirred in him a yearning for something unknown, and he found that fact unsettling.

He had goals. He had plans. And they didn't involve a gypsy impostor with fire in her hair and frost in her eyes. He should make some excuse to pull Angela away, find seats for them on the other side of the barn and forget he'd ever met her.

But he didn't.

Instead, he listened to the soft timbre of her voice as she chatted with Angela, liking the way she treated his sister with genuine friendliness. He had to admit, it was a sharp contrast to the condescending attitude Tianna often adopted around the girl.

And she knew horses. Her comments regarding each new entrant into the arena were intuitive. She had the kind of savvy gained from years of constant contact around them. He liked that.

Her earlier remark suddenly hit home. "Is your father Murdock Russell?" he asked, cutting into the conversation between the two women.

Jess looked at him, her features slightly wary. "Yes."

"I admire him," Adam said. "Doc Russell is one of the greats."

His tone was so openly sincere that Jess smiled. "He'll be pleased to know people still remember him."

"Is he retired now?"

"Just taking some time off."

Again there was *something* in the way she replied—a hint of evasion, perhaps. It puzzled him. If something had happened to end the man's career, surely he would have heard. Was Russell still with Carraway Hills?

Last year's Belmont favorite had been a Lexington colt from that well-known stable, but Adam couldn't recall the trainer's name. Not Russell, though. He'd have remembered that name. Adam realized suddenly that it had been years since he'd heard Murdock Russell's name mentioned in conjunction with any track winner, much less a Triple Crown hopeful. The idea that Jess Russell might be harboring a secret about her legendary father only intrigued him further.

And then abruptly, she was saying goodbye, wishing Angela luck in finding the proper mount. With a quick, dismissing smile, she jammed her hat on her head and turned from the railing.

Adam opened his mouth to stop her, then snapped it shut. What could he say? What right did he have to say anything? He watched her elbow through the crowd without a single backward look, that silly-looking straw hat tilting precariously on her thick curls. He let her go, feeling a vague sense of disappointment filter through him, annoyed because he couldn't account for it.

"She's very nice." Angela said. "Too bad she's not your type."

The comment made him unaccountably irritable. "What's that supposed to mean?"

Angela looked at him with weary patience. "Don't you remember last summer at the Stapletons' barbecue? I asked you what you saw in Tianna, and you said she was exactly the type of woman you were looking for. Tall, blond and beautiful, with enough power and backing to help make Rising Star what it should be.''

"I never said that."

"Yes, you did."

"Well, I never said it that way."

Angela gave him a look that spoke volumes.

He scowled. The words made him sound coldly calculating. But, hell, who was he kidding? He'd said it. Because even though he could never imagine loving Tianna Bettencourt more than she loved herself, someone who came with her family's connections could do Rising Star a world of good.

That kind of life—so long denied the Connors—was exactly what he wanted, for himself and Angela and the farm. He'd spent the last seven years working toward that goal. And nothing was going to stop him from reaching it.

His gaze unaccountably sought out Jess Russell in the crowd. He watched her leave the darkness of the barn and disappear into a bright shaft of sunlight just outside the door.

No. Nothing was going to stop him. Nothing, and *no one.*

JESS WAS ALMOST RELIEVED to be back in Zola's tent, back in the role of gypsy fortune-teller. Sequestered in this dark, warm haven, she wasn't likely to see Adam Connor again.

She liked Angela, but Jess couldn't say she felt the same about the girl's brother. He'd been as disturbing as she remembered. He watched her with an intensity that bordered on rudeness, silently analyzing everything she said. She didn't like that.

Shoving back the sleeves of her blouse, she lit the candles in the wrought-iron candelabra. As she set the match to the last wick, she heard the canvas flap slide back as someone entered the tent. Her heartbeat accelerated. *If it's him, I'm in big trouble.* That reaction bothered her, and she swung around.

It wasn't Adam Connor.

But she almost wished it was.

ADAM PURCHASED a gentle mare for Angela and made arrangements for its transport to Rising Star. He saw no reason to linger at the fairgrounds, but to his surprise, he discovered a sudden reluctance to leave.

"Would you like to stay a little longer?" he asked his sister.

Angela regarded him with wary excitement. "You mean it?"

He nodded. "I'll meet you in twenty minutes in front of the dart-throw game. We'll see how good your aim is. Okay?"

He handed her a twenty-dollar bill and watched her slip through the crowd. He noticed that the awkwardness of her gait seemed hardly noticeable today.

Turning, Adam headed for the fortune-teller's tent. On an intellectual level, he knew he was making a mistake. It would be better to leave well enough alone. Still, he owed her an apology, didn't he? He'd been out of line at the palm reading. Downright obnoxious. And Jess Russell had made it apparent she resented it. He should have made amends at the auction barn, but he'd missed his chance.

He told himself it wasn't too late—told himself there weren't any ulterior motives behind seeking her out now.

He reached the dusty canvas tent, but just when he would have pulled aside the flap, Adam heard voices coming from within. At first he thought she was with a customer, doling out one more laughable excuse of a fortune. Then he heard Jess Russell's low, abrupt tone and the snarling fury of a man's reply.

An argument. A heated one.

One peek through the slivered crack in the tent's opening and Adam summed up the situation immediately. He saw Jess, her features flushed with stubborn annoyance as she resentfully handed a refund to a customer. The burly giant, whose back was to Adam, didn't leave it at that. Swaying slightly, he let loose a string of epithets harsh enough to turn the air blue, though the slurring of his words made it clear he'd had too much to drink. Jess responded calmly, but her cool contempt for the man came through loud and clear.

Adam took a step back from the flap and heaved a disgruntled sigh heavenward. Terrific! His plan to apologize was one thing. But rescuing a damsel in distress could turn embarrassingly public if the guy refused to leave quietly. It could get *messy*. Adam couldn't afford messy. There'd been too much of that in his past.

He flashed a quick glance around, hoping to spot carnival security. Jess could handle the man, he told himself. Drunk or not, with a refund in hand the guy was bound to leave soon. Adam didn't have to get involved.

The customer's voice escalated, and Adam took another look through the opening. The man seemed determined to let Jess know just how pitiful a fortune-teller she'd been. He moved a menacing step closer in her direction.

Ah, hell. I knew it. Muttering a few curses of his own, Adam whipped the tent flap back and entered just as the farmer lunged toward Jess.

He heard a whoosh of air escape the man and realized that Jess's foot had connected with her attacker's belly. Hard. The kick sent the fellow barreling backward, colliding straight into Adam, who couldn't sidestep fast enough to avoid being carried along by sheer momentum. With grunts of surprise and pain, they fell into a tangle of arms and legs in the choking dust.

Stunned by this turn of events, Adam was dimly aware of Jess Russell standing in the archway of the tent. She looked at him in shock, then her eyes widened as her attacker came off the ground with an enraged roar. She took off down the midway, the sound of a hundred jingling gypsy coins accompanying her headlong flight.

No! Don't run! he begged her silently. *You'll only make it worse.*

Sure enough, the angry farmer thundered after her, through the crowd of astonished fairgoers, his meaty hands balled into fists.

Feeling as though fate suddenly had it in for him, Adam scrambled to his feet and ran after them.

FAIRGROUND SECURITY had a rickety trailer at the end of the midway. Jess headed straight for it, dodging in and out of the milling throng as though on a timed obstacle course. Her heart hammered. Behind her she heard the farmer close on her heels, breathing hard. The gypsy turban slipped off her head. Hair tumbled into her eyes, but she kept running. She might have made it, too. The man had been drinking, and his lurching gallop wasn't fast enough to catch her.

Until she lost valuable time by nearly colliding with a bunch of kids intent on their own race across the midway.

The man's hand landed heavily on her shoulder. He swung her to face him, reeling her in with a handful of her blouse. She landed against his chest with bruising force. He glowered down at her, so close she could smell peanuts mingled with the beer on his breath and see the burst blood vessels that mapped his nose.

He shook her. "I ought to whip your cheatin' little hide for trying to trick me," he shouted. "Who do you think you are?"

In her peripheral vision Jess was aware of the restive crowd surrounding them. Conversation dwindled. They were curious but unwilling to jump in and offer help.

She glared up at her captor. "You got your money back. Now let go of me, or I'll have you arrested."

The man's temper flared at her defiance. He swung his fist up in a threatening move, and Jess tensed, preparing herself for the blow. But in the next moment he went flying past her, tackled by a charging blur. It turned out to be Adam Connor.

Jess was astonished. She would never have guessed he could be so gallant, and certainly not on her behalf.

The size of the audience grew as the burly farmer threw himself at Adam. The man was bigger, more solidly built, but Connor moved quickly, with little wasted motion. He ducked a punch, then countered with one of his own. Jess yelled at them to stop, which appeared to be in exact opposition to the onlookers' wishes. They hooted and cheered the fighters on; even the carnival game tenders were shouting encouragement now.

Disgusted and embarrassingly aware that she was the reason behind this mess, Jess tried to find a hole in the crowd to slip through. The security tent stood less than two hundred yards away. Why hadn't someone heard the noise and come to investigate?

She shot a look over her shoulder, just in time to see the farmer find his opening and slug Adam. Infuriated, she ran forward without thinking and slammed her fist solidly into the man's nose. He bellowed in pain and took a wild swing at her, like a bear fending off a pesky mosquito.

Before the blow connected, Adam's arm shot out and swept her out of harm's way. The force sent her reeling backward.

She fell against the flimsy railing around the coin-toss game. The wood splintered and caved inward, crashing into the concession's platform where plates and saucers held hundreds of quarters tossed throughout the day. The dishes tipped, and amid the sound of broken glass, the money catapulted into the air.

For a few brief moments, it rained quarters like a sudden, metal hailstorm.

The crowd went wild. They stopped watching the fight and scrambled for the money.

The carnival workers yelled for them to stop and were ignored.

Fairground security finally appeared as Adam decked his opponent with two quick punches that set the man on his back, out cold.

Lying among the wreckage of broken plates, Jess watched Adam Connor crunch his way toward her, his chest heaving with exertion. Her ankle burned with knifing pain. Something was wrong there, she thought vaguely. But the sick, nauseated sensation in her stomach wasn't entirely the result of her injury.

He scowled down at her, then surveyed the frenzied scene around him. With his hands on his hips, he shook his head in disgust. His eyes were so dark they appeared nearly black. "I take it," he said in a clipped tone, "your fortune-telling hasn't gotten any better."

CHAPTER THREE

"HONEY, if you don't let me shoot another picture, the doctor can't give you an accurate diagnosis."

Jess gritted her teeth, trying not to lose her temper. She hated to be called "honey," especially by younger men. She hated hospitals. She hated being moved around like an inanimate object. And most of all, she hated this stupid hospital gown with its open back.

She leveled a look at the X-ray technician that should have chilled the blood in his veins. "The doctor already knows my ankle's broken. *I* know it's broken. You don't need another X ray."

"Only one more," he coaxed, then shot her a disparaging glance over the top of his monstrous equipment. "If you're afraid—"

"I've had busted bones before. I'm not afraid." She sat up on the table, trying to make the skimpy gown cover more than just her embarrassment. "Take another X ray if you like, but it's coming out of your pocket, not mine."

The technician obviously recognized the sound of trouble ahead. "Wait here. I'll get the doctor."

He left her alone. Alone with the too-cold air-conditioning blowing straight down her bare back, and the dehumanizing medical equipment standing guard. Jess hoped it wouldn't take him long to find the doctor who'd attended her when she'd first been brought to the emergency room.

Her departure from the carnival had been a humiliating ordeal. Ferried to the first-aid tent by security, fussed over by the nurse, then hustled into a waiting van and brought to the hospital, Jess felt as though she'd lost all control over her life.

Her injury wasn't that big a deal. She'd suffered worse breaks falling off horses. Even the doctor suspected a simple hairline fracture, and it had only irritated her further to have the carnival front office insist she have a full checkup for insurance purposes.

The shot she'd been given had killed the pain but left her with a headache. She wished she'd had time to call her father. Their budget couldn't stand a huge hospital bill. She wanted to go home to their trailer and lie down. Instead, strangers had poked and prodded and tried to take more X rays than she and Doc could comfortably afford. She felt disoriented and disinclined to play the cooperative patient any longer.

The technician returned and began setting up his machine for another shot.

"Well?" she asked when the man didn't volunteer any information. "What did he say?"

"The guy in your examining room says your bill is covered. Now lie back down."

"What guy? My father?"

The technician squinted through a small viewfinder on his equipment. "Not likely. A young guy. Black hair and a black eye to match. What did you two do, take on Rambo?" His head popped up as Jess slid off the X-ray table. "Hey, come back here!"

She ignored him. With one hand holding the back of her gown closed, she hopped out of the room. The movement jarred her ankle, awakening the pain, but she stumbled down the corridor until she reached the examining room and shoved the curtain aside.

She thought she'd left him behind at the fairgrounds, dealing with security reports. Instead, Adam Connor stood in the center of the room. His head was tilted back, and he held a blue ice pack against one eye. Hearing the low screech of protest as the curtain rings slid back, he turned.

He looked horrible. A guilty flush went through Jess as she noted the shirt flecked with blood from his nose, the rip in his sleeve and the bruise flowering on his chin. She felt terrible that he'd suffered so on her behalf, but that didn't give him the right to make decisions for her.

"What do you think you're doing?" she demanded.

"Trying to keep my eyeball from sliding out of my skull," he replied wearily. "What do you think *you're* doing? Why are you on your feet?" He frowned, then winced as the action pulled at his sore eye. "Sit down, for God's sake. Before you fall down."

The room began a slight spin. Jess hopped forward, making a grab for the examining-room table. The tissue-thin paper covering it rustled noisily against her fingers. "Did you tell the X-ray technician you're taking care of my emergency-room bill?"

"Yes."

"Why?"

He sighed heavily. "Because this isn't a Turkish bazaar where you can haggle over the cost of medical care. You need the X ray."

"I can't affor—"

She snapped off the words, but he knew what she'd been about to say. It didn't take a brain surgeon to figure out she wasn't rolling in dough. The carnival probably paid peanuts, but if she was living with her father, money shouldn't be that much of an issue. Trainers were well paid for their knowledge and expertise. Of course, from what Adam could piece together, Russell wasn't training anymore.

But why not?

Adam searched Jess Russell's face, but her tightly set features offered no clues. She was deathly white; the smattering of freckles stood out on her pale cheeks like cinnamon sprinkled on flour. Her fingers curled in a vise-like grip along the Naugahyde edge of the table, and she wavered on one foot like a drunken stork. She might not have much money, but this woman had enough stubbornness for two people.

He tossed the ice pack on the stainless-steel counter and went to her side.

"Look, if I hadn't shoved you, you probably wouldn't have gone sailing through that railing. So it's really my fault you're here." When she opened her mouth to voice further complaint, he added, "Could we straighten this out later? Right now I feel like that farmer ran me down with his truck, and you can't tell me you feel any better." When her knee buckled a little, Adam slid his arm around her. "Oh, hell, you have less sense than a newborn foal."

She looked up into his face and frowned. "I'm fine," she protested weakly. "Really."

"Sure you are."

Adam lifted her to the examining table, shocked by how little she weighed. Her head lolled against his shoulder. The tangle of red curls momentarily blocked his vision. He ended up half on the table with her, his arm wedged under her back, their faces only inches apart. She blinked rapidly. Her lashes moved like copper crescents against her cheeks, thick, spiky and dusted with gold at the fringed edges.

Poor little fortune-teller. Her ankle had swollen to the

size of a grapefruit, and the shapeless hospital gown had stolen her dignity, but she was trying hard to hang on to pride as well as consciousness. His heart twisted a little in sympathy.

"I don't need your help," she said softly. "I'm really all right."

She was so appealing. So small. Beneath the thin gown he felt the underside of her breast, the hard rhythm of her heart pounding against her rib cage. She suddenly caught her bottom lip between her teeth, then moistened its fullness with the tip of her tongue. Adam's breath went shallow with the quick longing to meet those lips with his own.

He jerked his head back, disengaging his arm from beneath her. He was behaving like a damned fool. Rescuing homeless kittens had always been his sister's specialty. He didn't have time for such nonsense. This woman had brought more unwanted excitement into his life in one day than he'd seen in years. Excitement he didn't need. Besides, something told him this kitten could scratch.

"Tell me something, Madame Fortune-Teller," he commanded in a low, gruff voice. "Are you always this much trouble?"

JESS CAME AWAKE struggling to sit up.

A hand, firm yet gentle, pushed her back down. "Lie still," the masculine voice commanded.

She closed her eyes and took several calming breaths, reaching the conclusion she'd fainted—an act she regarded as weak and stupid. Turning her head on the pillow, Jess opened her eyes, certain whose face she would see, but hoping it wouldn't be Adam Connor's.

Rats! It was him, all right.

He straddled a stool next to the table. Behind him stood

his sister, her fine, thin features pinched with concern. At Jess's feet, the doctor prepared her left leg for a cast with bored efficiency.

She came up on her elbows to view her ankle. Elastic bandaging hid the discoloration, but her foot had swelled to grotesque proportions. The doctor layered plaster across her instep. She grimaced and fell back, envisioning awkward weeks ahead in a cast. "Don't make it too big," she directed.

The doctor didn't respond, but she heard Adam give a short laugh. "Don't worry. He doesn't charge extra for using more plaster."

She turned her head toward him. "That's not what I meant. I just don't want something cumbersome." A moment later, she added, "And there's nothing wrong with not liking to see money wasted, you know."

She jerked her eyes to the ceiling, annoyed with herself. Why had she felt the need to justify thrift to this man? Just because Adam Connor obviously had money to burn didn't give him the right to ridicule a more conservative lifestyle.

Her hair spilled down the side of the table. From the corner of her vision, Jess saw Adam's hand stretch to capture a red lock. Slowly he slid the curl back and forth between his fingers, as though testing its quality. She felt the lightest tingling pull against her scalp. Her body tensed in instant response. Her eyes met his.

"Frugal Scots, huh?" he commented in a wry voice.

His disturbing, penetrating gaze made her feel as though he could see right into her soul. She didn't like it, and she looked away.

Angela Connor peeked at her from behind her brother. She asked solicitously, "Does it hurt a lot?"

Jess was glad for the distraction. "Not too bad."

"I couldn't believe it when I saw Adam flatten that guy. My brother—brawling! He never gets involved in that sort of thing."

Jess could tell by his frown that big brother didn't like Angela's observation on his behavior. His eyes strayed to Jess's fingers, which clutched the edge of the stretcher.

"How's your hand?" he asked.

Jess wiggled her fingers. "All right. How's your eye?"

Gingerly he touched the purpling bruise that lay beneath his indecently long lashes. "Strange. I haven't had one of these since I was a kid."

"You were both so brave," Angela commented.

"I asked carnival security to find your father," Adam interrupted before his sister could elaborate any further. "He should be here soon."

"Thanks," she said softly, touched by his thoughtfulness.

He gave her a slight smile, the first one she remembered seeing on him. It transformed his features, making him look boyish and uncertain. Maybe he wasn't such an overbearing stuffed shirt, after all. Coming to her rescue like Saint George out to slay a backwoods dragon. Good grief, had she even apologized for getting him into all this?

Jess cleared her throat. Apologies were something she didn't do often or very well. "I'm sorry you got mixed up in this mess," she blurted quickly.

"Have you ever considered a new career?"

"I was just helping out. I tried to tell Zola I'd make a lousy gypsy fortune-teller, but I never thought that guy would react so violently."

"The police were here," Angela told her, with a whisper of respect for authority.

Adam added, "I told them I had no interest in pressing

charges. I'd like to avoid any publicity if possible. You, of course, may feel—"

"I just want to forget it ever happened," Jess said with a frown. "But what about the farmer?"

"He could be arrested for public drunkenness, disorderly conduct. I doubt if he's interested in making any more trouble."

Angela insisted on hearing the details of the fight. Reluctantly Adam offered an abbreviated account. He made light of his intervention and then good-naturedly criticized Jess for arguing with the man.

They laughed together, and it had a nice, companionable ring, like a private joke. Jess wondered if Adam found many reasons for laughter in his life. His laugh had a rich, resonant strength, but there was a certain stilted quality, as though it didn't come easily and saw little use. Under her lashes she observed him, finding other things she liked: the way his hair gleamed with blue-black highlights under the bright hospital lighting, the soft twist to his mouth when he wasn't trying so hard to be overbearing or gruff.

Some of her tension slipped away. "Why did you come back to the tent?" she asked.

She regretted the question immediately. Their easy camaraderie suddenly died. Adam Connor's cool facade didn't return, but the wariness came back to his eyes. It was obvious the query made him uncomfortable. She wasn't certain what he thought of her, or even why he continued to remain, when he could so easily have found an excuse to leave.

Slowly he said in a low voice, "I wanted to apologize. I came on pretty strong earlier today, and I'm not usually like that. I gave you the wrong idea."

Angela glanced at Adam in surprise. Jess stared at him

in hypnotized fascination, not certain what to say or how to respond to the quiet intensity in his eyes.

The doctor saved her from having to say anything.

"You'll have to sit up now," he said. "I need to make sure your foot is in the right position."

She nodded and moved to rise, but Adam's hand was suddenly behind her, levering her upward. His fingers touched lightly at her back, against her bare flesh where the hospital gown had separated. The contact startled them both. He withdrew his hand the moment she found her balance.

Jess was grateful the cautious movements of her injured foot had made her sudden intake of breath seem natural. She frowned and tried to concentrate on the doctor's instructions, but her thoughts continued to stray to Adam Connor's touch and the absurd, irrational sensations it had produced.

"If you're not really a fortune-teller," Angela interrupted Jess's thoughts, "what do you do for the carnival?"

"I run the pony-ride concession and take care of the carnival livestock. I plan to be a vet someday since I have a pretty good way with animals. At least, that's what my father tells me."

"Your father travels with you?"

Jess stopped watching the doctor's manipulation of her ankle and met Adam's eyes with a level look. "He has an act with the carnival. Russell's Racing Pigs."

His eyebrows rose in astonishment. "Murdock Russell races pigs now?"

It gave her a sense of ridiculous pleasure to hear no censure in Adam's voice, only mild curiosity. "I told you, he's taking some time off from horse racing."

Voices drifted in from the corridor, one of them too

loud in the hospital environment, and Jess recognized her father's burr. A moment or two later, he barged into the examining room like a ship under full sail, flushed and slightly out of breath, his eyes shadowed with concern.

"Pony-girl!" he exclaimed, charging across the room with arms outstretched. "Are you all right, lassie?"

He was a big man, with a permanently ruddy complexion that came from many years spent working outdoors, and red hair that always seemed to need combing. Jess liked to think that he had kind eyes and a smile too wide and generous for a man, but most of the young trainers who had worked for him were scared to death of Doc. He had hands strong enough to calm the most recalcitrant beast, and a voice that could boom across a paddock. Jess submitted to a bone-crushing hug, noticing that all eyes in the room were fixed on her father. Even the doctor had stopped torturing her foot.

Enfolded in her father's embrace, she inhaled deeply. A dull lump of uneasiness settled in the pit of Jess's stomach at the smell of mint. Doc hated hospitals, forever associating them with his wife's death. She should have known he wouldn't be able to come without a fortifying drink or two, the smell of it carefully concealed behind the sweetened scent of breath mints. She glanced worriedly into his face.

She inched out of his grip. "I'm fine, Papa."

He pulled back, looking down at her. "Are you really? Took a year off my life, it did, when they told me you'd been taken to the hospital."

The emotion in his voice was so strong and heavy with paternal feelings that Jess blushed in an awkward mixture of embarrassment, annoyance and love. She felt every person in the room watching them with curious interest. With the sure knowledge that her father would continue in this vein unless she did something to distract him, Jess took refuge in introductions.

"Doc, Mr. Connor is the one who—"

"Oh, I've heard all about you, laddie," her father interrupted, pumping Adam's outstretched hand. "From the tales making the rounds at the carny, 'twas quite a fight."

"Adam, you're a hero!" Angela exclaimed.

Her brother frowned. "Don't make a big thing about it. It wasn't that much, and hopefully, the talk will die down quickly."

"Don't be so modest," Doc remonstrated gustily. "I wish there were some way I could repay you. I'm eternally in your debt for saving my pony-girl here."

Jess suppressed the urge to tug viciously on her father's shirtsleeve. As much as she loved Murdock Russell, at times he proved capable of making her feel six years old again. Hurriedly, she introduced the emergency-room doctor, whom her father greeted with respect, if considerably less enthusiasm.

"Could I speak to my father alone for a few minutes?" Jess asked.

The doctor agreed on a five-minute respite before the next layer of plaster would have to be applied.

Adam turned to his sister. "Come on, Angel. I'll buy you a soft drink."

They left the room, the slight dip of Angela's limp more noticeable now.

"Nice people," Doc commented when they were alone.

"Very nice."

"Are you sure the doctor's not just an intern? I don't want anyone practicing on you."

Jess glanced into her father's face. His tired eyes were lit with concern. She took his hand, her fingers stroking the familiar bumps and ridges formed over a lifetime of handling horses. "It's just a hairline fracture, Doc. Please stop worrying." She wobbled his hand, forcing his eyes to hers. "Are you sure *you're* all right?" she asked, knowing he would understand her meaning.

He nodded sharply. "Getting there. You know I've no liking for these places. 'Twas your mother who was always the backbone in such matters." He glanced around the room, the look in his eyes a little wild.

"Doc," Jess said, anxious to displace memories she saw forming in her father's head, "get me out of here."

"All in good time. We can't be taking a chance with your health, lass."

"The only chance we're taking is with our bankbook. We can't afford this."

His eyes found hers, full of sorrow and regret. "I've let you down these past two years, haven't I, pony-girl?"

"Don't say that," she commanded roughly. Her hand reached out to brush back a strand of fiery hair from his forehead. "You're not responsible for me."

He shook his head. "You should be in that vet school. Not baby-sitting an old wreck like me."

"You're not an old wreck. You're my father. And I'll enroll in that school when you return to Lexington. You know the breeders up there would welcome you back with open arms."

"I can't go back," Doc said gruffly. "Too many memories."

"Good memories as well as bad," she said gently.

"Aye, but even the good ones carry pain, lass. I miss my Beth. I see her ghost in all the places she used to be."

As always, her father's grief was an impenetrable wall of frustration for Jess. Aloud, she said, "Doc, I want to help you, but I don't know how."

Her father seemed to sense her despair and tried to

lighten the mood. "I'm not the one who needs help right now. Let's spring you from this dreadful place. You can put your foot up, and I'll even run those cursed ponies for you until you feel more like your old self."

"I'll be back on my feet tomorrow."

He scowled. "We'll see about that. I'll settle up and be right back." With his usual brisk, hearty way of moving, her father turned and strode toward the door.

"Doc," Jess called after him, "make sure they charge us for only *two* X rays."

THE DOCTOR RETURNED and spent the next twenty minutes fussing over her leg. He insisted on demonstrating the proper way to use crutches. Jess informed him she already knew how to use them. He ignored her.

Eventually she was left alone to wait for her cast to harden. No one returned to keep her company.

She hoped Doc wasn't still waging war with the bookkeeping department, but there'd been no distant bellows of outrage to indicate problems in that area. She wondered if the Connors had gone. Surely Angela would have insisted on popping in to wish her well before leaving.

Feeling unwanted and lonely, Jess sat on the stretcher and brooded about Adam Connor. She couldn't help being intrigued by him. He was like no one she'd ever met before. Undoubtedly he could be a harsh, demanding man, but he knew how to be gentle and kind, too. Since arriving at the hospital, he'd shown nothing but concern for her welfare, so much so that even his sister seemed surprised.

The amazing thing was it made no difference whether he treated her with that snobbish, abrupt attitude or looked at her with tender regard. Her reaction was annoyingly the same.

He caused a stomach-tightening awareness within her

that endangered self-control. She had the dreadful feeling that the longer she stayed around the man, the more difficult it would be to make the rational part of her brain function.

Jess shook her head in disgust. It was a very good thing, she reflected, he'd be out of her life soon enough, and she'd never have to see him again.

The curtain at the doorway slid back on its rings and Angela Connor entered, her face full of excitement. She crossed the room and grasped Jess's hands in hers. "Guess what? You're coming to stay with us!"

Jess's mouth dropped open. "What!"

Her eyes traveled to the doorway where Adam Connor had suddenly appeared. While she stared at him in disbelief, he folded his arms across his chest and leaned against the doorframe, the expression in his eyes unreadable.

"Put your crystal ball in storage, little gypsy," he announced. "You and your father are spending the next eight weeks at Rising Star."

CHAPTER FOUR

"HOW COULD YOU AGREE to such a thing?" Jess demanded.

It was the third time she'd posed the question to her father since leaving the carnival. She wasn't surprised when he didn't answer, but instead continued to maneuver their battered pickup through Ocala's downtown area, heading toward the interstate. For the past half hour he'd remained mulishly silent, but a rose flush of temper had turned his cheeks into twin warning flags. The traffic on the road wasn't tangled enough to account for his brooding reticence, and Jess suspected his sulky anger was directed toward her.

I'm the one who has a right to be angry, she thought, and settled back with the same sullen expression her father wore. They'd hardly spoken two words to each other since they'd left the hospital yesterday.

She couldn't help feeling betrayed. What possible reason could her father have for accepting Adam Connor's outrageous offer? And without even consulting her! It was nothing more than charity. Where had all the Russell pride disappeared to?

She'd gotten used to her simple existence, and now it had taken another drastic turn. They were bouncing along toward Rising Star Farm, a place they'd never seen, to be the guest of a man they'd known less than twenty-four hours. It was just too humiliating.

The truck lurched forward as Doc downshifted, grinding the gears so abominably that Carmen, Yum-Yum and the rest of the girls squealed a protest from the back of the pickup. Her father's driving ability always deteriorated when he was angry.

Jess hid a rueful smile. The strain of being at odds with him was too great to be maintained for long. "You don't have to take out your anger on the truck," she said, retrieving her crutches from against the dashboard. "I suppose we should discuss this calmly before we get to Rising Star."

Doc gave her a stiff nod. "Fine. If you think you can stop fussing at me long enough to listen to reason."

She took a deep breath, then let it out slowly. "I'm listening."

"I accepted Adam Connor's invitation because I honestly thought you'd be pleased," he grumbled. "You've been badgering me for months to get back in the business."

"And how is working at Rising Star getting back in the business?" she countered.

"For your information, lass, Adam Connor knows what I can do for him. He lost his second trainer six months ago, and it's beginning to show on the two-year-olds. With training season a month away, he can't afford to let them slip. He's agreed to pay me—a grand sum, I might add—on a consulting basis." He sighed. "The whole idea just came up in conversation. It seemed like a bonny plan."

Jess stared at her father's profile as he turned the pickup onto the interstate, heading toward horse country. He looked determined and confident, more so than he had in a long time. Had this agreement with Connor done that for him? The job might be temporary, but it might also prove to be the first step on the road to recovery. If so, how could she withhold her support? She should be glad he'd come to this decision; and yet the idea of staying at Rising Star for eight long weeks made her feel edgy and uncertain.

Her fingers clenched the armrest of one crutch. "All right," she conceded. "But what about our commitment to the carnival? Bailey's not likely to appreciate our leaving on the spur of the moment like this."

"He's still upset over the dustup you caused on the midway yesterday. Says in all the years he's owned the carnival, he's never had to consider calling in the riot squad. Zola thinks it wouldn't hurt us to take some time off and give him the chance to cool. The ponies will be fine without you, and my little girls—" he jerked his thumb toward the back of the truck "—should enjoy the break."

"And Adam Connor agreed to keeping pigs on his farm?" She couldn't prevent the skepticism from coloring her voice.

"He needs my help badly enough that he's willing to put up with them."

The self-assurance in her father's tone made her feel churlish for trying to deny him this opportunity. Chewing her bottom lip, she stared out the window at the rolling countryside. Miles of white fences. Grassy pastures of tall Bahia glaring brightly in the summer sun. The waving green carpets were dotted here and there by small herds of grazing broodmares and frolicking offspring. The scene was familiar to Jess, like a homecoming.

If the sight of all that sleek, splendid horseflesh could produce this vague sense of delight within *her,* Jess reasoned, what must Doc be feeling? Excited? Nervous?

With the exception of his time at the carnival, her father

had always worked around horses. He could observe a line of colts at the track starting gate and tell which one would try to jump the count. He knew when a mare would reject her foal and when a stallion had developed an unreasonable dislike for its exercise rider. His co-workers at Carraway had called his ability to read an animal's mind brilliant, but uncanny.

Did he still have the magic touch with horses? Could he bring to Rising Star what he had brought to Carraway Hills? Or had his drinking diluted that gift?

Since Doc did not consider his drinking an issue, it seemed unlikely he'd mentioned it to Adam Connor. Should she? In all fairness to the man, he ought to know about any potential problem. But how could she undermine her father before he'd even started? Maybe this job really would put him back on the right track, and she'd be voicing concerns that might never materialize.

Can you do this, Doc? Are you really in control?

She stole a look at her father, but his expression gave away nothing.

"What am I supposed to do for eight weeks?" she asked at last, voicing one of her worries.

"Rest up. Study those books you're always lugging back and forth to the library. What letter are you up to?"

"The *M*'s. I've just started *The Merck Veterinary Manual*."

Four years of veterinary college waited for her sometime in the future. In every town the carnival set up camp, she immediately paid a visit to the library, borrowing books on animal husbandry, biology and zoology. She was systematically working her way through the alphabet, so that by the time she started school, she would be well prepared.

"If you take advantage of the next few weeks," Doc

said, "you'll know more than a vet by the time you get that cast off."

Jess tapped the top of her cast. "I've had these before, remember? It doesn't make me an invalid." Settling her head against the back glass of the truck's cab, she focused her eyes on the dome light. Her hat lifted slightly from the top of her head. "Eight weeks," she muttered. "I'll go crazy."

"You'll be fine. And I won't have to worry about you clomping around the carnival in that thing. Or cooped up in the trailer. It's the perfect solution, lass."

"Perfect," she echoed.

The disbelief in her tone wasn't lost on her father. He shot her a narrowed glance. "Is there something you're not telling me?"

"No, of course not."

"Don't you like the Connors?"

"Angela seems a sweet girl."

His head tilted in her direction. "Her brother's a handsome laddie, wouldn't you say?"

"I suppose so."

Damn. Was it only her imagination, or had her heartbeat accelerated? With unexpected clarity, the memory of Adam Connor's hand pressed against her bare back intruded. She shook it away. What had gotten into her?

"This will be the longest eight weeks of my entire life," she said in a soft whisper.

"STEATITIS IN CATS and Other Fur-Bearing Animals" was a miserable chapter to get through. Jess closed the book with a dull snap. Using one crutch as a lever, she worked her way off the low couch and hobbled to the kitchen to check on the pot of chili she'd made for Doc's lunch. He'd be back from the exercise track soon, hot and tired and no doubt more animated than she'd seen him in months. Even the bottle held less appeal for him lately.

She hated to admit it, but living and working at Rising Star agreed with Doc.

She wished she felt the same.

Their two-bedroom guest cottage boasted a sunny, eat-in kitchen, handwoven rugs and comfortable furnishings. It was far nicer than the rented trailer they'd made do with at the carnival, but since their arrival a week ago, Jess had felt as though she were confined to a pretty prison.

Except for a few expeditions to the barns to view the Thoroughbreds, and her twice-daily trek to the pen to feed Doc's pigs, she'd been left on her own. Angela visited every day. Jess liked the girl, but her conversations had a teenager's one-sided shallowness and seemed to center on her attraction to Tim Rogers, one of the young grooms at Rising Star. Listening to her describe this hunk of male perfection, Jess realized it had been a very long time since she'd been sixteen.

She hadn't seen or spoken to Adam Connor since that day in the emergency room. Angela said he was busy, and Doc conferred with him every day, but he'd yet to make any attempt to seek her out. He hadn't even been there on their arrival. The farm manager, Bill Page, had settled them in the cottage that sat a stone's throw from the main house, a huge white structure that could have passed for a movie studio's idea of a Southern antebellum mansion.

She didn't know why Adam Connor's indifference should bother her, but it did.

Feeling bored and restless, Jess picked up the dog-eared copy of the veterinary manual she'd been studying, pulled one of her sun hats off the coat tree and left the cottage. The crutches stayed behind. Walking without them meant she had to bring her cast-covered leg forward in an awkward swinging motion, but she could move faster without them. And outside on the uneven ground, they were nothing but a nuisance.

A crushed-shell path lined by old railroad ties connected the main house to the cottage. Mattie, the Connor's housekeeper, was in the garden beside the house, and Jess smiled at her as she clomped past. The older woman waved her clipping shears and returned to decapitating roses.

Jess headed toward the front pasture where a stand of gnarled oak trees offered shade and solitude away from the hum of activity around the barns. Her father had told her the stable staff numbered between thirty-five and fifty, depending on the season, but that every employee here kept a quick pace.

Rising Star wasn't nearly as extensive as Carraway Hills. There were six barns in all, laid out in long rows of white cinder block, their tin roofs painted green. Remembering the austere, military look of Carraway, Jess thought Adam Connor's spread boasted more personality. Someone had taken the time to hang pots of brightly colored mums at regular intervals along the overhangs, and miniature birdhouses that matched the barns had been erected to keep the swallows from nesting under the eaves.

When her ankle began to ache, she cut under the white fence into the pasture. It wasn't hard to manage since it was only a three-plank fence. She smiled to herself, remembering how her father had always disdained breeders who surrounded their pastures with four- and five-plank fences. Why would they want more boards to paint and repair? her father complained. In Doc's opinion, owners who spent so much money on multi-planked fences were more interested in getting their farms photographed for magazines than in training Thoroughbreds to win races.

A few broodmares had been turned out for the day and stood grazing five hundred yards away. They regarded her passing with a moment of flared nostrils and erect ears, then settled back to cropping sweet grass, the sun bouncing off the sleekness of their coats.

The sunshine felt warm and wonderful on her shoulders, like a healing balm. With a sigh, Jess decided to forgo the shade. Awkwardly she settled herself in the grass. It was thick and springy beneath her, prickling against her bare thighs where her shorts had snuggled against her bottom. She dragged off the hat to shake her hair free, locked her elbows behind her, then lifted her face to absorb the heat.

Thirty minutes later she gingerly turned on her stomach. Indulging in lazy luxury, she rested her chin on her folded arms. The turf tickled against her cheek as she watched a ladybug explore a blade of grass, and her nostrils twitched at the rich smell of earth. Closing her eyes, she tunneled her nose deeper into the silky greenness, imagining herself back in Lexington, back at Carraway Hills...

The land had been hilly in Lexington, and one particular pasture of rolling emerald velvet had always been a favorite spot. On numerous Sunday afternoons, her mother would pack a picnic lunch, her father would scoop up his portable cassette player and a handful of their favorite opera tapes. Then the three of them would settle under the dark canopy of a shady tree to enjoy the music and watch the horses.

Her mother would always translate the words of any aria Jess didn't understand; her father always praised Beth Russell's fried chicken and potato salad as though he'd never enjoyed such a wonderful banquet before. Sooner or later Jess would realize that her parents' conversation had gotten softer, more intimate. Eventually she would go off in search of that disrespector of horses, the groundhog, whose burrowing holes could so easily break a Thoroughbred's leg.

Sometimes she'd look back at her parents and notice that they had moved closer, and occasionally she'd catch them in a quick kiss.

Now she smiled at that memory and wondered if during those times her parents had ever wished her farther away. Probably. In all her growing up years, she'd never known either of them to be shy about displays of affection. They hugged. They touched. The house she'd grown up in had been filled with lively chatter, spirited debates and boisterous laughter. Her parents had lived life to its fullest, and never been cowed by it.

Right up until the day her mother had been killed.

EVERY TIME ADAM DROVE under the wrought-iron archway that announced the boundaries of Rising Star, he experienced a feeling of comfort, as though the farm offered a safe and quiet haven from the outside world.

It was strange, really, because it hadn't started out that way. Seven years ago, after the death of his father, he'd left the law firm in town and come home. Since that time, the stables had been an all-consuming drain on his energies, like a demanding mistress who was never satisfied. It had stolen his parents and exhausted his bank account.

The farm still sat within the shadows of its notorious past, but soon, all the years of rebuilding would pay off. Sun Devil and Angel's Bet showed definite potential, and Midnight Star had proven remarkably blessed with the same fine qualities as his forefather, Faelen's Star. If the colt was as good as Doc Russell believed, a claiming race wasn't far off. It would be a good test of the animal's ability, and give Adam a chance to officially introduce Star to other contenders.

He drove slowly, his mind preoccupied by thoughts of how clever he'd been to snare Russell's assistance. The reasons behind Doc's defection from the world of horse racing still nagged at Adam, but the Scotsman knew Thoroughbreds. His training methods were legend; half the farm was already in awe of him. If there was a problem in the man's past that could create trouble for Rising Star, the feelers Adam had put out with his contacts in Lexington would soon reveal it. In the meantime, he needed Russell.

He fingered the slight discoloration under his eye, the only remaining sign of that ridiculous fight at the carnival. Too bad he had to take the daughter in order to get the father. Now *there* was a distraction he didn't need.

Since her arrival, Jess Russell had kept a low profile, yet he'd become increasingly aware of her presence. Angela talked incessantly about her, as though she'd found a long-lost sister, and on two occasions he'd glimpsed her at the barns, making her way through the crowded work area like a queen surveying her subjects. This, in spite of that hobbling gait brought on by her cast and the silly hats she seemed to love squashing over that glorious red hair.

He hadn't approached her. He had, in fact, found excuses to stay away, behavior that puzzled and annoyed the hell out of him. He preferred not to dwell on the knowledge he found her attractive. She was, after all, a good-looking woman, and he a healthy adult male. But thank God he had enough sense to recognize she wasn't his type.

The long, straight driveway dipped, then rose to a gentle slope. Adam glanced across the pasture to his left, his gaze assessing the appearance of the broodmares. Most had been bred early last March and were just now becoming round-bellied with foal.

He caught sight of a splash of blue in the long grass, and alert for any intrusion, Adam slowed the convertible. The form took human shape. With a start, he realized a person lay out there, facedown and unmoving. He recognized Jess Russell from the long stretch of white glaring in the sun—her cast-covered leg. A moment later he had pulled the car off the road and was vaulting over the pasture fence.

His mind began an endless chase of questions and answers. What trouble had the woman gotten herself into now? Had she come too close to one of the mares and been kicked? Surely she'd have enough sense to keep her distance. But as he jogged nearer, he saw she was still sprawled inelegantly on the ground, her arms stretched over her head.

When he reached her, Adam was so worried he forgot to test gently for injuries. He bent down and made a rough grab for her shoulder, yanking her over. He didn't know whether he was more shocked or relieved when Jess came struggling upward into a sitting position. One look at her face told him she hadn't been hurt.

"Hey! What do you think you're doing?" she demanded.

"Are you all right?" he retorted.

"Of course I'm all right. Why shouldn't I be? I'm just relaxing."

"With your nose buried in the dirt?" he asked in an incredulous voice. "I thought you were unconscious. You scared the hell out of me."

"Oh. Sorry about that." She tossed wayward curls back

over her shoulder. "Do you know you need more protein in your soil?"

"What?"

Her features were deadly earnest. "If you can't grow blue-grass here, you need all the protein you can get, at least eighteen percent in the blade. You should seed with more Bermuda. Ask my father."

He wanted to choke her. She sat there lecturing him like a college professor about the content of his pasture grass, while he stood over her, his heart still hammering in his ears. The slight breeze had disordered her hair as though a lover's hand had run through it, and a flush of color lay across her cheekbones. The sun had brought out the freckles on her nose, and along that stubborn jawline was a smear of dark earth.

Go back to the car. She's all right, and there's no reason for you to stay. Instead, he lowered himself beside her, sitting cross-legged.

"What are you doing out here? Besides inspecting my grass?"

"Relaxing. Reading." She gave him a quick glance. "I wasn't bothering the mares, but I won't come out here if you don't want me to."

He dismissed her fears with a shake of his head. "I don't suppose there's any harm, as long as you don't get too close. You know, if you're looking for a place to relax, you're welcome to use the pool behind the house."

The cotton shorts she wore had rucked up to her hips, leaving her strong thighs exposed. Her trim body would look terrific in a bathing suit, he realized, discovering how easily he could picture it.

"I don't swim very well," she replied, then rapped her knuckles along the top of her cast. "And how long do you think I'd stay afloat with this boat anchor?"

"I meant you could lie out in a lounge chair."

"Not for more than thirty minutes or I start to freckle."
She bent her head, pressing a fingertip against the flesh
just over her heart, then lifting it. The skin whitened momentarily, then pinkened with color. "I've probably gotten too much already."

Adam couldn't stop himself. He watched, transfixed, as
the gentle rhythm of each breath she took carried her
breasts upward against the edge of her scooped-neck
blouse. The soft swell looked warm and dewy from the
heat of the day. A flicker of exciting fire burned a path
along his insides. He pulled his eyes away in irritation,
wondering if the woman had deliberately set about capturing his interest.

She lifted her gaze to his, and though he searched for
it, he could find no coquettish teasing in the cool, gray
look she gave him. All he saw was the offer of open and
honest friendship, tinged with the slightest bit of wariness,
as though he were a stray she was determined to feed from
her hand. He thought of all Tianna's flirtatious manipu-
lating of the men around her, her haughty self-assurance,
and realized that this woman didn't have a clue how to
use her power.

He was appalled by how much that knowledge pleased
him.

The moment his eyes met hers, Jess realized she'd
made a serious mistake. However awkwardly she'd have
managed it, she should have hobbled up from the grass
and returned to the cottage. Sitting this close to the man,
nearly thigh to thigh, only confirmed her impression that
she'd be well advised to keep her distance. His dark, probing look studied her features with an embarrassing intensity. She shifted, uncomfortably aware of her disheveled
hair and wrinkled shorts, disliking the way he could so

easily make her nerves sprint with anticipation toward an unknown goal.

"Is that the reason for the hats?" he asked at last.

"Pardon?"

"Nearly every time I see you you're wearing some sort of hat. Because of the sun?"

Relieved to be sidetracked by an innocuous topic, she replied with enthusiasm, "Oh, no. I just like them. And it's easier to hide my hair than try to make it behave." She raked her hands through the shining mass. "I keep telling myself I'm not a kid anymore. I should get it cut."

"No, don't," he objected quickly, then frowned. What did he care whether she cut it or not?

"Why not?" she asked, looking a little surprised by his outburst.

"It becomes you," he found himself adding suddenly.

"Thank you," she said, knowing her cheeks darkened with the unexpectedness of his compliment.

She watched as he lifted his hand, and for a brief moment she suspected Adam intended to touch her hair. Her stomach tightened. But in midair he stopped, and instead, his fingers found her book where it lay in the grass.

"What are you reading?" He turned the book over and read the spine. "*The Musculoskeletal System of Sheep.* Fascinating." He looked at her askance. "I know the local library is small, but surely it can do better than this?"

The militant heartbeat he'd produced only moments ago had yet to be cudgeled into submission. She replied testily, "I don't have time for fiction. I told you, I'm going to be a veterinarian someday." Briefly she explained her study habits.

"Why don't you just enroll and get it over with?"

She couldn't share with him her concern for Doc's stability. Adam was a businessman who had to make hard decisions in order to ensure the success of Rising Star. Training Thoroughbreds required providing a consistent routine that didn't waver. He'd never permit her father to stay on the farm if he thought Doc's performance could be affected adversely by drink.

She still felt guilty about holding back the truth, but more and more her father seemed to be getting better. By giving Doc this job Adam was partly responsible for that improvement, but he was benefiting from it too, wasn't he? His runners had never been in better hands than Murdock Russell's. Searching for an excuse, Jess looked away, plucked a handful of grass, and idly watched the blades sift through her fingers. She shook her head. "The timing's not right just now."

He was silent for a long moment. When he spoke at last, his voice was softly textured with compassion. "You could probably get a student loan."

Jess gave him a sharp look. "Money's not the issue. It isn't everything, you know."

He gave a short laugh, a sound that held no merriment. "Perhaps not in your world. But definitely in mine."

"Then maybe you're in the wrong world."

He seemed to give that some thought, then sighed and said slowly, "Sometimes you don't have any choice."

She wanted to refute that. In her mind, there was always a choice. But she heard regret in his voice and knew instinctively he wouldn't appreciate her thoughts. She looked out into the pasture, concentrating on the movements of a lone black mare amid a cluster of bays.

"How's the ankle?" he asked suddenly.

"Coming along. It doesn't hurt anymore unless I overdo. Getting unpacked the first day was the worst, but Angela's been very sweet, helping us get settled. And the cottage is lovely, by the way."

"Our mother designed and furnished it."

"It's very homey. She should be an interior decorator."

"She died six years ago."

"I'm sorry."

Adam squinted into the sun. "My father died the previous year and Mother never seemed to get over it. She wasn't a particularly strong person, so her heart attack didn't really surprise anyone. Angela believes she willed it to happen." His voice was dispassionate, as though that time in his life no longer had the power to hurt him, yet she was aware of an underlying bitterness.

"But you don't?"

"My sister's full of dreamy nonsense like that."

"You don't believe in great love?"

He gave her a drop-dead sexy smile that nearly took her breath away. "I believe in great steaks, great sex and great horses. I'll let Shakespeare handle the great-love part."

"Such a pessimist," she accused with a laugh.

"A realist," he corrected. "I take it you disagree?"

She thought of her father, still lost in his memories of Beth Russell, and nodded. "If the feelings are strong enough, I think love can subjugate all common sense."

Adam made a derisive sound. "Romantic psychobabble. Where did you hear that? Some daytime talk show?"

"Haven't you ever been in love?"

"Of course. I'm very wise in matters of the heart."

"How old are you?"

"Thirty last May."

"You're awfully young to sound so jaded."

"And you're awfully old to still hold on to fantasies."

It occurred to Jess she was enjoying this conversation. Perhaps too much for her own good. "I think I'll hold on to them all the same,'' she said and made a clumsy attempt to rise.

Adam came to his feet quickly, offering a hand up. His warm, dry clasp encircled her fingers. She lifted her head, just enough to meet his eyes, wondering what he was thinking—this strange, handsome man who could be so charming when he chose to be and so irritatingly arrogant when he did not. For a long time they simply stared at each other.

Her hand was still in his. She saw the spark of interest flare in his eyes and felt her own body respond with sensual delight. ''I'd better be getting back,'' she said.

He nodded absently and released her. But a moment later her escape was halted when his hand curved around her bare arm. ''Jess, wait a minute.''

She looked up at him. His breath flowed softly against her cheek as he studied her features one by one, then brought his fingers to her jaw. Lightly he let his thumb stray back and forth across her chin for slow, mesmerizing moments.

''Such a small, determined chin,'' he murmured huskily.

And then suddenly, his fingers stumbled to a halt. His eyes shifted to a dark expression of doubt and conflict. The peculiar intimacy between them vanished on the hot summer breeze.

He rubbed vigorously along her jaw, in the brisk, matter-of-fact way of a mother tidying a naughty child. In a practical tone he said, ''A woman so set on finding true love shouldn't walk around with dirt on her chin.''

CHAPTER FIVE

IN A BLUR OF MOTION and thundering hooves, Midnight Star flew past the railing, moving so fast that a hot breeze fanned Jess's cheeks. Beside her, Doc snapped off the stopwatch, then gave a whistle of excited pleasure. The morning times had been encouraging, and watching the animal, Jess could understand why the horse was considered the stable's best hope for the future.

"He's a beauty," she observed. "Can he go the distance, do you think?"

"He's got the heart for it," Doc replied. "Connor would like him brought up to speed for a claiming race come November."

Jess ducked her head to hide her delight. They'd been at Rising Star nearly three weeks, and she had never seen her father look better. He glowed with good health and self-assurance. There was a jauntiness to his step that she hadn't seen in ages. More important, to her knowledge he hadn't had a drink since their arrival. Maybe now she could relax and shake the guilt she felt about not telling Adam about Doc's problem.

"You're enjoying this, aren't you, Papa?"

He gave her a considering look and then nodded. "I'll tell you the truth, pony-girl. It feels good to be back with the 'breds. Even better than before. Do you remember my last year at Carraway when we had four hundred in training? You run that many and you don't have time to appreciate the potential you find in a particular horse." He removed his pipe from his mouth and tapped it against the white railing to clear the bowl. "But here you get to know the individual animal, and it means more to you when they start to prove out."

"You were right about coming here. This is the kind of environment you need."

"Perhaps," her father conceded. "But I do long for a good game of poker with Zola and the boys. These barn lads have no head for cards. They're only interested in fighting little space invaders on their computer games.

"Maybe I should ask Zola to come for a visit."

"Oh, aye, that'd be grand. I've missed the old girl."

The note of enthusiasm in her father's voice made Jess look at him sharply. "Do I sense a special interest in the thought of seeing Zola again?"

Her father blushed and eyed her with a trapped expression. "The woman has a good heart, and she fancies herself my protector. But there's no sense in matchmaking, pony-girl. I don't think of her *that* way."

Jess wasn't convinced. From watching the two of them at the carnival, she knew that Zola and her father had shared a certain closeness. Although the woman looked nothing like Beth Russell, Zola's zest for living was amazingly similar. She didn't pass through life, she grabbed it by the throat. Doc had spent many evenings in her trailer good-naturedly arguing everything from politics to whether aromatic therapy really worked. Sometimes he had come home in a royal snit, claiming the fortune-teller was hopelessly inflexible and deliberately provoking. But Jess wondered if her father was aware of how often he said those words with a twinkle in his eye and the beginnings of a smile playing along his lips.

For now, she decided not to push the issue. She made

a mental note to send an invitation to the fortune-teller as quickly as possible. Shading her eyes against the bright sunlight, Jess squinted across to the far side of the track, where several of the barn boys were walking Thorough-breds. Angela's favorite, Tim Rogers, was among them.

She motioned toward him. "What kind of fellow is Tim?"

"As a worker, or as a boyfriend for the young miss?" Doc inquired with a wry smile.

"Both, I suppose. Angela's completely besotted with him."

Her father frowned. "I've seen the looks that pass between those two and suspected as much. That's no good, lass. The boy shows promise, but he needs to keep his mind on his duties, not the owner's sister. Connor's not likely to appreciate his interest."

"Why?" Jess asked, dragging her attention quickly away from the line of sleek horses so she could focus on her father's response. For some reason, it made her uncomfortable to think that Adam would object to his sister's fledgling romance with the groom.

"You know how it is between breeders and barn help. 'Tisn't done," Doc replied obliquely.

"Those archaic class barriers went out with the Nehru jacket."

"What's this? No one wears Nehru jackets anymore?" Doc commented. He inspected the bowl of his pipe and grimaced.

"I'm serious."

Doc cocked a bushy red eyebrow her way. "So am I. You know the unspoken rules these breeders play by. It's no different here than it was in Lexington. I'll keep my eye on the lad, and you should encourage Angela to turn her attentions elsewhere."

"Doc..."

"Gibson!" Doc called toward the exercise rider on Midnight Star. "Come 'round, lad, before you take the quarter turn."

Jess watched her father walk along the railing to meet the horse and rider halfway, still thinking about their conversation. Was Doc right about Adam's reaction to a romance between Angela and Tim?

Growing up in the close-knit environment of breeders and trainers, Jess had been conscious of a tacit understanding between those who could afford the finest horses money could buy and those who trained and cared for them. Owners worked closely with the hired help, but they seldom socialized with them, and the transient, distracting nature of "barn romances" had always been considered undesirable by both sides. But those days were over, weren't they? And even if there were a few old-fashioned holdouts among the breeders, surely Adam Connor wasn't one of them.

She thought of how protective he was of his younger sister. And the conversations they'd shared had left her with the impression that he was a man who cared a great deal about reputation and appearances. Perhaps too much. The thought left her feeling unaccountably morose.

Motioning the exercise rider back to the track, her father returned to her side. Jess envied Doc his ability to find contentment at Rising Star, something that seemed to elude her completely. She'd written three letters to Zola, worked her way through the *P*'s at the public library, and taken up knitting with disastrous results. Her leg itched in places she couldn't reach—even with an unbent coat hanger—and she felt awkward and humiliatingly unattractive clomping around in the cast. Most of the time she was either grumpy or bored or both.

"Doc, what's Adam Connor like to work for?" The question seemed to pop out before she realized she'd spoken.

Doc didn't hesitate. Removing his pipe from between his teeth, he used the stem to stress his opinion. "Good with the horses. Fair with his men. He's more intense about producing a winner than some I've trained for. Probably because he's got more to lose than the syndicate that owned Carraway. The barn boys say he's determined to make a name for Rising Star."

The exercise rider brought the big black horse to a halt beside the fence. In a soft, even-tempered voice, her father explained the mistakes the man had made in handling the animal. Midnight Star danced and threw his head, as though agreeing and anxious to prove he could do better.

When the man had kneed the Thoroughbred away from the railing and cantered down the track, Doc cocked a look her way. "Why do you ask?"

"Just curious, I suppose."

"You may not work for Rising Star officially, but the same rules apply. Don't set your cap for that one, pony-girl."

"For heaven's sake, I'm not setting my cap for anyone." Unaccountably annoyed, Jess turned her head down the track and squinted into the morning sun. "I'm certainly not in the market for a man," she felt compelled to add.

"Never met a woman who wasn't in the market for a man, if the right one came up for grabs."

"Well, I'm not. But why do you think I shouldn't be interested?"

"You're asking just out of curiosity, of course," Doc said with a smile.

"Yes."

"I don't know exactly what Adam Connor is out to prove to the world about Rising Star, but a man with that big a commitment about something doesn't have time to woo a woman. Not proper-like. And not like my lassie deserves." He tapped his pipe against the railing again, then looked up from under his bushy red eyebrows to eye her closely. "Don't let him break your heart, lass," he said softly.

"He can't break my heart, Doc. He doesn't even know I'm alive."

"Ah, don't be too sure. I said the man's committed. Not dead."

She laughed and gave him a peck on the cheek. Telling herself that so much thought about Adam Connor was a waste of time, Jess gathered the items she'd collected in a bucket that morning from the cottage. She left the training track and headed toward the hay barn. Doc's pigs had found a roomy, well-shaded home in a small pen behind the building. Hog heaven, Jess thought with a smile.

The sows greeted her with grunts and squeals of welcome, trotting close for a handout. She fed them apples before getting down to business, and she had just finished tying a plastic garbage bag around her cast to keep it from getting wet when Angela came around the corner of the barn, dressed in one of her favorite purple T-shirts.

"Here you are!" she exclaimed. "I've been looking for you."

"What's up?"

"Would you like to come up to the house for lunch? Adam should be back from town soon. It's such a gorgeous day, I thought we could eat out on the patio by the pool."

The last thing Jess wanted to do was sit beside Adam Connor dressed in her cutoff jeans and faded T-shirt. She shook her head. "Sorry. I've got work to do. The girls need a bath."

"You're kidding. I thought pigs liked to wallow in mud."

"Not all the time. Actually, I think they enjoy the scrubbing more than the bath. Except for Carmen, they're pretty cooperative."

"Can I help?"

Jess looked up from the bucket where she was working water into soapsuds with a garden hose. "Are you sure you want to? It can get pretty messy."

"Sounds like fun. 'How I Spent My Summer Vacation,' by Angela Connor. The kids at school will love it."

Jess shrugged and handed the girl the hose. "Suit yourself. Just try not to get me wetter than the pigs, and don't squirt them unless I tell you to."

They worked together as a team. Jess soaped each sow, then scrubbed it briskly with a stiff brush. Angela refilled the bucket and rinsed off the animal. Musetta, the least assertive, submitted to the washing with only a few grunts of displeasure. Nedda trotted playfully out of reach when it was her turn and had to be captured by Angela. By the time they got to Carmen, both women were tired and soaked to the skin from trying to hold on to the wiggling, slippery porkers.

"Not as easy as it looks, is it?" Jess commented, trying to keep Carmen's sharp back hooves from spearing her thigh.

"Next time I'll ask Tim to help us."

The pig squealed in outrage as the first soapy brush hit her haunches. "How's the romance of the century going?" Jess asked. "Has he asked you out yet?"

Angela shook her head. "I can't even get him to notice me."

"Well why don't you ask for help with your riding lessons?"

Angela's eyes slid away. She squirted water into the bucket. "I haven't started lessons yet."

"Why not?" Jess knew the gentle mare Adam had bought Angela had been delivered to the stables the day after she and Doc had arrived.

"Maybe it wasn't such a good idea, after all," the teenager said. "Adam's been too busy to push me, but the more I think about it, the less I want to ride."

Jess stopped running the brush back and forth across Carmen's shoulders. She gave the young girl a sharp look. "Angela, are you really that terrified of horses?"

Angela nodded with a slight look of embarrassment.

"Why?"

"I fell off once. That's how I hurt my leg." Her features twisted in frustration. "I want Tim to notice me, but every time I think about getting close to a horse, I feel like I'm going to faint."

"Maybe I could help. I'm bored to tears here. Teaching you to ride would give me something to do. What do you say?"

"I don't know…"

"We can take it slow."

"You wouldn't make me do anything I really didn't want to do?" Angela asked hesitantly.

"Of course not. We'll go as slow as you want," Jess promised. Carmen grunted angrily and tossed her head, spraying soapsuds over them both. "I guarantee, hanging on in the saddle will be a lot easier than trying to hang on to Carmen." She slapped the recalcitrant pig on the rear end. "Hold still, you miserable swine, or you'll be Christmas dinner."

"Well," a light, feminine voice broke through their

laughter. "I don't remember *this* from the last tour you gave me, Adam."

Jess and Angela looked up quickly, surprised to find they were no longer alone. Adam had come around the corner of the barn, one arm entwined with that of a tall, good-looking blonde. Despite the heat of the day, the woman looked cool and elegant in a white silk dress that swirled in soft folds around her trim legs.

Jess straightened, embarrassingly aware of her own splotched and ragged clothing and the rustle of the garbage bag around her cast. With a gleeful squeal, Carmen saw her chance to escape. She slipped out of Jess's grasp to trot around the pen, trailing suds.

"Some project for summer school, dear?" the woman asked Angela. "Don't they do car washes to raise money anymore?"

The mocking tone in the stranger's voice made Jess glance at Angela anxiously. The girl made a low sound of dislike deep in her throat, and Jess knew that whoever this woman was, Adam's sister didn't like her. Her hand had tightened around the nozzle of the garden hose, and for one awful moment, Jess suspected the worst would happen. Then, thankfully, Adam stepped into the uncomfortable silence.

"You met my new consultant over at the training track," he explained to the woman. "This is Murdock Russell's daughter, Jess. Jess, I'd like you to meet Tianna Bettencourt, a neighbor of ours. And an old friend."

Jess shortened the distance between them by hobbling to the fence, her hand outstretched. But before she got even halfway there, Tianna backed away in horrified surprise and gave a quick shake of her head.

"If you don't mind... This is silk. I'd rather not risk a water spot."

Jess halted. She knew in that moment that she and this woman were not destined to be friends. "Of course. That's always such a worry with silk, isn't it?" She wiggled her bagged leg toward the woman. "You never have that problem with plastic. Nice to meet you."

She caught a twitch of amusement on Adam's lips, but Tianna barely acknowledged Jess had spoken. "Shame on you, Adam," she said in a well-modulated tone. She leaned against his arm and laid her hand against his cheek, a touch Jess assumed was meant to convey a reprimand. "I've spent years trying to turn Angela into a proper young lady. How could you let her backslide while I was in New York?"

"She's a teenager, Ti," Adam said mildly. "Leave her alone. She'll have to fit into the real world soon enough."

"It's never too early to start," Tianna returned. Her sharp glance raked up and down the younger girl. "When are you going to give up this ridiculous obsession with purple, Angela? It's simply not your color. And what in the world have you been doing? Rolling in the mud with these creatures?"

Angela's quivering anger was nearly palpable. "I like this color. And I'm helping Jess give her father's pigs a bath. It's called *work*, Tianna. Something you wouldn't know anything about."

The woman laughed at that. It was plain that this was an old feud between the two, though Jess suspected the animosity ran deeper on Angela's side. Uncomfortable, Jess looked to Adam to intervene, but his expression was one of weary detachment.

"Dear Angela," Tianna said, redefining a pleat in her sleeve with long, graceful fingers. "Haven't I explained the importance of appearances often enough? You're one of the owners of Rising Star. You don't wash pigs." The woman's cool blue gaze slipped to Jess, as if to imply she was somehow to blame.

Jess struggled to keep her irritation under control. Tianna's lightly veiled barbs couldn't hurt her if she didn't let them. While Adam's sister and the woman on his arm lapsed into another rancorous exchange, Jess hobbled over to the spigot to turn off the hose. Catching Carmen in a corner, she poured the remaining water from the bucket over the pig, rinsing off the last of the soap.

Pushing wet tendrils of hair out of her face with the back of one hand, Jess straightened. She stretched to pull the kinks out of her spine—and found Adam watching her. Faint humor lifted the corners of his mouth, and the look in his eyes made her breath catch in her throat. Self-conscious, she jerked her gaze away, finding sudden interest in collecting the brush and soap.

Carmen was still squealing with displeasure, trotting around the pen and flinging drops of water everywhere. Tianna backed away from the fence quickly. Her lips curled in distaste. "My God, Adam. Pigs! Have you lost your mind? You've turned Rising Star into a sharecropper's dream."

This accusation stretched the last of Jess's patience. She let the bucket slip from her fingers. With as much dignity as her cast allowed, she strode to the fence, her insides churning.

"Miss Bettencourt," she snapped with barely suppressed fury. "Mr. Connor was kind enough to provide a home for these animals while my father is employed here. In my book, that makes him generous, not insane. And while I'll admit they're not as noble-looking as a Thoroughbred, it's a proven fact that a pig is smarter than almost any other animal. And maybe even a few humans I've met," she couldn't resist adding with a pointed look.

There was a moment of stunned silence. Then Angela laughed out loud. Jess waited in dread. Since it was obvious Adam cared for Tianna, she expected a curt reprimand. When it didn't come, she lifted her eyes to his and saw an odd, speculative interest.

Meanwhile, Tianna's vivid red lips were parted in surprise. She regarded Jess with renewed interest and the slightest hint of unease. Clearly, she hadn't given Jess much consideration in her continuing verbal battle with Angela. Now she favored this new adversary with a slow, calculating look, like a boxer sizing up an opponent.

She smiled, a faint pretense, and laid her head against Adam's arm and addressed him. "My apologies, darling. You know I love to tease you. But it's much too hot to be wandering around down here. Let's go up to the house for a swim." She rubbed her cheek against his shoulder with all the subtlety of a kitten begging its owner for a scratch. "I spent a small fortune in New York with you in mind, and I've got a new swimsuit I'm dying to model for you."

Before Tianna indulged in full-blown purring, Jess turned her attention elsewhere. She nibbled at her bottom lip uncertainly, watching Carmen undo all her hard work by rolling in the dirt. She wished Tianna and Adam would go. Why didn't they? Obviously there was nothing here that could interest either one of them.

Feeling Adam's stare, Jess turned her head. Their eyes met in a brief flicker of private understanding while Tianna finished playing out her scene for Angela's benefit. There was a new warmth in his steady regard, a touch of mischief in his glance, and Jess found that suddenly her heart seemed to be taking up an uncomfortably large portion of her chest.

Shaken, she sucked in a labored breath and found refuge in trying to corner Carmen once again. Eventually, Adam and Tianna moved away, and from beneath lowered lashes Jess watched them depart. They moved with the ease of experienced lovers, their similarity in heights emphasizing their suitability for each other. Tianna's blond delicacy was a striking contrast to Adam's dark handsomeness. Jess had to admit, they were an attractive couple. Perfect for one another.

Beside her, Angela released a low sound of hissing dislike. "That witch."

"She *is* a little..." Jess searched for the right word, careful to avoid adding fuel to Angela's fire. "Condescending."

The younger girl made a small huff of frustration. "She's a vain, egotistical viper. I'll never understand what Adam sees in her."

With a laugh, Jess picked up the bucket and bent to gather her supplies. "You can't? Open your eyes, Angela. She's beautiful."

"Not inside, where it counts. Do you know what Tianna's nickname is?" When Jess shook her head, she said, "Iwanna. As in, 'Iwanna new car—Iwanna trip to Paris—Iwanna husband'!" Angela imitated in a grating whine. The teenager dropped beside Jess. Her voice went conspiratorially low. "And I think I know who she's decided she wants."

Jess turned a glance toward Adam, who at that moment had lowered his head to catch his companion's words. He nodded, and though Jess couldn't see his face, she wouldn't have been surprised to find an indulgent smile pasted across his lips. "Your brother didn't look like he'd mind."

Angela frowned and turned to watch Adam and Tianna

disappear around the corner of the barn. "That," she said grimly, "is exactly what worries me."

THAT EVENING after dinner, Jess left her father snoring softly in front of the television and hobbled out to the barns. The quiet of the summer evening folded around her like a steamy cloak. The air was heavy, humid, and the enormous oaks near the cottage rustled and creaked against one another, fretted by a stiff breeze that promised rain.

The farm's pleasure mounts were quartered in Barn Four, a structure older and smaller than the others. The wide door scraped on reluctant hinges as she entered. Light bloomed in golden pools along the walls, cast by old-fashioned carriage lamps that caressed the fine wood in a mellow glow.

Jess closed her eyes and let the smells and sounds of the barn fill her senses. She had always found a homey, simple enjoyment in the mingled odors of horses and hay, hand-rubbed leather and the sweet richness of grain laced with molasses. She heard the dull thud of a stamped hoof, the restive movements of one of the six horses that occupied the barn, and thought of her childhood with nostalgia.

These horses couldn't match their expensive, pampered counterparts in the other barns, but they were good-tempered animals and willing to perform well for the right master. Jess located the stall where Angela's new mount had been boarded. As she approached the cubicle, the mare, a pretty gray with black-dapple haunches, lifted her head over the half door and offered a welcoming whinny.

Dipping into the pocket of her jeans, Jess fished out several pieces of carrot. While the mare lipped the treat off her hand, she stroked the animal's neck and crooned softly in ways learned at her father's knee. The gray listened attentively, her ears flicking forward and back against her head.

"Oh, you're a sweetheart, aren't you?" Jess praised. "You'll be a good girl for Angela. You wouldn't hurt her, now, would you?" The animal nudged Jess's arm, searching for more carrots. Brass winked a dull gleam along the mare's leather halter, and in the dim light Jess tried to read the name plate attached there. "What's your name, sweet one?"

"Misty Lady," a voice behind Jess supplied, and she whirled to find Adam Connor standing across the corridor in the doorway of the barn's small tack room. "She's as pretty as her name, don't you think?"

In the lamplit shadows, his features seemed softer, the stern harshness in his manner replaced by a gentle warmth. He wore age-polished denims with athletic grace and overpowering masculinity. Jess's heart leaped. With acute, sudden perception, she faced the inescapable fact that no matter how she felt about this man—no matter how he might perplex or annoy her—her body would always be willing to respond to the incredible force of his presence.

She drew a nervous breath as he uncoiled from the doorway to approach her. He stopped only a foot away, so close she could see the golden flecks dancing in his brown eyes.

"You look pale," Adam said. "I didn't mean to frighten you."

Still stroking the mare's glossy neck, Jess shook her head. "You didn't." Actually, he did frighten her. A lot. But not the way he meant. "I just wasn't expecting anyone to be out here."

"We'll have rain later tonight and the wind's kicking up. I like to make sure everything's buttoned down."

"Don't you have night watchmen in the barns to see to that, and keep an eye on your mares in foal?"

"Only one. We're not big enough yet to warrant more. But to tell the truth, this is a habit of mine that refuses to die. I like checking up on things after everyone's called it a night and the barns are quiet."

Lamplight gleamed on a lock of hair spilling across his forehead. Jess struggled against the urge to lift her hand and sweep it back into place. In an effort to divert her mind from such foolishness, she commented, "You have some beautiful horses here. Do you get much chance to ride?"

"Not as much as I'd like to." He shook his head regretfully. "Too busy."

"What a shame."

"Some sacrifices can't be avoided if I'm going to make Rising Star what it can be. What it was *meant* to be," he amended. "Do you ride? What am I saying? Of course you do. You're Murdock Russell's daughter."

Murdock Russell's daughter. That name had always implied knowledge and skill, and complete trust as well. Did it still? She wondered what Adam would think if he knew the truth about her father. Would he despise Doc...and maybe her as well? She shook off the unpleasant thought and forced her lips into a smile. "I rode before I could walk. By the time I was Angela's age, I had a two-year-old running in a stakes race. A bald-faced filly named Pie in the Sky." The suggestion of sorrow touched her lips as she sighed. "God, I loved that horse."

"How'd she do?"

"Ran fifth—consistently. It broke my heart when she had to be sold, but you know how it is when you have an animal that doesn't produce. We weren't in a position to keep her.''

Adam nodded in understanding, and a long moment passed as they both stroked Misty Lady's neck from each side. It was a thoughtful, companionable silence, broken only by the sound of wind whipping around the eaves of the barn, making the dark beams overhead groan and creak.

Adam went inside the tack room, came out carrying a large horse blanket, then moved to a nearby stack of baled hay. ''Why don't we sit awhile? We can talk.''

''What about?'' she asked uneasily.

He gave her a distinctly challenging glance. ''Does there have to be a specific topic?'' He spread the blanket over the hay, then patted the seat next to him. ''I won't bite.''

She did as he asked, though not without some misgivings about the advisability of sitting so close. There was no hint of snobbery or cynicism in his features, merely the gentle offer of friendship. He smiled at her as she settled beside him, and the sheer force of that smile rocked her.

Together they sat in the warm cocoon of the barn and listened as outside, thunder rumbled, making one of the horses along the line of stalls snort and paw nervously. Jess watched as Adam rose and moved to the animal's box, stroking the neck of a black gelding and talking to it in a low, soothing voice. She could see he had a way with horses himself; after a time, the animal blew lustily and went back to munching hay from the overhead rick.

''Vadar doesn't like storms,'' Adam said, returning to her side.

''You're very good with them.''

''That surprises you?''

She gave him a noncommittal smile and turned her head away. Yes, it did surprise her. She'd expected him to be too businesslike, too practical to realize there were times when a kind word was as important to an animal as the most determined discipline. Adam didn't seem the type of man to indulge a fanciful fear of storms.

He raised an eyebrow in her direction. "There's a lot about me you find surprising, isn't there?"

"I beg your pardon?"

"You don't like me very much, do you?"

She paused long seconds without speaking. Jess had no desire to quarrel with the man. "I don't know you well enough to answer that. You've certainly been very kind to my father."

He dismissed her response with a quick frown. "Kindness didn't enter into it. It made good business sense to take advantage of an opportunity that presented itself."

"I'm sure there are many nice things that can be said about you."

"Such as…"

"Your sister adores you."

He shrugged. "Not much of a surprise since I'm the only family she's got."

"My father says the men respect you."

He nodded. "I pay well."

She floundered under his expectant gaze. With a touch of asperity, she said, "Look, if you'll give me a couple of days, I'll work up a list of your good qualities and slip them under the front door."

He laughed. "Sorry. Did it sound like I was fishing for compliments? I wasn't. I was merely trying to figure out why—given your rather skeptical opinion of my character—you were so quick to jump to my defense this afternoon."

"I don't recall that I did."

"I do. Quite vividly. Tianna can be…undiplomatic at times. But with the exception of Angela, I don't believe anyone's ever tackled her head-on before, and certainly not for my sake."

"I was defending Doc's pigs," Jess explained, shifting uncomfortably on the hay. "Not you."

A smile hovered at the corners of his mouth. "I see."

Time moved slowly. Jess cleared her throat and tried to ignore the knot of apprehension that tightened within her. She didn't want to discuss his good qualities or why a man like him should feel the need to cater to a she-wolf like Tianna Bettencourt.

In an effort to change the subject, she said at last, "I was wondering if I could speak to you about Angela."

Adam's eyebrows nudged together as he turned to look at her. "What about her?"

"She's hoping you'll forget about those riding lessons."

"I suspected as much, but I've been so busy I haven't had a chance to encourage her. Buying Misty Lady was her idea, and I can't let the horse just stand idle. By the end of the month, she'll be so barn sour we won't be able to get her out of the stall."

"I could teach Angela to ride."

He inclined his head toward her cast. "What about that?"

"It's inconvenient, but I've ridden in a cast before. If you'll loan me the use of a mount, I could start tomorrow. Angela's willing."

Adam seemed to give the idea serious consideration. At last he said, "It won't be easy."

"I think I can help her overcome her fear."

His gaze met hers, questioning, and in his eyes Jess

saw a momentary hesitation and then a touch of guilt. "Did she tell you how she got that limp?" he asked slowly.

"No."

"It was my fault." A heavy sigh escaped his lips, and he fixed a stare down the barn's long corridor. She watched a muscle bunch and roll at the side of his jaw, testimony to the sudden tension within him. Quietly he said, "I was fourteen when Angela was born. I'd given up hope for a brother or sister, so by the time she came along, I was so excited that it didn't even matter she was a girl." His lips curved into a smile. "She was beautiful, and so small. I loved her right away, and amazingly, by the time she was two she was following me everywhere. I couldn't wait until we could ride together."

His hand moved to pluck at the ragged edges of hay captured in a wire-bound bale. "One day I took her out to the front pasture and put her on my horse. It was an adolescent, foolish thing to do, but I was excited, you see, thinking she would love it. Being so high off the ground. On a horse—just like big brother. Stupid," he said with a vehement shake of his head. "So stupid.

"We walked around the pasture and I had a pretty solid hold on the back of her shirt. She loved it. And then my horse started to dance around a little, just enough that I couldn't control him and keep a tight hold on Angela. She slid off and landed awkwardly. Her leg was broken in two places, and it never healed properly."

"You must have been devastated," Jess stated in a strained whisper.

"It was so sudden, I couldn't believe it happened. My mother cried for days. Until her dying day she blamed me for ruining my sister's life."

"But it was an accident!"

Adam shook his head, crushing the golden shafts of hay he had pulled from the bale as he made a tight fist. "Didn't matter," he said, his voice scraping low. "My recklessness, my impulsiveness, kept my sister out of everything from ballet to cheerleading. That day taught me a lot about thinking things through. I don't make many rash decisions anymore."

Jess sat very still, studying Adam's stony profile. Compassion flowed through her, making it difficult to hold on to indifference toward him.

"Are you always so hard on yourself, Adam?"

He turned to look at her. The relaxed lines of his mouth tightened, and an odd despair stole over his features.

"I'm afraid that I'm often…not nearly tough enough," he replied in a slow, quiet tone. He reached out, stroking a line down the length of her cheek with one lazy finger movement that seemed to take her breath with it. "Oh, Jessie…" His voice came deep and throaty, yet her name held the reverence of a prayer. "How can you present such a big problem?"

Her chest constricted as Adam's warm touch caused reason to slip from her control. A surge of excitement sent crisp shivers down her spine. "I—I don't understand."

"Neither do I." His fingers found her chin, cupping it with care as he returned her gaze. Adam's lashes swept down, and the heavy-lidded sultriness in his eyes brought an answering clamor of blood in her veins. "I just know you make me long for things I have no business longing for."

"What sort of things?" she whispered.

He touched her lower lip with the light, tender quest of one finger. "Kisses, my sweet gypsy-witch."

Dipping her head, she caught the tip of his finger with her teeth. She nipped it playfully, then released it. "For heaven's sake, Adam, a kiss isn't a lifetime commitment. Sometimes it's just...a kiss.''

He frowned. "And if one isn't enough...?"

A strange, hungering frustration she could not explain overtook her, and she heard herself say, "Kiss me and find out, Adam. For once, obey your impulses."

He frowned at her, clearly unconvinced about the advisability of such actions. But before he could formulate a refusal, she leaned forward and brought her lips against his.

She had intended it to be only a small kiss, a quick demonstration of what he might be missing. He was far too serious for his own good, and it couldn't hurt to melt some of that stuffy reserve of his. Just a little. *Just once*.

She could tell the kiss surprised him. She felt the tension in his body, but only for a moment.

In the blink of an eye his lips went from cool and unresponsive to warm and welcoming, and then *she* was the one left wondering about the advisability of indulging impulses. He stroked and nibbled, encouraging her to taste him by lingering degrees. In no time he reduced the air in her lungs and made her breathing difficult.

She felt his mouth curve upwardly against hers as he smiled, and she opened her eyes, caught between astonishment and pleasure. There was a hint of challenge in his gaze.

She pulled away.

Adam straightened, and she realized that his breathing was no steadier than hers. She watched a tight smile of regret drift across his lips before he shook his head. "I had hoped that one would be enough," he said in a voice hardly more than a whisper. "But it's not going to work, is it?"

CHAPTER SIX

By morning Jess was half convinced she'd imagined the whole episode. The rain had died in the night, and by eight o'clock the sun was already climbing up, promising another hot, summer day. In the bright familiarity of the cottage, that moment of warm intimacy in the shadowy barn held a dreamlike quality. Maybe it had never happened.

Oh, right, Dorothy. Now click your ruby slippers and see if you can whisk yourself back to Kansas.

It had been real, all right. Delightfully real.

Unfortunately, it had also been embarrassingly apparent that she had handled the retreat from that kiss with far less composure and grace than she'd approached it. She'd meant it to be light. Fun. At the very most, nothing more than a little lesson about finding enjoyment in the things life offered. No big deal.

Instead, she had jumped down from the hay bale, trembling like a frightened rabbit. Without a single backward glance, she'd left Adam alone in the barn. There had been a momentary howl of protest as she wrested control of the wide wooden door away from the wind, but Jess had hardly noticed it. Her mouth had still been moist from his kiss, and her heart...well, her heart had been spiraling into a whirlpool of tumbled emotions.

She wished she'd had the courage to stay behind and confront him, demand to know the meaning of his words.

What sort of problem did she present? What wouldn't work? As usual, the confusing man created more questions within her than he answered. But there had been another part of her, the cautious, cowardly part, that shied away from that knowledge. Some things, it warned her, were far better left undisturbed.

She set the breakfast dishes to soak in the sink and found herself dwelling on the sweetness of Adam's lips, the softness of his breath as it had coasted along her cheek. Her fingers lifted to trace the path he had followed along her flesh. His touch had been gentle, caring. An exquisite tenderness completely unexpected in such a man.

And far too desirable.

Pouring herself a cup of coffee, Jess tired to reason with herself. This was silly. She was placing far too much importance on a little kiss. She ought to pretend it had never occurred, which was probably what Adam was going to do. After all, it appeared he could count on Tianna Bettencourt for as many kisses as a guy could want, and as the daughter of a fellow horse breeder, she'd be a lot more desirable than a trainer's daughter—no matter how lofty Doc's reputation.

Besides, Jess remembered with a twinge of guilt, she was still withholding the truth about her father. Dishonesty wasn't a very admirable way to start a relationship.

She wasn't fool enough to say she was sorry Adam had kissed her. Or to deny that his touch hadn't brought an impassioned response shuddering through her own body. But for the sake of her emotional well-being, she couldn't dwell on it.

A knock at the door interrupted her thoughts and she opened it to find Tim Rogers standing there. The boy handed her an envelope. She recognized the Rising Star emblem in the top left-hand corner.

Squaring her shoulders, Jess slid one finger under the flap and read the bold, masculine script quickly.

> Jess,
> I've instructed Bill Page to put Vadar at your disposal. He'll give you a good ride as long as you keep him out of storms. You seem to have a natural instinct with animals and people. I trust your judgment to find a way to get Angela on Misty Lady.
>
> A.

Absently she folded the letter and returned it to the envelope. She cleared her mind, forcing herself to think of nothing except how pleased she should be by the prospect of teaching Angela.

And if, in some quiet corner of her brain Jess wondered how Adam chose to remember last night, she now had her answer. He, too, was going to pretend it had never happened.

OVER THE NEXT THREE WEEKS she took a deeper interest in her veterinary studies, concentrated on improving her culinary skills and spent hours with Angela in the paddock. The riding lessons progressed well, although it had taken some time before she was able to coax the teenager into sitting on Misty Lady while Jess led her. Considering the depth of the girl's fear, she showed remarkable perseverance. In time, they advanced to slow rides along the dirt trails that wove throughout the property and surrounding woods.

She had not spoken to Adam again, though she saw him on two occasions. Once, he nodded curtly to her as he got into his convertible. A second time she discovered him watching her as she finished a lesson with Angela. He stood at the railing, making no attempt to call out a greeting or approach them. A short time later when Jess looked up, he was gone.

From Angela she learned that Adam had been away from the farm a great deal. He worked closely with the Florida Thoroughbred Breeders' Association, lobbying for more support for the state's breeding industry. Even so, Jess suspected she would have seen little of him had he been at the farm every day. It was evident he simply saw no reason to seek out her company.

So why couldn't *she* forget that kiss? More and more she found the memory of it hovering at the edge of her conscious thoughts, peppering her dreams at night and stealing into her waking moments with the most disconcerting frequency. It was damned irritating.

And the knowledge that Adam Connor obviously had no problem chasing that memory out of his thoughts only made matters worse.

AFTER CONTINUAL URGING from Jess, Zola came to Rising Star for a short visit. She claimed she wanted to check on her sister, who lived in the area and had been recuperating from gall bladder surgery since the day Jess had been coerced into that disastrous stint as carnival fortune teller.

But secretly, Jess wondered if the older woman's sister wasn't just a handy excuse. During their numerous letters back and forth, Jess had repeatedly extended an invitation. Zola had never agreed to come...until Doc had added a postscript to one letter: *What are you waiting for, wretched woman? An engraved invite? I miss you. Come see us.*

Within a week, the fortune teller had called to say she would.

Jess found it very interesting that, in spite of a hectic training schedule, her father found the time to meet Zola's bus at the Ocala station. She noticed too, that, when the front door of the cottage banged open and the woman entered in a blur of long, flowing hair and glinting bangle bracelets, Doc was laughing, in a deep, hearty way she hadn't heard in a long time.

During Zola's stay she became aware of other things, too. Little clues too meaningful to be ignored. The tender smile that came to the older woman's lips as she watched Doc work. Zola remembering how Doc liked his tea sugared—one level spoonful slipped over the ice before pouring the liquid in. And unexpectedly, the realization that Zola occasionally cheated at cards—in her father's favor!

In Jess's mind, it all added up to one thing—love. But every time she tried to pin the woman down about her feelings, she outmaneuvered her with vague comments and mysterious smiles. It was infuriating.

Finally, on the morning of Zola's departure, they stood at the track fence, watching Doc give instructions to a couple of exercise riders. Unable to bear it any longer, Jess turned her head toward the fortune teller and pierced her with a determined look.

"Are you in love with Papa?" she asked.

If she had expected to unnerve the woman, she was disappointed. Zola watched the action on the track for a long moment before she met Jess's gaze. "I wondered if you would finally find the courage to ask."

"Well?" she prodded amicably. "Are you?"

"Of course," Zola responded with a smile. "Your father can be a very charming man. Who would not love him?"

Jess frowned. "You know what I mean."

"Did that seem an evasive answer to you? It was not. Murdock's skill and powers of persuasion are not reserved solely for horses and the men who work for him."

The exercise boys finished their runs and brought their mounts cantering back toward Doc. He met them halfway, moving down the track with the purposeful strides of a man half his age. The stiff morning breeze had raked his red hair into wild disarray, and Jess was struck by the thought that her father was ruggedly handsome. He could have been a Highland chieftain marching across a battle-field. Zola would make a good match for him. But would *he* ever see that?

"Have you told him how you feel?" she asked.

"I did not have to. He knows."

"And what does he intend to do about it?"

"Do?" Zola repeated. She turned her attention to Jess once more. "Why, nothing. How can he? Your father is still married. To a ghost."

Jess felt her heart tighten in sympathy for the other woman. She knew the truth in those words—and it was so unfair! She saw the translucent beauty of Zola's features, knew the decent, loyal strength of her character. Why couldn't her father see what was right in front of his nose?

"Oh, Zoe," Jess said around the constriction in her throat. "I'm so sorry."

Zola met her somber gaze. "Don't be. The day will come when he leaves the past behind. I have 'seen' it. There is a future for us together, and when the time is right, it will happen. Until then, I will be patient."

Did the fortune teller really believe that? Or was she simply putting on a good front for Jess's sake? Knowing there were no easy solutions to be found, Jess tried to offer a hopeful smile of her own. "I'll do everything I can to help. I want Papa to be happy again."

The woman nodded agreement, and they dropped the subject. For the next few minutes they watched as Doc sent one of the exercise riders back to the stable and issued a new set of instructions to the one remaining. The boy slid out of his saddle and rushed away. Doc snagged the Thoroughbred's reins and walked toward the fence where the two women waited. The chestnut colt snorted in displeasure and pulled against the bit, but her father's hold was unbreakable.

"Raymond's going to get a pair of blinkers," Doc explained as he ran a calming hand down the colt's neck. "Could be he's just afraid of the rail and he'll do better if he doesn't see it."

Zola reached over the fence to place her hand on the animal's velvety nose. "What is this horse's name?"

"Kokomo. Connor bought him last week at an auction in Saratoga. He was fine until we started legging him up on the track."

Zola nodded and continued stroking the animal's head. In contrast to how Kokomo had behaved while he was being ridden by Raymond, he seemed content to stand still and accept the fortune teller's touch. When the exercise rider returned, and the new bridle with blinkers had been placed over the horse's head, Doc sent them back to work.

They disappeared down the track, and Doc turned toward the women again.

"So you're leaving us already," he said to Zola.

"Yes."

"I can't convince you to stay a little longer?"

"No. There will be other visits."

"I'm counting on that," he said, and although Jess was pleased to think that he sounded sincere, she found herself irritated with him, as well, for being so oblivious. Really, she wanted to shake him.

"I'll get the keys to the truck, and we can have breakfast in town before you go," Jess spoke up abruptly. "No sense standing around here."

She left them and headed in the direction of the cottage. Frowning, Doc watched her go. "I guess someone fell out of the wrong side of the bed this morning," he commented.

"She is unhappy here."

"Why?" he asked in some surprise. "I thought she'd love it. It's so much like Lexington. Better in some ways."

"Give her time. She has yet to understand her purpose here."

"And you know what that is, I suppose?"

She cocked her head at him. "Of course."

Her arms rested on the top rail of the fence. He placed his hands over hers. "Zoe, I never know when to take you seriously."

"You must always take me seriously, Murdock."

Grinning indulgently, he lowered his gaze. Zola's fingers were long, the tips blunt, and he realized how different they were from Beth's who had always complained that her hands were too thin and delicate to manage a horse properly.

He turned his attention back to the track and scowled. The blinkers were doing little good. Raymond was having a devil of a time getting the colt to focus. Twice the animal broke stride, and as they passed the gap in the fence that led toward the barn, the Thoroughbred tried to exit the track. It took all the boy's strength to turn the colt back.

Doc gave Raymond a waving arm signal that indicated

he should take Kokomo around a second time. "We don't have time for this," he muttered in sour annoyance. "If he doesn't cut out this nonsense, he'll be finding himself a new home."

"He is frightened," Zola said in a low, mysterious tone.

"Aye, he ought to be."

"I mean it, Murdock. Something has frightened him."

He couldn't help giving her a skeptical look. "Taken to reading hooves, have you?" he said with a snort of disbelief.

To his surprise, the woman straightened and favored him with a look she'd never given him in all the time he'd known her—disappointed irritation. Her lips compressed into a flat line, and she started to walk away. He leaned over the rail and caught her arm to bring her back to face him.

"My apologies, madame," he said quickly. "That was uncalled for. Please tell me what the poor beastie's got to be so upset about?"

He was relieved that she seemed willing to forgive him his rudeness. He had few friends left in his life, and he would not want to lose such a valuable one.

She shrugged. "I don't know. That is for you to find out."

"All right," he conceded. "I'll look into it."

They observed the horse and rider together in silence. In a few minutes, Jess pulled alongside the railing and honked the truck's horn.

Zola touched Doc's hand. "Till the next time, Murdock."

He watched her go, and realized suddenly that their relationship had undergone some subtle changes with this visit. He was beginning to appreciate her on a new, unspoken level. Maybe he missed having her around more than he knew.

She was halfway to the truck.

"Zoe!" he called after her.

She turned. Her long, flowing skirt caught in the morning breeze, swirling the material into a kaleidoscope of color. For the first time he noticed that she had good legs for a woman her age, and that momentary thought was so unbidden, so foreign to him, that he ended up frowning at her instead.

"Could you really 'read' that horse?" he asked gruffly.

Her mouth quirked into a smile. "Animals are easy, Murdock. They can't hide the truth." She had the most expressive dark eyes, and the look in them now left Doc feeling off balance, and suddenly vulnerable in an odd way. There was silence for a long moment, and then she added, "It's people who are the difficult ones. They cannot admit when they have a problem."

IT WAS LATE AFTERNOON by the time Jess and Angela rounded the curve in the road that led back to Rising Star. Tired and covered with trail dust, they'd ridden longer today than ever before. Jess was pleased. Though she doubted the younger girl would ever come to love riding, she felt certain Angela was making real progress.

The house came into view, sparkling in the summer sun like a jewel. Misty Lady and Vadar pricked up their ears and blew lustily, knowing an extra ration of oats awaited them.

Angela lifted her spine and drew a deep breath. "Hurrah! Home sweet home. I'm dying for a bath."

Jess slipped her hat off and slapped it against her thigh. A cloud of dust lifted off her jeans. "A bath sounds heavenly. I can't wait to get this cast off my leg and have a real soak.''

"What do you mean?''

"I've had to make do with sponge baths the past few weeks. There's no shower in the cottage, and as pretty as that old-fashioned tub is, it's too deep. I tried hanging my cast out of it and nearly drowned trying to get back up.''

"When does the cast come off?'' Angela asked.

"Not a moment too soon for me,'' Jess replied with a groan. She ran a finger around the sweaty collar of her blouse. "Don't ever break a bone in the summer. It's miserable.''

"Hmm.'' Angela looked thoughtful for a moment, then flashed Jess a huge grin. "I've got a wonderful idea.''

THIRTY MINUTES LATER, Adam pulled into the driveway in front of the house. He didn't glance in the direction of the barns and guest cottage but, instead, took the three front steps in a single leap. Normally, he couldn't resist standing on the porch and letting his eyes rove over the acreage that comprised Rising Star. It irritated him to realize that he'd altered an insignificant habit because of what he'd come to regard as "this foolish obsession.''

Kissing Jess Russell had been a big mistake. Better to have gone to his grave never knowing what her sweet lips could offer than face the knowledge that now made sleep impossible—the fact that he wanted more. The memory of that kiss had plagued him for weeks. He was tormented by a need he'd steadfastly refused to acknowledge, a need he'd foolishly tried to quench with one experimental kiss.

Exasperated, he'd driven himself hard these past few weeks, concentrating on worlds he could control and avoiding those he could not. He made vague excuses for long days and nights spent at the breeders' association office, discovered a sudden renewed interest in tennis at the club and even let one of his fellow breeders set him up on a date with a visiting board member of the racing commission.

The woman was attractive, poised and had seemed genuinely interested in his opinion of the latest regulations Florida had proposed to the commission. By the end of the evening, when he returned her to her hotel, she made no bones about the fact that taking her to bed would not hurt his standing with the board.

He couldn't do it.

In her company, he envisioned only the free-spirited charm of a woman who claimed pigs were as noble as the costliest racehorse, who thought nothing of lying face-down in his pasture to sniff the grass and who considered old hats the height of fashion. Jess Russell was fun, sensitive and—damn her to hell—she was ruining him for other women.

Lately he couldn't even seem to concentrate on the future. A future he'd been planning for seven years. The farm was all that mattered. All that *should* matter.

He ought to quit torturing himself and order her off Rising Star. Knowing she'd be out of his reach for good would go a long way toward easing her out of his thoughts. Except if *she* went, so did Doc Russell. And that he could not afford right now. So for the sake of Rising Star's future, she had to stay.

But for the sake of his own sanity, he'd have to keep away from her.

What a damned mess! he thought with a grim shake of his head as he entered the house. A prisoner of his own emotions. And there seemed to be absolutely nothing he could do about it.

He crossed the cool, tiled foyer, heading up the stairs

to change clothes. Maybe an afternoon swim would clear his head.

At the doorway to his bedroom, he ran smack into Angela, who blocked his way with arms crossed over her chest and stunned surprise hovering in her blue eyes. She looked worried, and, as he watched, her lower lip disappeared between her teeth.

Adam knew her too well not to recognize that tiny habit. His sister was in a panic about something and trying to work up the courage to do battle.

"What are you doing home?" she asked in a light tone that didn't hide her nervousness.

"I live here. Remember?" Not in any mood to play games, he crossed his own arms over his chest. "All right, Angel, what are you up to?"

"Nothing." But when Adam made a move to slip past her into his bedroom, her arm descended across the doorjamb like an iron bar. Fierce determination danced in her eyes. "Don't go in there."

"Why not?" he demanded.

"You'll spoil my surprise."

"What surprise?"

"What surprise," she muttered. She blinked several times, and her face suddenly lit with enthusiasm. "It won't be a surprise if I tell you, will it?" She gazed at him with a trapped, hopeful look. "Could you just go downstairs for a few minutes and wait for me? No! Out by the pool would be better."

Frowning, Adam studied her face, then decided he wasn't feeling generous enough right now to let her off the hook that easily. "I'm not going anywhere, and you have two seconds to start talking. What mischief are you up to?"

"I'm not up to anything," Angela objected hotly. "I

didn't think you'd be home for hours. You've been working late so much. It seemed like a perfect solution at the time and I didn't see the harm—''

She broke off this rapid litany of excuses as a tortured wail drifted out to them. It came from behind his closed bathroom door, an ominous succession of sounds both eerie and painful to the ear. No longer amused, Adam lifted his sister's arm out of the way and entered the room. Angela launched herself into his path, tugging on his arm.

He glared at her. ''What the hell is that?''

''It's Jess. She's taking a shower.''

''What?'' It was Adam's turn to look stunned. Unprepared for that answer, he sagged against the door.

Gradually he realized the sounds he heard were not the tormented noises of a wounded animal, merely the pitiful attempts to punish unschooled vocal cords into performing an operatic solo. Up and down the voice went, the subtle, melodic nuances of the piece reduced to wild plunges and shrill squeaks.

Adam hated opera.

''She's singing,'' Angela offered meekly. ''She likes opera.''

He winced as the woman hit a note that left his ears vibrating. ''Sounds like the barn cats fighting.'' He scowled at his sister. ''Why is she doing *that* in my bathroom?''

''You promise not to get mad?''

''I'm already past mad.''

''It was my idea.''

''Tell me.''

''Well...we had a long ride today. Jess says I'm really getting quite confident on Misty Lady.''

''Angela...''

"All right. But it's not Jess's fault. I know you don't like her, but this really was my idea."

Adam's eyebrows lifted at his sister's words. "What makes you think I don't like Jess? Did she say that?"

"No. But it's pretty obvious. You never bother to talk to her, and every time I mention her name you change the subject."

"I see. Go on."

Hesitantly, Angela explained about Jess's difficulties in taking a bath at the cottage. "So I suggested she tie a garbage bag over her cast and use your shower since it's so big. She didn't want to, but I convinced her you weren't coming home till late." The teenager favored him with a coaxing smile. "See? No big deal." The smile dimmed a little. "You're not mad, are you?"

The corner of his mouth lifted with the first genuine amusement he'd felt in days.

THE SHOWER FELT wonderful.

Exhausted from the long ride with Angela, Jess had turned the tap on full force, letting needles of hot water beat down into her stiffened shoulder blades and the cramped muscles in her forearms. Vadar gave a good ride, but he had a hard mouth, and it took all her upper body strength to keep the horse under control.

As much as Jess hated the thought of invading Adam's territory, his sister's idea had been too enticing to resist. For the first time in weeks she began to feel truly clean and refreshed as steam rose to surround her in a warm, hazy mist. She worked shampoo into her hair, letting the water sluice down her body into every tired, aching pore.

Invigorated, she burst into song—Violetta's farewell aria from *La Traviata*. With the tiled walls of the shower offering the proper acoustics, her voice didn't sound half-bad.

Not wanting to keep Angela waiting, Jess twirled the knob to the off position and scraped water out of her hair. Through the moisture-covered glass of the shower door she saw obscure movement. She opened it a crack and accepted the fluffy towel Angela offered her on one finger.

"Thanks. I'll be out in a second," Jess said with a contented sigh. She pressed the material to her dripping face, then frowned.

The hand offering that towel...had definitely been... *masculine!*

It can't be, Jess thought with a sinking feeling in the pit of her stomach. With the tips of her fingers, she swiped a patch of moisture from the glass and squinted out into the bathroom.

Adam Connor peered back at her, a smile stretched ear to ear on that smug, arrogant face.

Jess slammed the shower door shut. She clutched the towel to her body and stood dripping, her mind tumbling erratically to find some graceful way out of this predicament. Where was Angela? Why had the teenager abandoned her? A full minute of silence passed while she cursed her luck and the man who stood between her wet, naked body and fresh, dry clothes.

"Aren't you getting a little chilled by now?" Adam's voice broke the silence at last.

"No."

"Wouldn't you like to come out of there?"

"Yes."

"So why don't you?"

"Will you go away?"

A delighted male chuckle reverberated off the shower

walls. "No. Not a chance. In fact, I'm seriously considering joining you. It *is* my shower, after all."

Embarrassment helped her find her anger. Winding the towel around her body, she popped the shower door open just enough to stick her head around the edge. Adam leaned against the bathroom counter, arms crossed over his chest.

His smile broadened.

"You are no gentleman," she accused.

He laughed, an annoyingly superior sound. "I don't believe I've ever claimed to be."

They gazed at each other while the steam trapped in the bathroom swirled softly, caressing their bodies with its heated, gentle touch. The look in Adam's eyes held that same heat, and Jess felt goose bumps rise along her arms.

"Where's Angela?"

"After reassuring her for the tenth time that I wasn't angry, I sent her off. Next time you plan an escapade, don't pick a teenager as your accomplice. They tend to be easily intimidated."

No help from that corner. She swallowed, knowing that if the hot water hadn't already turned her skin pink, her embarrassment would have. "I suppose you want an explanation."

He shrugged. "Not really. I've already gotten a pretty detailed one from Angela."

"Then what do you want from me?"

His eyes flicked down her body, then back up. Passion glowed in their depths, igniting heat within her. "I'm not sure," he said with a momentary frown. Then his mouth lifted in wicked amusement and soft invitation. "But it might be entertaining to find out."

Jess gave him a "fat-chance" look meant to whittle

away some of his smugness. "I'm not here for your entertainment."

"Oh, I don't know," he said nonchalantly. "I think this is pretty amusing. A naked woman in my shower sure beats the stripper Angela sent me for my birthday." He frowned again. "But please don't sing anymore. I thought someone was being murdered in here."

That was the final blow. "Look, I *am* getting chilled. If I catch pneumonia, I'll sue your socks off, so you'd better let me get to my clothes. They're on your...bed."

He waved his hand in front of her path like an old-world courtier spreading his cloak over a mud puddle. "Be my guest."

She caught the sparkling challenge in his eyes and knew he expected her to balk. Jess's lips flattened into a thin line. She wouldn't give him that pleasure. Inhaling determination with a deep breath, she stepped from behind the shower door and headed out of the bathroom. She kept her head high and her gaze fixed firmly ahead.

Clean clothes lay in a tidy pile on his bed—salvation so near and yet so far. She hobbled quickly toward them.

The bulky, wet plastic of the garbage bag made any kind of grace impossible and it clutched her good leg like the tentacles of an octopus. She made a short attempt at kicking the bag away, then bent to detach it, but realized that she couldn't unless she let go of the towel wrapped around her body. And *that* she couldn't do.

Adam was suddenly in her path, and she halted.

"Hold still," he commanded. "Let me get you out of that thing before you fall and break something else."

For one horrible moment, she thought he meant the towel, but in the next second he was kneeling in front of her, working at the knot she'd made in the plastic. She had tucked the bag into the top of her cast, and when his hand brushed the underside of her knee, she couldn't help her jerking response to the warmth of his fingers.

"Stick your leg out," he said. "You can use my shoulder for balance if you need to."

She swung her leg forward, but she would have swallowed fire before she would place her hands on him. He was so close she could smell his warm masculine scent. His head was bowed over her leg, and Jess had to acknowledge a decidedly feminine reaction to his silky dark hair, only inches away from her hand. His shoulders were wide and moved beneath his shirt with beautiful male fluidity and strength.

Jess bit her lower lip, suddenly finding the far wall very interesting.

"You tie one heck of a knot," he said, his fingers still working on the wet plastic and sending little tingles up her leg. "Where'd you learn it? Let me guess. Before the carnival, you had a tour in the navy."

There was a lump in Jess's throat that threatened to choke her. Good grief, was that her stomach starting to tingle now?

"Just rip it," she told him between clenched teeth.

"And fling water everywhere? I don't want to get your cast wet."

"I don't care."

"I do."

The towel around her body slipped a little, and Jess clutched the two ends of it tighter over her breasts. The movement threw her off balance and instinctively she thrust one hand out. Her fingers clutched Adam's shoulder as she realized that his hand was pressed firmly around her thigh now, and a slow fire suddenly seemed to be burning there.

"What are you doing?" she demanded.

He didn't look up. "Just making sure you don't fall."

Oh, but it was too late for that, wasn't it? Her knees were gelatin, and in another moment she was going to go down like a house of cards.

"Adam…"

"Yes?" Without releasing her, he rocked back on his heels. The mischief dancing in his eyes confirmed her worst fear. He was completely aware of the effect his touch was having on her.

She gasped as his fingers slid to her inner thigh. She tensed, as if a hot brand had been placed against the cool flesh. "I don't think you should be doing that," she managed to get out.

"Why not?" In a smooth voice tinged with amusement, he added, "Aren't you the lady who thinks I ought to listen to my impulses? I'm getting one right now. Want to guess what it is?"

"Yes. No. I mean—I don't care."

"Oh, come on, try. Here's a hint. The shower's big enough for two."

"I've already had my shower."

"But suppose you missed a spot?"

"I didn't."

Rising, he kept her body loosely captured by placing his hands against her hips. He cocked his head as though trying to see past the overlapped edges of the towel. "You wouldn't consider letting me check that out for myself, would you?"

Jess began to see the absurdity in her situation, the futility in fighting fates that seemed determined to throw stumbling blocks in her path. Besides, how could she stay angry with a man who insisted on looking so infuriatingly attractive? She'd grown up around men on the farms—a lot of young, athletic men with well-developed male bodies. She just couldn't remember the last time she'd been this close to one.

Spying the amused tilt to her lips, Adam drew a soft, sudden breath and shook his head. "Don't do that, Jess."

"Don't do what?"

"Don't smile at me like that. Not if you're really determined to keep me at a distance." He drew one finger along the slope of her shoulder, down the length of her arm. His eyes followed the spreading beads of moisture that lay against her skin. "A nice, safe distance," he added.

Her face lifted to his. For a long, long moment neither spoke, neither looked away. Then finally, Jess said softly, "I'm not sure distance is what either of us want right now."

He stared at her in astonishment. He hadn't expected that kind of response, but he couldn't pretend he wasn't delighted by it. Poorly functioning common sense told him this playfulness had gone far enough, but even as he had the thought, he pulled Jess's body against his.

He heard her startled, uncertain gasp as his lips found hers, yet she made no move to slip away. He stroked her lips with his in a light, flirtatious kiss. But when she pressed upward for more, Adam forgot about being gentle and patient. He tunneled his fingers into the wet tangle of her hair. The clean, wonderfully feminine scent of her drifted into his senses. She was still wet from the shower, and holding her, he felt the cool dampness of contact with her flesh, the ridged hardness of her knuckles against his chest where her fist continued to clutch the towel between them.

Breath became precious, and he lifted his mouth, but only long enough to whisper his delight, only long enough to find the silky, warm curve of her throat with his lips. Torn with passion, his resistance stretched and shattered.

Crazy. He must have been crazy to have ever believed one kiss from this woman would suffice.

In defiance of conscience he brought her closer to him, rotating his hips with slow, erotic intent, eager for Jess to know how much she aroused him. His fingers slipped beneath the hem of the towel, cupping her buttocks. The smooth muscles tightened as he kneaded and stroked. She was no meek creature demanding to be wooed in slow, careful ways. She groaned with wild pleasure and nipped playfully at his earlobe.

Her breath came hot and ragged against his ear. "Adam," she whispered in a dazed tone. "Adam, please."

When her knees weakened, he pressed closer, pinning her against the low mahogany dresser. Their sudden, fevered movements jarred every item on it. Adam was only marginally aware of the sound of brushes scattering across the smooth surface, small change rolling to bounce on the carpet. The framed picture in one corner smacked facedown, then slid over the edge. The leaded-glass frame shattered into a spiderweb's pattern.

Conscious of Jess's bare foot, Adam let his eyes follow the sound of tinkling glass. He nudged the pieces away with his shoe, and in that moment, in spite of the desire that threatened to eclipse everything else, in spite of the sensual pitching of his heart…he stopped.

Faceup, the picture lay undamaged beneath the cracked glass, a casual study of two old friends—his father and Faelen's Star, the forefather of Midnight Star and every damned horse worth anything in the stable. Faelen Connor was beaming proudly, holding on to the colt's halter as though parading a Triple Crown winner before the crowd.

Maybe he thought he was. The picture had been taken four months before the Thoroughbred's first win, but already there was an arrogant tilt to Star's head, the promise of greater things to come.

The dreams of glory captured in that picture hadn't happened. His father and that glorious, promising creature—both of them were gone now. No more than bitter memories for Adam and the stuff of rainy-day gossip at the horsemens' club.

Gossip only *he* had the power to change.

"Adam?" Jess murmured against his cheek, then lifted her head. She'd sensed his sudden change of mood and now searched for the reason behind it.

He turned his face away, dipping his head low because he didn't want her to see the regret he knew must be in his eyes. He wasn't ready to let her go. Not yet.

He hugged her to him, listening to her breath settle and waiting for his pulse to do likewise. Gritting his teeth, he closed his eyes to banish the shattered picture from his sight, wishing he could as easily silence the voices in his head.

But he couldn't.

His hands shaped her face. He forced his gaze to remain steady on hers. The ache of longing in her smoky eyes was full of intoxicating promise. He'd brought her to this, savored the magic as much as she.

He thought about what he *had* to say.

And suspected she'd never forgive him for it.

"What is it?" she asked, frowning.

"Jess, I want you to understand something," he replied. His voice came rough as sandpaper. "There isn't anything I want more than to make love to you right now. I've probably wanted it from the first moment I met you. But I can't. I just...can't."

She shook her head fervently. "I don't understand."

"I'm not trying to hurt you. But we're just not...meant for each other." He saw the color rise in her face and knew he'd failed miserably. "Please, let me explain."

She stared at him, shocked and hurt. Her mouth, so moist and love-bruised only a moment ago, tightened into a thin line. With her free hand she pushed against his shoulder, anxious to put distance between them. He knew she struggled for control. He could almost see the fine quiver of restraint that somehow held her together.

"Don't bother to explain," she snapped. "I'm not completely stupid. I get the message."

He willed her to comprehend. But in the molten steel of her gaze, there wasn't an ounce of caring left. "You don't understand. I want—"

"I think I understand all too well," Jess cut in. "Now, if you're through showing me exactly how incompatible we are, I'd like to get dressed."

He looked at her solemnly, then sighed, a weary, miserable sound. "I'll leave you alone to change."

He turned to walk out of the bedroom.

Before he reached the door, her voice came to him, strained and shaky, but filled with such dislike he wondered how the heat of it kept from singeing his flesh.

"Just leave me alone. Period."

CHAPTER SEVEN

JESS'S EXPERIENCE with men had been limited to two serious relationships, neither of which had been particularly romantic, both of which had ended amiably by mutual consent. No man had ever caused her breath to quicken in her lungs with a mere touch. No man had ever caused her heart to accelerate with one look.

And no man had ever rejected her so completely as Adam Connor had.

It stung to realize she'd been the one to initiate her own downfall. She'd kissed him in spite of her father's warning; in spite of knowing the torments a relationship with a man like Adam could cause. She should have known better.

He had behaved like a heartless bastard. She didn't know which was worse—thinking that he'd been playing with her emotions, making her respond to him only to prove he could. Or fearing that he truly was one of those uptight, arrogant breeders who still clung to the old class barriers between owners and hired help. She wanted to hate him. In theory, it should have been easy.

So why couldn't she?

For the next two weeks she suffered from a peculiar restlessness. She wanted to leave Rising Star—with or without her father. Once she even began packing. She unpacked just as hastily. She'd be damned before she'd let Adam think he had chased her away from here.

So she stayed, emotionally weary and filled with a keen frustration that grew with every passing day.

In direct opposition to Jess's own life, her father's experiences at Rising Star seemed to fill him with new self-respect. She often saw him around the farm, standing tall and confident, issuing instructions to the exercise riders. Or in quiet consultation with the farm manager, Bill Page. Hearty laughter came easily and more frequently to him now, and Jess began to believe that Doc was putting the past behind him.

There was only one relapse. He and her mother had always enjoyed opera, and Jess saw it as an encouraging sign that lately he'd begun to listen to his and Beth's favorite records once again. But on her parents' wedding anniversary, Jess returned from a trip to the library to find Doc listening to the final tragic act of *La Bohème* in total darkness.

As the orchestra pounded out the fortissimo chords that announced Mimi's death to her beloved Rodolfo, Jess flipped on the living-room light switch. There in one of the chairs sat her father, a near-empty bottle of Scotch cradled between his legs and tears streaming down his face.

Jess hurried to his side as quickly as her cast would allow her, then knelt awkwardly. She pulled him against her. He smelled of cheap liquor but of horses and pipe tobacco and old times, too. So much so that her eyes dampened with remembrance of better, happier moments.

He moved restlessly, a pathetic attempt to recapture control. She hugged him tighter. "It's all right, Papa. I know it hurts."

"I try to forget, lass. And sometimes I almost...I almost succeed. But not on days like this. Your mother loved this piece." Heavily slurred and accented, the words were difficult to decipher. His voice sounded as though it had been placed in a strangling vise. "Do you remember when I took her to the Met? Our twentieth anniversary, and she looked like a bonny new bride."

"How could I forget? Mother talked about it for months. And I can still hear her scolding you for spending the money."

"Your mother was more frugal than any fellow Scotsman I ever met. On our first date I took her to the fanciest restaurant in Lexington. The Pavilion. Do you remember it?"

"Yes, I remember."

"I wanted to impress her, so I insisted on lobster and wine. I was just a barn boy back then, and your mother knew that dinner would cost me a week's wages. When the dessert tray came around, Beth reached out and put a hand on my arm. 'Murdock,' she said. 'Do you really want to stay any longer in this stuffy place and eat overpriced food? Wouldn't you rather take me up to Cumberland Bluff and tell me how you ended up in Lexington? I want to see Scotland through your eyes.'" Doc turned his watery gaze toward Jess. "I promised to take her there someday. Show her all my old haunts."

"I know."

"I didn't keep my promise. And now I'll never have the chance."

"Papa..."

Violently, Doc Russell shook his head. "Don't ever fall in love, lass. It can tear the heart right out of you."

Commiserating, Jess stroked her father's cheek, trying to find the right words to soothe him. And wondered why in those moments she suddenly thought of Adam Connor.

She was able to get Doc into bed without much difficulty. Emotionally and physically exhausted, he was snoring loudly five minutes after she tucked the covers under his chin.

Jess was the one who tossed and turned all night.

MIDMONTH Tim Rogers discovered an outbreak of hoof thrush in Barn Two, and by the end of the day every horse on the farm had to be treated preventively for the fungus. Jess knew from her growing-up years in Lexington that it was backbreaking, messy work, but breeders lived and died by the old adage, "No Hooves, No Horse." Every hand that could be spared would be expected to pitch in and help Bill Page's barn crew accomplish the task of getting ornery, skittish Thoroughbreds to accept treatment they clearly had no interest in receiving.

Doc had already headed over to the barns. Slipping into a ragged pair of jeans and her least favorite T-shirt, Jess planned to join the men. Back at Carraway Hills she'd been known to wield a thrush brush better than anyone— fast, with little wasted motion. The men here knew she had good instincts around horses, and she expected no argument for the offer of an extra hand.

What she *didn't* expect when she got to the stall that they'd set up for treatment was to find Adam Connor there, disheveled, his clothes already splattered with oily thrush liniment, and about two thousand pounds of horse-flesh trying to escape the grip he had on its back hoof.

She hated the timid voice inside her head that advised her to back out of the stall and hope no one had seen her. What was Adam doing here? None of the Carraway Hills breeders had ever so much as passed a water bucket to their animals for fear they'd get their cashmere jackets wet.

Did Adam own a cashmere jacket? If so, he wasn't wearing it today. He'd cut the collar and sleeves out of a sweatshirt, exposing some lovely arm and neck muscles. And his jeans were as worn and torn as hers, though they were low-slung and clung so nicely to his narrow hips that she might have missed the comparison if she hadn't been so determined not to care one way or the other.

Rats! Why did I even have to notice?

"Pony-girl, you're just in time!" her father called from his place at the colt's head, where his hands were tightly wrapped around a nose twitch. Pinching a horse's sensitive nose, the twitch was supposed to force the animal to a standstill. Only, some horses didn't know that, and evidently this recalcitrant beast was one of them. "Adam can't keep a solid hold and slap on the oil, too. Come paint for us."

Adam had glanced up at her from his stance by the horse, and Jess's stomach lurched. If she had wondered what kind of welcome she'd receive from him, she didn't have to wonder any longer. He was frowning. Darkly.

Tough, she sent the message across to him. *I'm still around, and you're just going to have to put up with me.*

"This is no place for her, Doc," Adam said over his shoulder. "She could get hurt."

The colt chose that moment to kick outward, trying to loosen Adam's grip on its back leg. Adam hung on with both hands, but the thrush brush he'd been using to swipe medicine across the animal's upturned hoof pirouetted across the stall.

Jess hobbled across the dirtied straw floor and picked it up. "I'm not a novice at this sort of thing. I've probably coated more hooves with thrush mixture than you have. Haven't I, Papa?"

"True enough," Doc replied.

She could feel Adam's eyes on her. Ignoring him, she dipped the brush into the can of treatment medicine. Approaching the colt from the side, she slid her free hand along its back and down its rump. Nerves quivered under the animal's silky flesh.

"Who is this?" she asked Adam. "Sun Dancer?"

"Eclipse," he answered tersely.

She came around him and bent forward, so that their faces were only inches apart. "If you can hold him still," she told him, "I can finish the job."

"You have to be sure to paint the entire—"

"I know what to do. You just do your part."

Neither of them said anything for several seconds. The stall felt much too warm. Jess noticed a pulse working wildly at Adam's jawline, and his stare definitely challenged, but she couldn't tell if he was annoyed or uncomfortable or both. She wasn't too comfortable herself, but she'd be damned if she'd let him see it.

"Then do it," he said, the words seeming to come with effort. "Just don't get any closer to the hooves than you have to. Pay attention, and you won't get hurt."

Jess covered a secret smile of victory by bringing the brush closer to her nose for a sniff. "I see they haven't improved on the smell. The stuff still stinks."

"Try not to get more of it on me than you get on them."

"If you two are finished comparing lesson notes," Doc called from Eclipse's head, "I'd like to get this scurvy beast back in his box before he pulls my arm out of its socket."

Abruptly, the tension broke, and they settled down to do the job. As Bill Page and his crew brought each animal in for treatment, and Doc positioned them in place, she and Adam worked as a team. Jess stood back out of the way, waiting patiently until he had a tight hold on each fetlock and could lift it. Once he had the leg raised, she darted forward to paint the hoof as quickly and efficiently as possible.

By the end of the day, there were only one or two horses left to be treated, and she knew the men considered the day a success. There had been few mishaps.

Midnight Star had kicked Tim Rogers in the leg before getting settled, Doc had been nipped in the hand a couple of times, and one of the barn boys suffered a broken toe when he'd tripped over his own feet trying to avoid flailing hooves.

Jess's back and shoulders were aching, she couldn't smell anything but the thrush mixture and her cast-covered leg was starting to throb. She didn't think Adam felt any better. He was sweaty, dirty, and for the past thirty minutes he'd groaned a little every time he bent to pick up a horse's hoof.

The two of them were poised over Sidewinder's left back hoof when Jess realized Adam was laughing.

She tilted her head up and frowned at him. "What's so funny?"

Both his hands were clamped around Sidewinder's upturned hoof. He shook his head, and tendrils of damp hair sifted around his head. "I can't see to hold him steady," he said, squinting as perspiration runneled from his forehead into one eye. "Sweat keeps running into my eyes. I feel like a blind man trying to hold on to a fire hose."

Slipping her brush into the hand holding the treatment can, Jess pulled the towel from the waistband of her jeans. She frowned. That wouldn't do. It had been used to wipe excess liquid off the horse's hooves.

Impulsively she moved closer to Adam, yanked the tail of her T-shirt out of her pants and covered her hand with the stretchy material. "Hold still," she told him.

While he held on to Sidewinder, she brought the cotton

shirt against his eyes and matter-of-factly wiped away the
moisture obscuring his vision. A second later she had
stepped back and returned to her duties. It was insignificant, she knew, but she was acutely aware of the cool
wetness of Adam's sweat against her bare midriff.

"You're doing it on purpose, aren't you?" Adam
asked.

She jerked her head up to find him looking at her in an
odd way, the slightest stretch of a smile across his lips.
"What?"

"Pretending that this isn't getting to you, while I'm
about ready to drop in my tracks."

"Ha!" she conceded with a tired laugh. After the long
day, she realized they were both feeling giddy with wea-
riness. "I can barely lift my arm."

"How many have we done now? A thousand? Two?"

"Hooves or horses? Enough of both to outfit Custer's
entire cavalry division."

"You're all right, Russell. You know your stuff."

Thank goodness Sidewinder took that moment to try to
jerk free. Adam had to turn his attention to hanging on to
the animal's hoof as the horse threw him off balance.
Otherwise, Jess was sure he would have seen how much
his praise affected her. She could feel the heat stealing up
her neck, and a little tingle of pleasure tweaked her insides.

Stop it! she scolded herself, aware that being this close
to Adam created the same unfortunate reaction within her
that it had on the first day she'd met him. Paralyzing and
thrilling. She tried to concentrate on the job at hand, but
aware of Adam's eyes on her, she stopped and lifted her
head.

His features had shifted into an intense, grave study of

hers, and Jess's nerves stretched and threatened to shatter as she realized that his thoughts had shifted, too.

Into dangerous territory.

His lips seemed so close…and the hungry, feminine part of her willed them closer. She wondered what she could say to her father if Adam suddenly turned loose of Sidewinder and yanked *her* to him instead. If he kissed her. Really hard. Really deep.

She recovered from this temporary insanity as Bill Page appeared in the stall doorway. His hand was looped around the lead line of a pretty chestnut filly. "Last one," he announced.

Feeling as guilty as a child caught with her hand in the cookie jar, Jess quickly slapped the brush across Sidewinder's hoof, and without a word, Adam dropped the animal's leg and indicated Bill should bring in the last horse.

IT WAS CLOSE to sundown by the time Doc headed back to the cottage. He was exhausted, but looking forward to Jess's promise of chicken potpie for dinner. He'd told her not to bother with anything fancy, but she'd insisted that she'd done all the work before their marathon day of thrush treatment. He couldn't help hoping she'd remembered the biscuits for sopping up the gravy. No one had ever been better at baking than his darling Beth, but Jess, bless her, had been trying hard lately to duplicate some of her mother's best recipes.

She was such a bonny, loving girl. So much like her mother. Doc wondered if she was even aware of her feelings for Adam Connor, the softness that came into her eyes every time she looked his way. As her father, Doc didn't want to see her hurt, and falling for the head of the farm—there lay trouble if ever he had a nose for it. But she had to find her own way, didn't she?

Still, he wished he could convince her it was time to go back to college. She didn't need to fret and fuss over him so. She needed to get on with life. Just as he…well, as he was finding *his* way back.

The long, productive days at Rising Star were working magic on his soul—keeping the dark, lonely nights at bay and giving him hope for some sort of future without Beth. Never the golden, loving days he'd known with his wife. Never that. But something…acceptable. Manageable.

Ah, Beth, I miss you, luv…

He sighed, looking forward to the prospect of a hot bath before dinner. Maybe after he had scrubbed the last of the day's messy work off his skin, he'd give Zola a call. She might be tickled to know her instincts, prediction—whatever she called it—about Kokomo had been right.

It had taken a few more times on the track before Doc had figured out the problem, but eventually he came to the realization that the Thoroughbred was scared to death of Raymond, the exercise boy who rode him most of the time. After a couple of telephone calls to the animal's previous owner in Saratoga Springs, Doc learned that the horse's first "hacker" had been fired for abusing the animals under his care. As it turned out, Raymond physically resembled the fellow. Once Kokomo was reassigned to another lad, the problem of skittish behavior on the track ceased.

He smiled, thinking what Zola would make of that news. He was in for a haughty, I-told-you-so time of it, that was for sure.

He passed the grooms' quarters and heard the sound of boisterous laughter coming from within. The lads had done an exceptional job today. Working together like a well-oiled machine. Never losing their tempers or patience. Tim Rogers would make Bill a good assistant someday. The stouthearted fellow hadn't missed a beat, even when Midnight Star had balked at treatment and walloped him in the shin.

Thinking he might check on the boy, Doc cut back toward the dormitory-style building that housed the barn crew. On a Friday night it was nearly empty. No doubt, in spite of an exhausting day, the lads were off to town to relax and meet their girlfriends. Such energy, Doc thought with a wistful sigh.

He found Tim in the shower room, slipping into a clean pair of jeans in front of the row of metal lockers that held personal items.

"How's the knee?" he asked as the boy turned to see who had come in.

Tim shrugged. "Nothing I can't live with. That's not the first time Star's tried to bust my chops. He's a temperamental devil."

"The best ones are, lad."

"He can do it, can't he, Doc? He can take the big races."

"I've never seen a colt who had a better chance."

The groom slipped open his locker door. Removing a brush from the top shelf, he ran it through his damp blond hair. "This is gonna sound dumb, but every time I see Star run the practice track, my heart just about leaps out of my chest. Watching that baby hit those morning times..." Clearly embarrassed, the boy tossed the brush back on the shelf and closed the locker door. "Oh man, listen to me. I sound like such a track rat."

Doc smiled, pleased by the boy's enthusiasm. He remembered what it had been like for himself as a young groom, filled with the love of horses, the feeling of awe and admiration for such magnificent, tightly leashed power. A true horseman needed that kind of zeal.

"You've got good instincts, Tim. Bill and I have noticed that the other young bucks look up to you for guidance. 'Tis a good thing to start making your mark here."

Tim looked pleased. "I don't intend to be a groom forever."

There was a bench in front of the lockers and on it lay a neatly folded shirt. Beside it sat a pair of expensive-looking sneakers, and Tim picked one up and began fiddling with the laces.

"You won't be. Give yourself a little time. You have a gift with horses."

"Right now, I just hope I've got a gift with women."

"Big plans for the evening?"

"The biggest. I've been waiting a long time for tonight."

His hand swooped down to pick up the shirt. There was a clatter as something fell out of the front pocket and skittered under the bench. Tim bent to retrieve it, and when he straightened, Doc saw that he held a small lavender box in his hands. A deep purple ribbon kept the lid secured.

"It's a gift for my date," Tim explained. "Lavender sachet. I think it's too flowery, but you know how girls love that sort of thing."

"Indeed," Doc said with a lift of his eyebrows. At least, after listening to Jess talk about Angela Connor, he knew how *one* girl felt about it. "That's a very pretty box, too."

"Yeah. Girls are crazy about purple."

"I notice the young Miss Connor is particularly partial to it."

"Is she?" Tim remarked absently as he slipped the box back into his pocket. He patted down his jeans, obviously searching for keys. "Sorry, Doc, I gotta go."

"Tim, can you indulge an old man for a few more minutes? I'd like to talk to you."

"What about?"

From beneath the bench, Doc bent to retrieve the second item that had slipped out of Tim's shirt pocket. Keeping his features as noncommittal as possible, he handed the small square to the boy. "I'm not a nosy fellow who concerns himself with another man's business, but I can't help thinking you might benefit from a word or two of advice."

Tim removed the foil packet from Doc's fingertips. He placed it in his back pocket, and Doc hid a smile at the flustered stain of red that crept up the boy's neck. Poor laddie. He was still young enough to be uncomfortable about sex. But it was the realization of what was evidently on the fellow's agenda tonight that worried Doc.

Apparently determined to brazen it out, Tim met Doc's eyes in a level stare. "I'm a grown man, Doc. And I'm not reckless."

"I don't doubt it. But if the lady you plan to meet tonight is the one I suspect, it's more than just *physical* caution you need to take."

"What do you mean?"

"Angela Connor's awfully young, and to her brother she's little more than a child."

"My mother was married to my father at her age."

"Aye, so was my ma. But do you think that argument will make a bit of difference to Connor? Touch his sister, and he'll bounce you off the farm faster than Star can take the quarter turns."

Tim folded his arms over his chest. "I can handle big brother."

"That's your mouth making promises your head can't keep, lad. Don't make the mistake of thinking you can trifle with the boss's sister and then have him bless the bed.''

To his credit, the groom looked offended. ''It's not like that. She's not just some girl I want to sleep with,'' he protested. ''She's special. I think I'm in love with her. And after tonight—''

''You'll not be any closer to knowing,'' Doc cut in quickly. ''Think, man! You could be throwing away a promising career to satisfy an urge that may bring you nothing but heartache. I know what I'm talking about. I was a randy stallion myself once, wanting a particular woman so badly I could taste her kisses on my tongue long before she offered them.''

Tim shifted his weight, but Doc was gratified to see that the boy didn't push past him and out the door. Maybe there was a chance he could get through to him. He had to try. He could imagine what a man like Adam Connor would do to a fledgling Romeo who dared to sully his sister. The man was fair and sensible, but he had a definite blind spot when it came to the young miss.

''Doc…''

''Listen to me. If Connor finds out—and he will—there will be hell to pay for this folly.''

''Angela knows her brother will be angry for a while. But eventually…''

Doc shook his head and leaned over to place his hand on the boy's shoulder. Giving him a hard look, he said, ''Laddie, the girl loves her brother dearly. She may care for you, but cause her to sever family ties for your sake, and she'll not thank you for it. Like as not, it will break her heart, and I've never known that to be a good way to start a relationship.''

Tim settled back against his locker. His eyes fastened on the ceiling as he seemed to give the matter serious thought. "I like it here," he said after a few seconds. "I don't want to screw up. But I do want to be with her."

"There's nothing that says you can't be," Doc was swift to reassure. "But take it slow. Win her brother over and I'll wager the girl can be yours with his blessing."

"Do you really believe that, Doc?"

"Aye, I do."

They were silent for several long moments. The boy's breathing was audibly rough, harsh with suppressed longing. Finally he spoke. "She's waiting for me at a girlfriend's house. Her brother thinks she's at a slumber party."

"Send her the gift as an apology. Tell her you can't make it because you have work to do here."

"I'm finished for the day." He gave the older man a faint, bleak smile. "At least, I thought I was."

"I can change that," Doc said with eager determination. "I can keep you so busy you won't have time to think about anything except when you'll be able to get a good night's sleep."

"Why should I prefer that?"

Doc grinned and clapped him on the shoulder. "Because it will give your testosterone level a chance to settle down. It will make Connor that much more aware of your value and it'll keep your future in one piece. What do you say?"

"Angela is gonna kill me."

"But she loves you. Remember?"

"All right. Suppose you get me through tonight? What about tomorrow, and the night after that, and the night after that?"

"Leave it to me. First, tonight. Jess won't mind an extra plate at dinner, and afterward I'll teach you how to play canasta. Then we'll set you up in Barn Six to watch Majestic all night. The fool mare looks like she might drop her foal early."

"Oh, boy. Lucky me. And then...?"

"If you've still got an ounce of energy left," Doc began as the two headed out of the barn, "I'll tell you a story about a young man who came to this country fresh off the boat from Scotland and fell in love with a bonny lass. Only the girl's father thought she deserved someone better. You see..."

THE DAY THE COUNTRY CLUB chose for its annual summer golf tournament turned out to be unexpectedly sweltering. Eighteen holes were played with a decided lack of enthusiasm, the winner received a modest check amid only a smattering of applause, then everyone escaped gratefully to the refreshment tent that had been set up next to the Olympic-size swimming pool.

It was no better under the tent. Although the sides had been tied open, the heat seemed to be trapped inside. The band was playing lazy tunes to an empty dance floor; the floral centerpieces and food had begun to wilt, and even the guests seemed to be engaged in no more than the most desultory conversations.

Adam stood near the dessert table and let his gaze wander over the crowd. He hated golf and hadn't wanted to come today, but there were obligations to be met, opportunities he couldn't afford to let slip away. Most of these people were strangers to him, but he spotted a few of his fellow breeders busy glad-handing sponsors, currying the favor of potential backers and trying to wheedle newspaper coverage for their farms from the press.

What a circus, Adam thought. He tried to keep his features from revealing his disinterest, aware that many would find his attitude shockingly ungrateful. It had been only two years since the Connor family had been "allowed" to become a part of this kind of pompous production.

In his father's time there had been no country-club memberships, no society balls, no celebrity auctions. Rising Star had garnered its reputation through hard work and determination, and Faelen Connor had seemed to enjoy his standing as a bit of a loner in the Ocala community. The caliber of his Thoroughbred offspring, the wins on the racetrack would speak for him, he'd often told his son.

Adam frowned down into the bowl of his tropical drink, topped with its ridiculous tower of fresh fruit. His father would probably be disappointed to see him here, listening to advice from people he had no respect for, struggling to keep his boredom from showing, and above all, trying to seem unaffected by any indiscreet mention of Rising Star's sordid past.

Would Faelen understand Adam's need to be here?

Probably not. There were times when *Adam* didn't understand it.

Though he had often told himself these games were necessary, lately he thought longingly of a time in the future when he might not have to play at all. Russell was working miracles with the horses. Midnight Star and several of the others had such great potential, and once again, people in the racing community were beginning to sit up and take notice of the name Rising Star. The farm was creating its own momentum, and as long as he stayed focused...

He almost snorted aloud.

Focused? That was rich.

One hell of a word to be using right now, when all he'd been able to think about recently was how badly he must have hurt Jess Russell that afternoon in his bedroom. *And all the ways he could think of to make it up to her.* How hard he had wanted to ignore her presence in the stall the afternoon they'd treated the horses for thrush. *And how much he had wanted to kiss her instead.*

He muttered a curse under his breath and took a swig of liquor, then grimaced. It was cold and wet, but too damned sweet for his tastes. He looked around the tent, searching out the signs of an open bar where he could get something more to his liking. Although there were several waiters circulating, he couldn't spot a single bartending station.

His irritation rose. Everything was too lavish here, too crowded, too false. There was nothing that he wanted from this kind of gathering. Nothing to be gained by being here. Nothing.

What's your problem today, Connor? What do you want?

He knew the answer to that. When he was really honest with himself—in the quiet, thoughtful hours of the night when he lay in bed and ached with longing—*then* he could admit what he wanted. The bright glory of blue ribbons paled in comparison to desire. The shiny trophies became lumps of worthless metal held up against his longing for Jess Russell.

He wanted her. More than he'd ever wanted anything in his life. He wanted her sharing thoughts with him in the summer grass. Laughing with him. Openly, as he'd watched her laughing with Angela. And touching. The memory of her small hands against his chest, that velvety soft mouth welcoming him so willingly, anxious to please, eager to receive. He wanted to experience all those things again.

How had it happened? How could mere physical desire

make years of careful planning seem such a foolish waste of time? And that's all it was, wasn't it?

Physical desire.

Nothing more.

That question echoed and reechoed in his mind, making a mockery of all the cold, cynical plans that had demanded there be no room for joy. Was he thinking now as he had so often sworn he never would again—impulsively, recklessly? He didn't know. He only knew that nothing so rational as common sense seemed to be functioning for him lately.

What if he went to her? She'd probably already heard some of the gossip surrounding Rising Star. What if he told her the truth about what had happened seven years ago? Besides easing the burden on his shoulders, it would help explain his actions. Might help her to accept that he couldn't get involved right now. Not when Rising Star needed his full attention, when it was so close to recapturing everything it had lost. She might understand. She knew firsthand what it took to keep the stable up and running. That day in the barn, when they'd worked so well together. She'd been—

"Good heavens, Adam, just how horrible is that drink?"

He swung his head around. "What?" Tianna Bettencourt, the only person under the tent who didn't seem to be feeling the heat, had reached his side, along with her companion, a fellow breeder from the next county. "Oh, hello, Ti. Lorne."

She indicated the half-filled glass in Adam's hand. "You look like the bartender's tried to poison you."

"Sorry. Just thinking."

"About your latest entry at Winston Park?" Lorne

Vandivert asked. "Forget it, Connor. My colt has it in the bag, I'm afraid."

Adam smiled good-naturedly. "Don't spend that prize money yet."

Tianna gave her head an eloquent toss. "Oh please, let's not talk horses. Lorne, be a dear and get me a fresh margarita. This one's melted to syrup already." She plopped the glass on the tray of a passing waiter. "Damn Florida summers."

Looking more than agreeable to do Tianna's bidding, Lorne nodded and strolled away. A few moments passed while she and Adam watched him make his way through the crowd.

"Well...?" Tianna prompted at last.

"Well, what, Ti?"

She narrowed a glance at him. "You owe me an explanation. Showing up here when you specifically told me you weren't coming and couldn't escort me."

"It was a last-minute decision. Things have been hectic at Rising Star. I needed to get away for a few hours."

She sniffed and appeared slightly mollified. "I suppose you're forgiven. And anyway, Lorne's much more attentive to me than you've ever been." Casting Adam a closer look, she added, "And attractive, don't you think?"

Adam gave her a bland smile. Tianna never changed. Completely self-absorbed, she was as easy to read as a child's primer. "Are you trying to make me jealous?"

"Only if it works," she replied airily. "Does it?"

He expected the wicked twinkle in her eyes—Ti was a hopeless flirt—but something in the way she looked at him caught and held his attention. They had dated in high school, only to separate as they each went off to college. By the time Adam had come back to Ocala, Ti had been firmly entrenched as the reigning arbiter of fashion, form and social standing. An easy, bantering friendship had developed between them, but in spite of Angela's dire warnings about Ti's designs on him, and Adam's own theories about what kind of help he needed to make a success of the farm, he'd come to know Tianna too well to ever seriously consider deepening the relationship.

But was Ti satisfied with that? Looking into her perfectly primped and powdered features, he thought he suddenly saw something more, as though all her fragile coquetry was disintegrating right in front of his eyes, and she was allowing him to see her as she never had before.

His forehead knit in concern, and seeing it, Tianna gave a sound of exaggerated disappointment. "I'm beginning to think I may be wasting my time on you, Adam Connor."

"I thought you'd decided that already. Not enough money in Rising Star's coffers to keep you in style."

"That's true. And since Daddy threatens to cut me off without a cent every time I step out of line, I've got to make sure there's more than one bank account with my name on it. But you're awfully handsome, darling, and since we've known each other forever, you already know all my little flaws."

"And like you in spite of them."

She flashed a delighted look at him. "Such a sweetie. Why aren't you rich yet? Daddy thinks you're going to make something of that little farm of yours. Maybe I should work on him…"

"Don't, Ti," he said softly. Their eyes met, his solemn and sincere, hers seeming to struggle valiantly to remain nonchalant. "You know we make better friends than lovers."

There was a sudden pinkness to her cheeks, but after an uncomfortable split second, she sighed dramatically

and gave him a look that was pure Tianna Bettencourt—
vain, aloof and condescending. "Yes, I fear you're right,"
she said. "You're the most interesting man in three
counties, but I suspect I'll never get a ring from you. Still,
I'd like to think that if *I* can't get a commitment, no one
else can, either."

"Ti, I'm sorry," Adam began hesitantly.

Her chin lifted as she made a protesting sound. "Don't
you dare feel sorry for me, Adam Connor. Just help me
convince Lorne that I'm wonderful. Here he comes. Tell
him about all the days I've spent feeding poor lost souls
down at the homeless shelter."

"I didn't know you had."

"I haven't," she said with a rippling little laugh. "But
if he thinks I'm a saint for doing it, then I will."

CHAPTER EIGHT

SHE HAD CIRCLED the day on her calendar, and when it came, she couldn't wait to get to town. After eight long, miserable weeks, the cast was finally coming off.

Jess ambled over to the garage, only to find Doc's pickup propped up on blocks. Her father and Tim Rogers had become friends, and she'd forgotten that as a favor to Doc, the groom had volunteered to give the vehicle a tune-up.

Angela was with Tim, and neither of them heard her approach. The girl hung over the open hood of the pickup, watching the groom's every move as if he were a heart surgeon about to begin a delicate operation. There was a murmur of private conversation between them, then with a laugh, Tim reached over and brushed his lips lightly against Angela's mouth.

She blushed prettily. Then, as though sensing they were no longer alone, Angela looked up to meet Jess's glance. Her pale skin went beet red. "Jess, I didn't see you there."

Jess tried to keep her features uncensuring. When had the relationship between Angela and Tim reached the kissing stage? Did Adam know? She suspected not, and she doubted he'd approve.

"I forgot Tim was going to work on the pickup," Jess remarked casually, not wanting to give her young friend any cause for alarm. "I have to go into town. The cast comes off today."

"Why don't you take Tim's car?" Angela suggested a little too quickly.

"Angela," Tim warned.

Jess had heard that the boy was extremely proud of the souped-up convertible he'd labored over for two years. It was obvious he didn't want to let someone else drive it. She saved him the embarrassment of having to wiggle out of Angela's offer. "That's okay, Tim. I'm not sure I'd know what to do with all those knobs you've put in the thing, anyway."

"I'd be happy to drive you, Miss Russell," the groom said. "I can finish up here in a few minutes."

Jess watched Angela's smile fall a little as the girl saw her opportunity to be alone with Tim slipping away.

"Thanks, anyway. I can see you're in the middle of something important."

Something that might not have all that much to do with fixing cars, she thought with an inward smile and a knowing glance in Angela's direction.

"Take one of the farm cars," Angela persisted. "Adam won't mind."

Jess nearly choked. "The last time you said something like that, I ended up caught in your brother's bathroom. No, thanks."

"Still not going to tell me what he said?" Angela prodded. Curious to know, the girl had pestered Jess for days after the incident.

Jess shook her head. "Not fit for young ears."

"He said he wasn't mad."

There are some things worse than anger, Jess wanted to say. Much worse. Instead, she waved the subject away and turned to leave. "Don't worry. I'll find another way into town. You two have fun."

The city bus stopped only half a mile from the entrance of Rising Star. If she hurried, she figured she could easily make the connection into downtown Ocala. She plunked a wide-brimmed straw hat on her head to ward off the afternoon sun, scooped up a journal on the treatment of rabies and set off down the dirt lane that led away from Connor property.

Hoping for a handout, a few mares in foal wandered over to the fence to follow in her wake, then gradually returned to cropping grass. A slight breeze stirred sluggishly through the pines, fluttering the edges of the gauzy tunic blouse she wore. Overhead, clouds gathered with the threat of an afternoon storm, but she wasn't deterred.

The walk would strengthen her calf muscles, and maybe, just maybe, it would help to burn off some of the restlessness that had plagued her lately.

ADAM HAD BEEN PORING over the farm's expense books for hours, trying to make sense of Bill Page's handwriting on the feed bills, when he happened to look out his study window and catch sight of Jess Russell heading off in the direction of Ocala. Yesterday Doc had told him that she was excited about getting her cast removed today, but surely she didn't intend to *walk* all the way to town?

He pursed his mouth and stared after her, until she was nearly out of sight. Knowing her, she probably did. She wasn't the kind of woman to let a little thing like a ten-mile hike stand in her way. She was one of the most determined, stubborn women he'd ever met.

She was getting to him. Driving him crazy.

He had no misconceptions about her feelings for him. With the glaring exception of when they'd been thrown together to treat the horses, she'd obviously decided that he was beneath her notice. From the moment they'd parted in his bedroom, he might as well have ceased to exist. Oh, she was pleasant enough when she happened to run into him around the farm, but the increasing tedium of their cordiality, the bland indifference in her voice when she was forced to speak to him, was starting to grate on his nerves.

Tossing his pen on the desk, Adam rubbed his hand around his neck in weary frustration. He knew he should be glad she'd put up these boundaries. Hadn't he made it clear he wanted them, too? He shouldn't resent them. It shouldn't depress him. This hands-off stance made the most sense for both of them.

And didn't he pride himself on being, above all, a sensible guy?

"To hell with it!"

In disgust, Adam shoved back his chair and stood. Snatching his car keys off the edge of the desk, he bounded out of the study.

SHE HEARD THE CRUNCH of tires as a car slowly pulled alongside her. The hood of a cream-colored Mercedes entered her line of vision. She didn't have to turn her head to know who it belonged to. Her heart gave a furious thump, but she ignored it and kept walking.

"I heard you're getting your cast off today." Adam called out. "Need a lift?"

"No, thanks."

"It's a long walk into town."

"I'm only going as far as the bus stop."

"Might get soaked before then."

"I'll take my chances."

"Afraid to accept the offer?"

Jess's lips parted to refute that claim, then snapped shut. She wouldn't rise to the bait. She shrugged and continued walking. "Not afraid. Just not interested."

"I'd like to talk to you."

"Seems to me there isn't anything left to say."

"It's about your father."

She stopped and turned toward him. Seconds ticked away as she debated the wisdom of accepting his offer. She didn't want to be within a hundred miles of the man, but suppose he'd somehow found out about her father's drunkenness the other night...

Although Doc refused to believe he had a problem, he had agreed to talk to a professional. It was a step in the right direction. Jess couldn't take the chance of alienating Adam's willingness to help her father now.

Without a word she settled in the front seat of the convertible. She stared straight ahead, ill at ease and angry. No matter how she felt about Adam Connor, he still held their immediate future in the palm of his hand.

When the car continued its expensive, idling purr and Adam made no move, Jess looked at him. He was as attractive as she remembered, perhaps more so. She ordered her senses to stop taking note of that fact. "What are you waiting for?"

"Directions to the doctor's office."

"Oh."

She gave him the address of the orthopedic clinic, and waited nervously for him to bring up the subject of her father's drinking. He didn't. Not exactly. But he came close enough that she felt a flicker of unease steal up her spine.

"Your father's working miracles," he told Jess when she asked him what he wanted to talk about. "With both the crew and the horses. But Bill Page thinks Doc pushes himself too hard.''

''Papa takes his responsibilities very seriously,'' she replied evasively.

''I know he does. But yesterday he seemed...I don't know...not quite himself. A little frazzled maybe.''

''He has a lot on his mind.''

He took his eyes off the road long enough to give her a curious look. ''You don't have to get defensive. I'm not criticizing. I just want to be sure that you think he's physically able to hold up to the stress. I'm asking a lot, and your father's not a young man.''

''Doc can work rings around any man on the farm. Including you.'' The words sounded sharper than she'd meant them.

He smiled and held out a forestalling hand. ''All right, all right. I just want you to tell me if the day comes when the workload seems to be taking more out of him than it should.''

''Fine.''

They didn't say another word to one another until he pulled up to the front door of the clinic to let her out. Then his hand came across the seat to capture her wrist.

''I'll wait to drive you back.''

Her eyes, hard and rebellious, met his. ''That's not necessary.''

''I'll wait.''

An hour later, she came out of the doctor's office to find Adam seated in the reception room, staring out the wide front window. He looked pensive, and Jess felt her heart sprint along forbidden paths. She wrenched her thoughts back viciously, unwilling to invest any more time in foolish daydreams.

He glanced around as she approached and surveyed her unencumbered leg. "Free at last! How does it feel?"

"Great," she replied in a stiff, formal tone.

The coldness in her voice made Adam wince, although he couldn't say her attitude surprised him. But when he stood up, attempting to offer the faint touch of support at her elbow, he felt Jess's immediate withdrawal. Her back ramrod-straight, she strode away. He watched her go, his heart twisting with regret. This chilly indifference wasn't what he wanted. So what *did* he want? Suddenly, he made a decision. He had to make her understand.

The clouds were still swollen with the promise of rain, scudding across a gray sky. Adam put up the convertible top, and in an atmosphere of uncomfortable silence, they wound their way through traffic. Jess watched the road, her nerves stretched and frayed.

They reached the entrance drive of Rising Star. When Adam drove past, Jess jerked her head around to look at him. "Where are we going?"

"I'd like to show you something. And we still need to talk."

The Mercedes moved onward, past the far reaches of Connor property, then bounced onto a winding dirt road that ran between heavily wooded pastures. Here the Bahia was thick and high, undulating gently in the breeze. Thoroughbreds grazed in the distance, but Jess's trained eyes told her they weren't the farm's current hopefuls. They weren't lean enough, and they moved with the contented, lingering gait of animals past their prime.

The fencing curved into a half-moon clearing beneath tall hardwoods. Adam killed the engine and got out, indicating Jess should do the same. He walked a few feet ahead and stopped in front of a neatly manicured plot of ground. As she neared his side, Jess saw the small rectangular headstone and realized they'd come to a grave.

"Faelen's Star is buried here," Adam said quietly. "You've been at the farm long enough to know most of our yearlings carry his blood. Including Midnight Star. Watching that colt run is like stepping back in time."

Jess nodded, unsure why Adam had brought her here. She sensed a sudden anxiety within him. She glanced down at the simple marker with the animal's name carved into it. There was nothing unusual in an owner honoring a great horse this way. But intuitively, Jess knew there was more here than that. She stood quietly and waited.

Adam's gaze shifted to her face, and the expression in his eyes was disconsolate, filled with pain. "I know you're angry with me, you have every right to be. But I can't change the way it is for me. I've spent years working toward one goal. I can't—" He stopped, searching for the right words.

"Ruin everything by getting involved with me?" Jess finished. "I think you've already explained how unacceptable I am. I'd like to go now."

She turned, but he latched on to her arm. "Jess, wait."

His eyes were full of pleading, but she refused to acknowledge his needs. Not while her own heart throbbed this way. She snatched her arm from his grasp. The wind lifted strands of hair across her face and she swiped them out of the way. "There's nothing left to talk about, Adam."

She got into the Mercedes, and a moment later Adam followed. She realized her mistake instantly. She should have cut through the pastures and walked home. The interior of the car held all the intimacy of a lover's haven. She sat quietly with her head down, listening to the wind sift fretfully through the trees, her fingers twisting the straw brim of the hat on her lap into a shapeless mess.

Adam started the engine, then abruptly shut it down.

Jess's nerves, already strained to the breaking point, snapped. She couldn't take this. Adam was so close, so disturbingly close. She groped for the door handle.

His fingers fastened around her wrist. "Jess, no!" She threw him an angry look, and his eyes studied hers intently. "It's going to storm. Are you so anxious to get away from me you're willing to take the chance of getting caught in a downpour?"

When she didn't respond, he had his answer. With a weary sigh, he removed his arm and stared out the windshield. In the eerie afternoon light, his features were chiseled in sharp planes and angles. Minutes passed. Adam remained silent and seemed preoccupied, as though he had willed himself away from her presence. Numbed by the strength of her feelings, Jess tried to do the same.

And failed.

"Why *did* you bring me here?" she asked at last, no longer able to bear the silence.

"I wanted to try to make you understand."

"What is there to understand?"

He turned to face her, digesting her words for a long moment or two, his features disciplined and unreadable. When he spoke, his voice was a tight, rough rumble. "Seven years ago there was a fire at Rising Star that destroyed every barn except Number Four."

She lifted her eyes to his, stunned. The clouds scudding across the sky created running shadows against his face, so that for a moment she hardly recognized him.

"My father and twelve Thoroughbreds, including Faelen's Star, were killed."

"Oh my God," Jess exclaimed in a hoarse whisper.

She pressed her fingers against her lips. Every breeder feared fire, a disaster that could wipe out the hopes of a prosperous stable in minutes.

"Insurance investigators and the state fire marshal's office claimed it was arson. A fire deliberately set...by my father."

"Why?"

"Money, of course. Faelen's Star was heavily insured. He ran second at the Breeders' Cup as a two-year-old, but then won five consecutive races, including the Whitney Stakes and Hollywood Park. My father wasn't the only horseman who thought Star could take the Triple Crown." He paused, his mouth tightened into a grim line of remembering. "His trainer was aggressive, a man my father didn't always agree with. The man felt the horse needed more bottom before Churchill Downs, and he talked Dad into running Star in a small stakes race. Instead, Star came out of it with a splintered sesamoid. He got tripped up by a bumper from South America who was later disqualified."

Jess didn't have to ask what happened after that. That kind of injury was devastating. "That ended his career."

"Yes."

"But your father didn't put him down?"

"He couldn't do it. He loved that horse. Besides, there were still people who thought Star's offspring would have great potential. My father had him shipped to the best veterinary hospital in the country. They rebuilt his leg, and a year later we did the only thing we could to recoup some of our investment."

"You offered him for stud?"

He nodded with a weary sigh. "The first foals didn't have the conformation we expected. By that time, we'd spent a fortune on a Thoroughbred that couldn't be raced and wasn't producing worthwhile get.''

"But potential's often impossible to see in new foals," Jess protested. "Given a year or so—"

"We didn't have the chance to find out. By the time he serviced a second season of mares, Faelen's Star had been nicknamed Fallen Star by the Ocala racing community. The farm was mortgaged up to the eyeballs. We were on the verge of losing everything. When the fire occurred, it didn't matter that my father was one of the victims. Everyone thought he'd set it deliberately to get the insurance money and had somehow gotten trapped inside one of the barns."

Jess didn't know what to say. It was an unspeakable, unthinkable nightmare—a horseman accused of setting fire to his own barns. Any connection with such a crime could scar a breeder forever. Had Adam's father lived, he might never have been able to overcome the taint of suspicion. The fact that Adam had managed to rebuild the stable in the wake of such a loss was remarkable.

"Who do you think set the fire?" she asked softly.

"Three weeks before it happened, my father had to lay off half the barn crew."

"A disgruntled employee?"

"The police questioned them, but there was never any proof." His lips molded into a flat, hard line. "But I know my father didn't do it."

"Those days must have been unbearable."

"It was like a nightmare—one you can't wake up from. Mother was in tears every day. Dad was dead. The farm was in shambles, all the best stock gone and no money to rebuild. Angela came home from school crying because kids were saying horrible things about our father." He shook his head, reliving those difficult months. "I'd just graduated from law school and hooked up with a firm in town. They asked me to leave. Their best clients were breeders who didn't like the idea of associating with the son of a criminal.''

''How can people be so cruel?''

''Well, this is a small town. The breeders are close. What touches one touches all of us. And in the end, leaving the firm worked out for the best. I didn't want to be a lawyer. I like working with the Thoroughbreds.''

''You've done well in the last seven years. My father says he's never seen this much potential in a small farm.''

''It hasn't been easy,'' he said. ''I've sacrificed everything to bring us back to where we were before the fire. The other breeders have gradually come around. Since I took over, there hasn't been one whiff about wrongdoing, not a hint of gossip to harm us. I make sure of that.''

''I don't see what this has to do with me,'' Jess replied.

''Credibility, Jess. Positioning. In this town a stable's reputation turns on the smallest word whispered in the right—or wrong—ear.''

''And you think I'm some kind of threat to your hard-won reputation?''

''Yes, you are.'' He exhaled the words as though they were a burden. ''You make me want to do things that I can't.''

She swallowed around the lump of sorrow in her throat. ''You're talking nonsense. I can't make you *do* anything.''

''Don't you understand how easy it would be for me—'' He had twisted in the seat to face her, and now he withdrew, so that once again he stared out the windshield, putting more than just physical distance between them. ''I want to make love to you,'' he said in a low voice.

"But you won't," Jess said softly.

"But I *can't*. The Triple Crown is right around the corner. I have to stay motivated, focused. I have to give the racing community the impression that I'm in complete control. Millions of dollars depend on that—everything from syndicate backing to the two dollars a Sunday better plunks down at the track window." Their eyes met, held. "I can't afford to care about you."

Anger tingled along her spine. "Is that really the reason, Adam? Or is it because of who I am? A horse trainer's daughter and not a member of one of Ocala's finest families? Because I'm not Tianna Bettencourt?"

He seemed genuinely surprised by that statement. "No. Ti's got nothing to do with us."

"Doesn't she?" Jess countered in a bitter tone. She didn't wait for his answer. "I'm sorry about what happened to your father and the stable. Truly sorry. But don't pretend it's the reason you've decided to keep me at arm's length. You're right about Ocala being a small town, Adam. People talk. I know all about what you want out of life. And I know I'm not it."

"Jess…"

"Please take me back now."

In the gray light, the tight, cold lines of her features were so uncommunicative that Adam knew the conversation was over. Jess's anger and mistrust were still at the forefront of her emotions.

They made the short trip back to Rising Star in acute silence, the hostility of Jess's attitude warring with the disappointed determination of Adam's own—a quiet contest of battered feelings. The car had barely pulled to a stop in front of the cottage before Jess pushed open the door and sprinted out.

She did not look back.

With the afternoon workouts halted due to the impending bad weather, Doc met her at the door, exclaiming over her newfound freedom of movement, making her internal misery seem that much more difficult to bear. She settled her father in front of the television and began preparing an early supper of beef stew and corn bread.

Viciously she chopped carrots into the pot. Just what had Adam hoped to accomplish by taking her out to that grave and telling her about the fire? A play upon her sympathies? Justification for his rude behavior?

She nearly choked on the knowledge that even before he'd told her that story, she had been so eager to grant him a second chance. So willing to be persuaded his earlier actions had been some awful mistake.

Instead, he'd only reinforced what he'd said before. The old class-conscious barriers she'd witnessed in Lexington were just as prevalent here. She wasn't good enough, and there was nothing she could do to put it right. She'd failed miserably in areas totally beyond her control. She didn't have the money, the connections, the lineage to help Adam achieve his "master plan."

With dull fury she attacked a pile of fresh vegetables with her knife. He might try to put a more palatable spin on it by saying he didn't have time or energy for a relationship, but Jess didn't buy that for a minute. If Adam had *really* wanted her, he would have…

She snapped a carrot in two and tossed it in the pot. Why was she thinking along those lines, anyway? She had enough to worry about without getting involved in an affair that had no hope of growing into something more permanent, more wonderful. Adam was doing her a favor, really. She ought to be grateful. She ought to thank him.

"Like hell I will," she muttered.

Her father meandered into the kitchen during a commercial. Removing his pipe, he sniffed the aromas spiraling upward from the pot, but she didn't glance his way.

"Mmm...your mother's stew," he said appreciatively. "My mouth's watering already."

Jess nodded, her throat too clogged with emotion to speak.

"Something troubling you, lass?"

She smiled carefully and shook her head, then swiped the heel of her hand across her dampened cheeks. "It's the onion," she said in a fierce voice and tried to make herself believe it.

ADAM SLAMMED into the house, stripped off his jacket with irritated movements and tossed it over the foyer coatrack. It was still early, only four o'clock, but the house felt empty, cloaked in shades of gray because of the coming storm. The silence annoyed him.

"Angela?" he called loudly. "Mattie?" Neither his sister nor the housekeeper answered. He stalked into the study, snapped on a light and stopped in front of the cherry-wood liquor cabinet. "No one's ever around when you need them," he muttered, splashing a generous portion of Kentucky bourbon into one of his mother's precious crystal glasses. He drained it in one gulp, exhaling a ragged breath as the liquid cut a quick, neat path to his stomach. He sloshed another shot into the glass.

Bringing it to his lips, Adam frowned as he caught his own reflection in the mirror behind the cabinet. He looked out of control, a little wild. Definitely not himself. He drank more slowly this time, savoring the bite of the liquor. In the mirror, the light arrowed and flashed as it caught the cuts of the crystal. As with everything in his life, the glass bore the Rising Star emblem.

Behind him were the trophy cases, proof of the stable's

past success and hope for the future. Adam turned and leaned against the cabinet, his eyes moving over the wall of blue ribbons, the pictures that captured a lifetime of dreams.

His father's dreams.

His dreams, too.

Long ago he'd accepted that sacrifice was necessary to fulfill the destiny his father had envisioned. He'd always understood that. Why, then, had that sacrifice been so hard to accept lately?

Like a caged animal, he prowled the study, replaying his conversation with Jess in an endless litany of regret. All wrong. He'd sought her out, thinking that somehow he could make her understand how it was for him right now. But he'd been an idiot to think that. She was a proud, passionate woman. It was no wonder his clumsy attempts to explain had fallen on deaf ears.

You botched it, Connor. Looks like there can't be any middle ground between you two. It's either feast or famine with Jess, and boy, are you in for famine. She hates you.

Reason murmured he ought to be able to live with that.

Outside, thunder rumbled, making the glass panes of the trophy cases rattle for attention, as though to remind him of their importance in his life. Adam strode across the study, splaying his hands against the glass. For years this room, and all it represented, had been the focal point of his existence.

This is all that's important, he thought as he let out a slow, calming stream of breath.

"This is everything I need," he whispered, but the words had never sounded so empty.

CHAPTER NINE

UNBEARABLY RESTLESS, Jess left her father in front of the television and escaped to the horses. It was a familiar pattern in her life: when she was worried or sad or upset, she found solace in the stable.

She let herself into Barn Four. There was still an occasional rumbling growl of thunder and the misting rain seemed destined to last the night. Pushing the wide door closed, she leaned against it to catch her breath. Dressed in shorts and the same gauzy blouse she'd worn to the doctor's office, she shivered. The material clung to her body where icy raindrops had found a home, but she ignored the whispery cold that chased up her spine. The chill couldn't begin to match the frost surrounding her heart right now.

She moved down the broad corridor, pausing to scratch Misty Lady's nose and offer a piece of carrot she'd saved from the stew pot. Nearby, Vadar stamped noisily, a telltale sign the horse was nervous.

She reached his stall as thunder boomed outside. The black rolled his eyes as though he'd spotted a rattler among the straw, and backed restively, refusing to lip the carrot from her hand.

"Hello, Miss Russell." Tim came out of the tack room to investigate. "He's one scared fellow," he commented as the horse struck the back wall of his stall with his hooves. "Looks strung tighter than some of the 'breds."

"Has anyone ever tried working this fear out of him?"

He gave her a sidelong look laced with cynicism. "Worry about a kink in a thousand-dollar Sunday hack when we got million-dollar colts to train? Nah." When the groom attempted to place his hand against Vadar's neck, the animal swung its head wildly and tried to nip him. Tim snorted. "You black devil. It's a good thing Angela's gone to the movies with a girlfriend. If she'd seen you try to take off my fingers, you'd be supper for the dogs."

Jess glanced up at him, surprised by the depth of feeling she heard in his voice. Idly she remarked, "I've appreciated your help making Angela comfortable around horses, Tim."

He threw her a knowing look, one far more mature than she expected in someone so young. "She told me you saw us kissing today, Miss Russell. I don't want you to think we've been doing anything we shouldn't. I like her—a lot. But we're just friends."

"You haven't given me any reason to doubt that." She placed a reassuring hand along his arm. "And really, it's none of my business."

"She's just lonely, and it's good that you're around for her. She says you're easier to talk to than her brother, who doesn't understand her at all."

She smiled at that. "He's a man. He's not supposed to understand a sister, especially one who's budding into an attractive young woman."

"Yeah, she is, isn't she?"

Jess watched him make another attempt to coax Vadar closer. He held out his hand, letting the animal see that there was nothing to be afraid of in his palm. She suspected he had a natural way with horses. A gentleness. Angela would be safe with him. But would Adam ever sanction a relationship between them? Where would someone like a simple groom fit into all Adam's grand plans for the future?

"Tim, be careful with Angela, will you?" she found herself saying suddenly.

"Believe me, ma'am, right now I don't have any other choice," he grumbled almost to himself.

"I beg your pardon?"

Tim flashed her a brief smile. "Just thinking out loud. Nothing to worry about, Miss Russell. Between your father and Bill, I don't have time to do much of *anything* but work. But even if I could be with Angela as much as I want to, I promise, I'd never hurt her."

"I trust you. But—"

"Mr. Connor doesn't," he finished for her. "He's a good guy, but I know he doesn't approve of me having anything to do with Angela." He gave her a hopeful look. "I'm working on changing his attitude, though. Think I can succeed?"

She didn't put much faith in that, but she didn't have the heart to tell him so. "If anyone can, it would be you. Bill and Doc have made him very aware of your potential. I think Adam could help you get the experience you need, but you mustn't ever forget that when it comes to Angela he's a typical older brother."

She wondered why she felt the need to warn him about his employer and then defend the man in the next breath.

Irritated by such illogical thinking, she turned her attention back to Vadar. The horse sidled against the side wall, bumping it so hard that the boards sifted dirt onto the stall floor. "Angela's getting much more confident on Misty Lady, don't you think?"

The boy was more intuitive than most teenagers his age. He knew enough to let her turn the conversation to safer ground. "Yes, ma'am. Those lessons have really paid off. Mr. Connor says he's real proud of her. And he thinks you're about as sharp as your dad when it comes to horses."

Jess experienced a sullen resurgence of anger. Clever enough to keep his sixteen-year-old sister company. Just not acceptable enough to be seen in his.

Oh, she really didn't want to think about Adam Connor anymore. Suddenly catching the groom's arm, she said, "Tim, would you get a bridle and bareback pad out of the tack room?"

"Huh?"

"I'm taking Vadar out."

"Now?" Tim's eyebrows came together. "This rain isn't going to let up for a while, Miss Russell."

"That's what I'm hoping. Have you ever heard of a training discipline called 'racing thunder'?"

"No, ma'am."

"It teaches Thoroughbreds not to be startled by the noise of the starting gate or other horses coming up behind them in a race. We might be able to adapt some of that technique to Vadar here. It's just the racket he's afraid of. It's worth a try."

"I don't know, ma'am..." Tim hesitated. "Vadar's pretty worked up. Mr. Connor might not like it."

Tim had no way of knowing, but for Jess, those words settled the matter.

THE RAIN CONTINUED, accompanied by the sound of thunder that Vadar feared so much. Jess didn't mind. She needed it to bring the animal under control. In the distance, heat lightning lit up the gray sky but offered no threat in the immediate area.

She worked the gelding in the back pastures of the

farm. All her life Jess had watched her father around horses, dealing with every kind of quirk and bad habit, so many of which centered around the fear of loud noises. Vadar wasn't nearly as high-strung as the Thoroughbreds Doc trained, but surely her father's behaviorial theories could be adapted to fit the gelding's fear of thunder.

The horse made several attempts to unseat her, but as each thunderclap began, Jess grabbed his attention with a light smack between the ears, then set him into a controlled walk. While the heavens boomed and grumbled, she spoke in a low, soothing tone. Eventually, Vadar's ears swiveled to catch the sound of her voice as the horse worried more about what she would do next than what was happening in the sky.

Between drumrolls of thunder, Jess set her heels to his side, pushing him into an easy canter, forcing his attention off the storm. With each new thunderclap, she slackened rein and issued lavish praise.

After two hours, her arms and legs ached from the strength it took to keep Vadar from dumping her in the soggy grass. She was soaked to the skin and exhausted, yet exhilarated, too. Skimming her tongue over her lips, she tasted the rain's fresh sweetness and lifted her face to a cleansing stir of wind. The strong, elemental forces of nature appealed to Jess. It was a secret pleasure of hers to ride in bad weather. She loved the feeling of life and energy that spun through her veins.

She was pleased when Vadar showed definite signs of progress. A few more sessions and she felt certain he'd settle down. Her father would be delighted to see how well she'd adapted his skills to Vadar's problem. Angela would be in awe. Adam would think—

She turned her thoughts away from what Adam might think. She already knew. Only too well.

The light was nearly gone. Though reluctant, Jess wheeled Vadar back toward the stable. She wished she could think of a logical reason not to return. The past two hours had been a small respite from reality. A chance to escape the bitter knowledge that she'd been a fool ever to think a relationship with Adam was possible.

With a toss of her head, she set her heels into Vadar's side and the horse sprinted into a canter. *What does it matter?* she scolded herself severely.

Yes, she had found Adam attractive.

But she didn't need him.

She didn't love him.

What Jess couldn't understand was why she had to keep reassuring herself of that fact.

BEFORE HE LOST SIGHT of Jess completely, Adam kicked Keno into a plunging gallop. He'd been stunned into near speechlessness when Tim came up to the house to tell him that Jess Russell had taken out one of the pleasure mounts. Now, seeing the shadowy figure of horse and rider galloping along the crest of the hill, he couldn't believe his eyes. It was nearly dark and pouring rain, for God's sake! What could she possibly have been thinking? Only a lunatic rode in weather like this!

Adam watched Jess urge her mount into moves that seemed to serve a particular purpose. While he'd hastily thrown a saddle on Keno, Tim had tried to tell him some nonsense about "racing the thunder" and Vadar's fear of storms. He'd barely listened. He didn't know what harebrained scheme she had in mind, and he didn't much care. The liquor he'd consumed earlier had left him with a headache and little patience. The idea that she'd ridden out in such unsafe conditions had made him angry.

Flicking rainwater off the end of his nose, Adam bent

his head into the wind. Ahead of him, Jess was a slim silhouette, unable to hear his approach over the wind and thunder. When she suddenly whipped Vadar around to head in his direction, he had to bring his mount to a skidding stop to keep from colliding with her. Startled, Vadar reared, but in spite of her own surprise, Jess managed to force him down.

Knee to knee, they eyed each other as their horses capered in nervous attendance. In the fading light, Adam glimpsed bitter anger in Jess's face for a fleeting moment. Then her features became a cold, expressionless mask.

Her hair whipped away from her face, a dark red wet banner in the wind. With her body soaked to the skin, the gauzy blouse molded to her breasts more intimately than revealing lingerie. She looked beautiful, and he felt desire cast its tempting spell. If he hadn't been so annoyed by her careless disregard for her own safety, if he hadn't been so frustrated by her harsh indifference toward him, he might have lost all control.

Instead, he found refuge in outrage. "Are you out of your mind?" he shouted. "What in the hell are you doing out here?"

"Working on Vadar's fear of storms."

"Vadar has enough sense to be afraid of storms. No one in his right mind should be out in this."

"In Lexington I rode in the rain all the time. I like it."

There was a new harsh tone in her voice that made him long for the gentle friendship she'd once offered. He didn't miss the way her hands tightened on the reins, an effort for control that had nothing to do with Vadar straining at the bit.

"This isn't Lexington, it's Florida. Lightning hits the pastures all the time."

"There's no lightning now. If there had been, I'd have come in."

Fast losing patience, he leaned over and clamped a hand around Vadar's reins. The gelding's nostrils flared and he tossed his head, but Adam ignored the beast. His eyes fixed on Jess. "I didn't come out here to give you a weather report. Head in. Now. Or I'll pull you off and take you back upside down over my saddle."

She drew herself up, sitting so straight on the bareback pad that Adam thought her spine would snap. She threw him an icy, embittered look. "You're the boss!"

She wrenched on Vadar's reins, sending him into a run toward home.

They were no more than a mile from the stable, when a pounding torrent of rain brought visibility to zero and turned the rich pasture soil to clinging muck. The light was gone now, trees and fences and buildings reduced to varying degrees of wet blackness.

Catching up to Jess, Adam shouted over the downpour, "We'll have to sit this out! Head for the maintenance barn up ahead."

The words swirled away on a gust of wind, but she seemed to understand and nodded agreement.

The maintenance shed was a fair-size building, yet they nearly missed it in the dark. They slipped off their mounts even before the animals slid to a halt on the soaked grass. Adam tossed Jess his reins and tried the door, only to find it locked. He planted a booted foot against the padlock and kicked. The wooden doorjamb splintered, sending the door slamming back. He fumbled for the light switch, and a naked overhead bulb sprang to life.

He led his stallion to a shadowy corner, using a huge mower as a hitching post. A moment later, Vadar and Keno stood side by side, blowing hard and dripping water on the dirt- and hay-covered floor. While Adam tried to prop the door closed again, Jess pulled the bareback pad from Vadar's back.

She rooted around the equipment in the shed until she found a stack of ragged towels. Anxiously she ran a cloth over Vadar's quivering hide, hoping to calm his resurfaced fear. From the corner of her vision she saw Adam follow her example, removing his rain-soaked saddle and rubbing Keno vigorously.

Neither of them said a word. Her lungs still hitched for air, but she knew that wasn't the only reason she remained silent. She resented Adam's presence here and the highhanded way he'd ordered her back to the stable. Feelings close to the surface, she realized how easy it would be to vent her frustration.

She tried to ignore him, concentrating on the barn's rich smell of fertilizer and grain, machine oil and grass. Her eyes traveled over the starkly lit contents. The building housed more than farm machinery. It had been used as temporary storage for everything from paint cans to car parts.

Unfortunately, it didn't provide much warmth. By the time she'd finished rubbing down Vadar, she was shivering. If her jaw hadn't been clamped so tight with tension, her teeth would have chattered like castanets. She peeled her blouse away from direct contact with her body and wandered into the center of the barn, hoping to find something to warm her up.

Over Keno's back, Adam watched Jess. She looked cold and pale. Her legs, bare and shapely, were splattered with flecks of mud. He thought how pleasant it would be to play her rescuer. Drying her body with slow, sensuous movements, the only thing between his hands and her flesh the soft, fluffy warmth of a thick towel.

He frowned as he caught sight of her feet. "Where are your shoes?"

She jumped at the sound of his voice and turned. "I didn't wear any. I hadn't planned on doing any walking."

For no reason he could name, that response irritated him. He tossed down the rag and approached her slowly. "Do you ever *plan* anything? Is everything you do a spur-of-the-moment decision?"

Her chin climbed, and she eyed him with icy scorn. "Some things can be planned to death."

His own temper rose at the thought of how careless she'd been. Adam knew calm reason was the tack he should take with her, yet some self-destructive demon drove him to push past her attitude of haughty disdain.

While she stood and watched in sullen silence, Adam scooped littered hay into a pile. Without saying a word, he sifted through the barn's contents, finally locating a stack of worn blankets that were moth-eaten but fairly clean. With a snap, he spread one over the hay and sat down.

"Might as well get comfortable," he told her, extending an old stadium blanket. Over the sound of rain pelting the tin roof, he added, "This could last awhile."

Jess stared at him, then turned and moved back to the horses. Vadar stamped restively. She went to the horse's head, crooning soft words of reassurance.

Adam scowled at her thinly disguised snub. "You're wasting your time," his rough voice scraped. "He can't be hypnotized into losing his fear."

She turned so quickly that wet strands of hair whipped across her face. Her hot gaze raced over his features. "Don't tell me what to do."

"Vadar happens to be my property. If you ever pull a

stunt like this again, you'll be on foot for the rest of your stay here.''

''Fine. My stay shouldn't last that much longer.''

He sat up straighter. ''What in hell does that mean?''

''Just what I said. I'll be leaving shortly.''

''I doubt that. Your father's still got a lot of work to do.''

''Better check your game plan, Coach. I'm not part of it, remember? I'll leave when I please.''

There followed a tense, ominous silence. In the hollow of her throat, Jess's pulse throbbed. A dark, agonized look came into her eyes, which Adam was quick to note. He hated himself for reducing her to this, hated the way he'd once again bungled the conversation. What was it about this woman that brought out the worst in him?

Her shoulders sagged. Then, as though she couldn't bear to look at him any longer, she crossed her arms over her chest and turned her back on him.

He realized she was shivering, whether with cold or emotion he couldn't tell. Feeling like the worst kind of bastard, he was hardly aware of crossing the distance that separated them. He pulled her into his arms. She looked so unhappy. What was the point in arguing? Especially when that wasn't what he wanted to do at all...

In her soaked clothes she was almost naked against him. Immediately he felt the tingling thrill of holding her electrify his senses. He stroked her wet hair, then her chilled, pale cheeks, trying to impart warmth. But in another moment his hands slowed, until he was cupping her face, lifting her eyes to his.

''Jess, I'm sorry...''

As though suddenly coming out of a deep sleep, she jerked her head away. ''Just leave me alone.''

''I wish to God I could,'' he said sharply. And then,

almost without thought he shook his head and added in soft misery, "But I can't."

Her gaze swept back to find his. She froze, her eyes widening in sudden comprehension. "No."

"Jess—"

"No!"

She darted out of his grasp. Blindly, she headed for the door, found the latch and slipped it free. She stumbled out, running through the rain. Adam was only a step or two behind.

She didn't know where she ran. She was hardly aware of the cold, drenching rain that pounded against her skin. She only knew she had to get away from Adam...this cruel, clever man who used words to unbalance her.

His hand fell on her upper arm, pulling her up short. He whirled her around.

"Let go!" she yelled over the storm's racket.

"Did you hear what I said?"

"Yes. You're crazy."

"Crazy from wanting you, maybe."

"Stop!" She squeezed her lashes shut against him. "Stop saying that."

"Why? It's the truth. It's all right. We can work this out."

Her eyes snapped open. She put both hands against his chest and shoved. "Why is it all right?" she shouted. "Because you've decided it is? How fortunate for us both. Doesn't it matter at all what I think? I think—"

"Don't think. For the first time I'm not. I'm just feeling." He shook her, the wounded pant of his voice barely discernible over the roar of rain. "Dammit, Jess. Tell me this isn't what you want. What we both want."

"Maybe I thought so once..." Unable to control her

voice, she stopped, her heart locked in a vise of pain. She shook her head. "But not now. This isn't what I want."

He caught her face in his hands, forcing her eyes to meet his. In the silver wetness of the pelting rain, it was difficult to see. "Liar. Tell me any relationship between us will create difficulties. Tell me I'm a bastard for wanting to take this any further. But don't tell me you can ignore what's between us. Because I can't," he said raggedly. He shook his head. "God help me, I can't anymore."

He waited, expecting her to deny his words, expecting her to lash out at him once again. Instead, with relief he saw that she could do neither. Her features had crumpled and he knew that her tears ran freely, sliding down her cheeks to mingle with the rain.

With desperate hope he brought his lips to hers.

Rainwater coursed down their faces and between their lips. Wrapping her arms around his neck, Jess surged against him. She could feel his heartbeat, could feel the exact moment its rhythm shifted into a savage beating.

"Jessie," he breathed and swung her up in his arms.

They returned to the barn, but she was only dimly aware of the moment he laid her gently on the blanket-covered hay. She hardly noticed the prickle of straw against her back, the itch of the blanket he threw over them both. She was aware only of Adam.

Hurriedly he pulled the wet clothes away from her skin, skimming the soaked shorts down her hips until she kicked them away. The gauzy blouse offered greater resistance, but, no match for Adam's determination, it quickly landed in a sodden heap.

When his fingers grazed back and forth across her breasts, she writhed under the feel of his hand teasing her nipples to life, the tender abrasion of flesh against flesh.

With every reverent caress, he brought her closer to a quivering peak of excitement. Her breathing became hectic as his every move inflamed her.

She brought one hand to his face, her fingers mapping the interplay of muscle and bone, coming to rest against one corner of his mouth.

"Adam," she whispered in a shaky voice. "Don't regret this tomorrow. I couldn't bear it—"

"Shh... Don't talk about regret. There isn't any." He caught the tips of her fingers in his mouth, then pressed a kiss against her palm. A kiss that held a wealth of tenderness. "Not for me."

It was enough for now.

She gave herself over to the sensations his lips and fingers so easily aroused. Eager to touch him, she pulled at his clothes, tugging at shirt buttons until he chuckled at her impatience and pushed her hands away to finish the chore himself. After an endless time, he lay naked.

She lifted her head, then dipped it to flick her tongue boldly across the beaded point of one nipple. She heard his breath catch as her mouth played erotically.

Adam's blood pounded in his brain until he thought it would burst. Her lips were like satin against his flesh, and her hands... Oh...what was she doing with her hands? Down and down they went, smoothing against his hips, his thighs, then lower. Her fingers lingered there.

Rough.

Tender.

Incredible hands.

He groaned and tunneled his fingers into the wet satin of her hair. He pulled, just enough to force her head up.

Surprised and delighted, he met the sultry desire in her eyes. "We've waited too long to rush now," he murmured huskily.

With a muffled moan, part pleasure, part despair, Jess writhed beneath him, shaping and fitting her body to his aroused length. "Adam...please. Don't make me wait. I want to feel you...inside... I'm ready *now*."

And she was—hot and tight and ready.

He would go slow. He would make the pleasure last. But whatever noble, unselfish thoughts he entertained became impossible, became unthinkable, as her body lifted to thrust against his, asking for more.

Taking him deeper.

Higher.

He swallowed. His muscles corded with the strain of holding himself still, giving her time to adjust.

Jess moaned in pleasure, ardently accepting Adam's warm invasion. Faster and faster their rapturous dance went as spasms forged them into one being.

Pleasure exploded, so bright and wondrous a feeling she thought she might die from it. She cried out, wanting to hold on, wanting to bask in its glorious warmth, but already she was free-falling back to earth in a lazy, drifting tumble. But even that was all right, even that was good, because Adam was there to catch her, cradling her close and murmuring softly in her ear.

CHAPTER TEN

JESS LAY SHELTERED in Adam's arms, listening to the soft, even rhythm of his breath, a mist of warmth that stirred against her cheek. His scent seemed to permeate her skin. His fingers lay against her temple, stroking the damp red tendrils of her hair with infinite care.

Beneath Adam's slow, hypnotic movements, Jess's mind struggled to keep from sliding toward foolish possibilities. She stared up into the rafters, her thoughts drifting.

Did she love Adam Connor? How could she? It was an absurd idea.

Frightening. Unthinkable.

The touch of Adam's fingers on her chin startled her. "Where are you, Jess?" he asked in silken tones. "Come back to me. I miss you."

She answered him with a smile, and he wasted no time in brushing his lips to hers in slow, heady contact. His kisses held magic. She shivered to think how easily he could steal her soul.

"Are you cold?"

She shook her head and nuzzled into the warm cocoon created by his strong shoulder and muscular arm. Beneath her hand his heartbeat drummed deep and even, where once it had pounded and raced.

She *was* in love with him. No use pretending otherwise. Feelings she could not escape now held her firmly in their grasp, and if the truth were told, she was not surprised to find herself in this position. From the moment he had come to her rescue at the carnival to the moment he had looked at her when she'd offered that first teasing kiss in the barn, she had known this man had the power to capture her heart. His loving concern for Angela, his patience with the horses and his men—all of it had added to the conspiracy.

And as for what had just happened between them? It had seemed right and wonderful—there would never be regret in that. But could there ever be more?

It took less than a second to distinguish wistful thought from harsh reality.

Adam seemed to sense the sudden, bow-strung tension within her. She felt him stir, trying to find her features beneath the web of tangled hair that made such an effective shield.

"Jess?" He angled her chin upward with the tip of his finger. "What's happening here? What is it?"

"We should be getting back."

She moved to sit up, but with a tug, Adam easily brought her beneath him. She turned her face away, trying to think, trying to avoid the truth that wanted to break her heart in two.

"Don't shut me out, Jess."

"Adam, please..."

"Listen to me." He gave her a caressing smile, and his lips took on a self-deprecating twist. "No regrets. Remember?"

"Yes."

"Then what's troubling you?"

"I don't think we should...do this again."

The look in his eyes was dark and probing. "Why not?"

"You were right. This isn't what either of us needs right now."

He laughed at that, drawing her fingers down beneath the blanket. "You don't think so? Feel me. Tell me what I *do* need, then, if not this." He sucked in a quick breath as her fingers moved reflexively against him. "Oh, sweetheart, can't you tell that I'm ready for you again?"

She pulled her hand away instantly. "You know that's not what I mean. We both have responsibilities. "My father—"

"Is far more capable of managing his life than you give him credit for."

She bit her lip and looked away. Not in Doc's current state, he wasn't. Now would be the perfect time to tell him about her father's problem with alcohol, she thought, but the words stayed lodged in her throat. A queasy sense of dishonesty made her respond more sharply than she might have. "That's not the point. And what about my studies?"

"What about them? Study all you want, but we can still be together."

"I have plans, Adam. So do you. You have your hands full with the stable."

"I'll make time for you." His lips found the sensitized curve of her breast. "I'll always make time for you."

Before his lips could do any more damage to tremulous logic, she pushed upward, hugging the scratchy blanket to her breasts. Over one bare shoulder, she tossed him a defiant look. "That's exactly what I mean. You're too distracting. Neither of us would ever get anything accomplished."

He smiled wickedly. "I think we just accomplished a lot."

"You're not taking my objections seriously."

With a sigh he settled back against the hay, fingers laced behind his head. "Because they're not objections, they're excuses." He lifted himself onto both elbows. "Ah, hell, Jess, I can't explain what's happening between us. I just know that ever since you came along, nothing makes sense anymore. I can't eat. I can't sleep. I'm so restless I feel like I've got ants crawling under my skin."

She forced lightness into her tone by smiling ruefully. "Maybe it's a summer cold."

The hay shifted with a sudden rustling sound as he rose behind her. His hands settled on her shoulders. "Don't ever denigrate what I feel for you," he said. His words rumbled against her scalp as his lips sifted through her hair.

He lifted the heavy mantle of her hair. His breath flowed, a zephyr of sweetness, against the short, fine tendrils at the base of her neck. At last he turned her to face him. His mouth connected with hers. More than anything, she wanted to lose herself in his kisses. He chooses his weapons well, she thought with sudden, keen awareness. He had the ability to cause her such hurt.

She was beginning to feel as though they were locked in a contest of wills. But she had to be the one to win, she *had* to. Determinedly, she jerked her head away. "Adam, no! We can't do this. It's stopped raining. I want to go back."

"All right. But first, I want the truth. I'm not talking about all the excuses you've just given me. I'm talking about the reason behind the fear I see in your eyes."

Feeling desperate, she decided on honesty. "You hired my father, Adam. But I'm not part of the package."

He went still. "What does that mean, exactly?"

"I know you have a plan for Rising Star. My father can help you realize it, so you'll use him to get what you want. That's business, and nobody gets hurt in that kind of agreement." She swallowed hard, trying to dislodge the knot of pain in her throat. "But I know you have *personal* goals, as well, and until you've made up your mind who fits them, I'm not willing to be just a place holder."

He moved so quickly that she gasped. He rose and began to pace the straw-littered floor. She wondered if he was even aware of his nakedness. Then suddenly he wheeled around and stared at her. "So that's how you think I see you? Some sort of stand-in? The woman I want to have sex with until someone better comes along?"

"I'm sorry, Adam. But you've said yourself—"

He snorted and threw out a forestalling hand. "Yeah, I know what I've said," he replied, running a distracted hand through his hair. He bent to retrieve his clothes. "Don't apologize. I asked for the truth. I just didn't expect it to be so unflattering."

Following his example, Jess began sorting through the tumbled heap of her clothes. They dressed without a single word between them. Adam moved to the horses and began saddling Keno. Over Vadar's back Jess stole a glance at Adam's pale, implacable profile. He seemed completely absorbed in his thoughts, and his mouth was compressed in a tight, thin line that didn't bode well.

With a sinking heart she realized that this was for the best. He must know she was right. It could never work between them. Never. Better to end it now and move on, before either of them got seriously hurt.

By the time they had finished saddling the horses, a vicious wash of tears lay behind Jess's eyes. She wanted to be home. She needed to find some dark, quiet corner to retreat into.

She gasped when Adam suddenly came up behind her and turned her to face him.

"Okay, so maybe you're right," he confessed in a grim, low voice. "Lord knows I've spent enough years laying out the future I want."

So he agreed with her. She stood still, trying to regain some sense of dignity and wishing she could hate him for not loving her.

Trying for a nonchalant tone, she said, "Great. We're in agreement. You continue building your great master plan for life, and I'll...I'll..."

His eyebrows arched. "Continue tearing it down?"

Damn him! *I won't cry. I won't.*

"I'm not going to tear down anything," she said, hoping that some of the fire burning a hole in her heart could find its way into her voice. "In fact, I'll make a concerted effort to get out of your hair as soon as possible. It's settled."

"Settled, hell." With one finger he tipped her chin up so that their gazes met. "If it's so settled, how come you look as miserable as I feel?"

She pulled her head away, praying that if she remained silent he'd give up and get on his horse.

He didn't. Instead, he placed both hands against Vadar's bareback pad, trapping her within the circle of his arms. He leaned closer. "Answer me, Jess. If you're so damned happy—" his fingers reached out to touch the silver wetness that quivered at the corner of her eye "—why the tears?"

She was silent a long time. The rain had blown away, and the night breeze whistled through the Australian pines surrounding the barn. Not far away, she thought, the world is still intact. People are living normal lives.

But Adam didn't move, and finally there was nothing

else she could do, nowhere else she could look but at him. She wiped the moisture from her cheeks. "Because I'm not jaded or worldly enough to pretend that what we just shared wasn't special to me," she said softly.

He didn't move a muscle, but the full force of eyes so dark they seemed black continued to pin her with a bottomless gaze. The silence that came between them was unbearable, and she rushed to fill it.

"That doesn't mean I think we should ever do it again."

"Because you think you know what I want?" Adam asked.

"Yes." She bit her lip and decided to add weight to her argument. "And because I think I know what *I* want. It isn't this, Adam. What we shared was fun and a little naughty, but it wasn't *real.* We're adults, and there's no reason—"

He shook his head. "I don't feel like an adult. Right now I feel like a kid who's had Christmas snatched away from him. I'm not used to losing like that, and I'm not willing to chalk it up to lust and let it go. Let *you* go."

"It won't work—"

"Shouldn't we give ourselves the chance to find out? Listen—" He looked away for a moment, as though composing his thoughts, then back at her with new determination glinting in his eyes. "Suppose I'm wrong? Suppose we're both wrong? Whatever I thought I wanted doesn't seem to be working for me anymore. I don't know what's the right thing for either of us. I don't know if what we have together has a snowball's chance in hell of surviving. I only know that wherever we go from here, we can't go back. I want to be with you. And you can deny it all you want, but your body doesn't lie. You want to be with me."

"I'm not a casual-affair kind of person, Adam."

"I want you in my life, Jess. Even if you're not in my bed."

"And you expect me to believe you can be happy with that kind of bargain?"

"Hell, no, I won't be happy!" he said, grinning for the first time. "I'm a red-blooded American male. I'm going to do everything in my power to convince you that my bed is exactly where you want to be." With exquisitely tender intimacy, he suddenly lowered his head and placed his lips against the corner of her mouth. "And you can protest and deny me all you want..."

"I will," she promised on a whisper of breath.

She turned her head away and shivered as his mouth dragged across her cheek. "This is a mistake," she whispered. "We don't have a future together."

He laughed unrepentantly. "My beautiful little gypsy. When are you going to accept that your predictions just never come true?"

JESS PULLED HERSELF away from daydreaming long enough to glance at her watch.

Almost an hour since Doc had gone inside the Adult Counseling Service building. As grudgingly as he'd kept the appointment she'd made for him, she'd expected him to bolt out the front door about two minutes after he'd entered. But he hadn't, and she could consider that a good sign, couldn't she?

She wished she knew more about how places like this worked and what Doc would be willing to tell the counselors. Would they ask him about his drinking? Would he bring it up? She supposed all she could do was wait and see.

Settling back in the passenger seat of the truck, Jess

tipped her wide-brimmed hat over her eyes to block the sun glaring through the front windshield. The downtown Ocala street offered little of interest, and she closed her eyes with a sigh and let her mind drift once again.

It didn't have to drift very long. Adam's kisses—that's about how far her mind took her these days.

There'd been no repeat of those wildly passionate moments in the maintenance barn. But true to his word, Adam had begun a campaign to get to know her better. On several occasions he had joined the morning rides she and Angela took along the back trails. He'd invited her and her father and Bill Page up to the house for dinner and made a special point to include her in the conversation. He'd even asked her to one of the breeders' association functions.

She had refused, and, complaining that he must ease his disappointment somehow, he'd kissed her until she could hardly think straight. A consolation prize, he told her, and she realized he was very good at finding reasons to be consoled.

She smiled even now, thinking how wonderful Adam's kisses could be—

The driver's-side door opened, and Jess sat up in her seat abruptly. A long moment passed while her father fiddled with his keys, then started the truck. She tensed, struggling against the urge to batter him with questions about the session. Doc's features were pale and tight, and she knew him well enough to know that he wouldn't tell her a thing until he was good and ready.

He glanced over his shoulder to see if he could merge into the traffic. Then suddenly, he shut down the engine, smacked his hand against the steering wheel and turned in the seat to face her.

"They want me to come back," he said.

"What's wrong with that?"

"I don't want to."

Jess took a deep breath and tried to appear nonchalant. "Then don't."

Her father's eyes narrowed. "Don't act like it doesn't matter to you one way or the other. I know what's turning in that head of yours. It won't work, lass. I won't spill my personal business to a stranger."

"Maybe a stranger's the best person to tell your problems to. Someone objective—"

"I said 'personal business,'" her father snapped. "Not 'problems.'"

"Papa…"

"Aye, I know what you want. You want to know why I drink more than I used to. Why don't you just ask, if that's what all this counseling nonsense is all about?"

Doc seldom spoke to her so sharply, and his features were flushed. Aware that she'd struck a nerve, Jess realized that it was too late to turn back now. Maybe it was time for the truth. "All right," she said, biting her lips nervously. "I'm worried because your drinking seems excessive, unpredictable. When Mother was alive you hardly touched a drop—"

"When your mother was alive I had no need for it."

Jess looked at him, then quickly turned her gaze out the windshield. There was so much pain in her father's expression. "It won't take away the hurt, Papa," she said softly. "You can't drink to forget—"

"Is that what you think I do?" he asked quietly, then shook his head. "You're wrong, lass. When I drink I don't forget. I see your ma sharper than ever. Every turn of her head, every soft breath she took, every smile she ever gave me…even the last, when she knew 'twas her final moments on earth and me begging her to forgive me…"

His voice broke and the words trailed into the silence. Jess turned in her seat. She caught her father's hand in hers. "It wasn't your fault," she whispered.

He didn't seem to hear her. His face was turned toward the windshield, where the sun poured through with relentless, harsh brightness. When he spoke, the words were so soft he might have been talking to himself. "Sometimes the days get away from me, and I can't see her face in my mind so clear. I get scared, 'cause I think I've forgotten, that I'm losing her forever. But when I take a nip or two, she comes back to me, and I think she'll never leave me again. I need that. I need to keep her with me..."

Jess felt cold. Was that what her father really wanted? Never to get on with his life, but forever be mired in the past? How could anyone hope to reach him, then? The shock of his words made her move closer, until her hands found his shoulders. His features were a blank mask, and she shook him slightly to capture his attention. His head swung in her direction.

"Papa, you can't," Jess cried desperately. "You have to let her go."

He blinked rapidly and seemed to come to himself. Pulling away, he shook his head. "I don't know if I can, lass."

ADAM WATCHED ANGELA bounce up and down on the diving board. Her swimsuit was modest, but he noticed she'd begun to leave the gangliness of her teen years behind. Her slim, young body hinted at future beauty. In spite of the limp, it wouldn't be long before boys took a real interest.

He frowned. Hadn't one of the grooms been hanging around the house a lot lately? Possible trouble there, he thought, and made a mental note to talk to her about it.

She took a final hard jump and sent him a quick smile before she swanned into the pool. Adam swallowed a gulp of iced tea, then returned to the article he'd been reading. No, he didn't have to worry about Angela. His sister was a good kid. She'd follow his advice. She was manageable.

Unlike Jess Russell.

He shook his head, wondering how he'd had the misfortune to be attracted to such a stubborn, unpredictable woman.

By now the yearlings were in serious training. Midnight Star was slated for a maiden race in November, with Doc Russell proclaiming him to be a push-button runner. Excited by what a horse of that caliber could mean to his future, Adam should be ready to dive full force into the season.

Instead, he couldn't get his mind off Jess.

Since that stormy, magnificent night in the maintenance barn, they had agreed to give their relationship a chance to grow. Of course, making that kind of bargain had been easier for Adam when he'd been fairly certain he'd be able to entice Jess back into his bed. He was eager to share the subtle nuances of lovemaking with her, to bring her body to a quivering response in a dozen different ways. But had he?

No.

Jess Russell was the first woman he'd ever met who couldn't be persuaded, couldn't be bullied, couldn't be charmed into thinking he was...well...special. He'd always been somewhat successful with the ladies, but he hadn't really concentrated on one particular woman in...Lord, seven years. Maybe he'd lost his touch.

Ti thinks I'm a pretty good catch, he told himself.

Ti thinks anyone who compliments her wardrobe is worth a second look.

Damn! Maybe he *was* past his prime.

With an exasperated sigh, Adam tried harder to focus on the magazine article he was reading about Thoroughbred syndicates. *In the past ten years, the racing industry has seen a major shift in the number of—*

What was he supposed to do? Blame this mismatched romance on bad timing, bad planning, bad...*vibes?* Move on? Forget her? Revisit all the plans he'd made seven years ago until he believed every stinking word again?

He almost wished he could.

But with every passing day, that seemed less and less of an option. To his increasing consternation and surprise, he had discovered an irrational determination within himself to alter Jess's feelings.

It was crazy. He should have been delighted that she placed no restrictions on him, demanded no more attention than what he was so embarrassingly eager to give. His game plan for the future remained intact, and not once, not once had she made the suggestion he change it.

Any other man might have told him he should count himself lucky. She did not cling or pout or beg for attention. Yet it chafed to know that, while the white-hot passion that had burned between them that one time was something neither could discount, his enjoyment of it seemed to far outweigh Jess's own.

And even now, when he was pulling out all the stops to please and impress, he often felt her withdrawal. He tried to deny it. He tried to ignore it. He wanted to battle it openly, but he wasn't always sure what caused it, much less where the front lines lay.

God, the woman had him tied up in more knots than a windblown mane!

"You haven't heard a word I've said," Angela's voice intruded.

Adam glanced up to find his sister seated in the opposite patio chair, her wet hair dripping on the table as she poured a glass of iced tea. He thought how nice it would be to share one of these summer days with Jess here beside the pool, how attractive she'd look in a swimsuit now that her cast had come off. But unwilling to draw attention to their relationship, she had refused to come.

She had told him one day that she couldn't identify with his life of charity balls and tennis tournaments. She was a homebody at heart who liked old movies and board games and pizza. Hell! He liked pizza. Maybe if he tried harder to become a part of *her* world...

"Stop pretending you're reading, and listen to me," Angela demanded.

"I want to finish this article."

"It's two columns long. You've had your head buried in that page for forty-five minutes. You're not reading, you're thinking."

"So let me think in peace. Finish your tea."

"What are you thinking?"

With an aggrieved sigh, Adam tossed the magazine to the table. "I'm thinking how lucky only children are because they don't have brothers and sisters to drive them crazy."

Angela smiled and scraped water out of her hair. "Be serious. I need to talk."

"All right," Adam conceded, folding his hands over his chest. "You're not going to leave me alone until you get what you want. What's the problem?"

"I don't want to go to Palm Beach next month."

He shook his head. "Sorry, we have to go."

"I hate polo."

"Geoffrey Wilson was Dad's friend. You might be too young to remember, but he was one of the few men who stood by us when everything hit the fan. He's invited us to this charity match, and we can't disappoint him.''

''So why can't you go and leave me here?''

''Geoffrey specifically asked about you. He can't wait to see how much you've grown. Stop fretting, Angel. You'll have fun.''

''I won't. There won't be anyone there even close to my age.''

''You don't know that.''

''I do,'' she retorted with a petulant curl to her lips. ''I'll have to stand around and listen to a bunch of old people talk about horses and the stock market.''

''Not everyone's like that, Angela. Ti will be there. God knows, she doesn't care a thing about the stock market unless it affects her personal bank account.''

Angela's expression became incredulous. ''Oh, now there's a good reason to go. Iwanna and I have *so* much in common.''

''So invite a friend. Geoffrey's place is huge. He won't mind an extra guest.''

''Adam, this isn't a rock concert we're talking about. I don't have friends who'd want to go to a polo match.'' She straightened in her chair as inspiration struck. ''How about Jess? I could ask her.''

''I already—'' He broke off, not willing to admit that Jess had already turned him down. Flat. ''She wouldn't be interested,'' he amended.

''I bet she'd go if I told her I'd be nervous around all those horses.''

That was an angle he hadn't considered. He rubbed his jaw and gave Angela a slow, speculative glance. ''She might.''

''What's going on between you two?'' she asked with sudden boldness.

"Nothing you should concern yourself with, brat."

"I wish you two—" Angela stopped and tilted her head to look past Adam's shoulder.

Adam turned in his chair to find Jess striding toward them. The determined expression on her face, the crispness of her walk said this wasn't a social call. He took one look at the oblong white box she carried, the gift he'd sent to her door that morning, and didn't have to guess the reason for her obvious displeasure.

She halted beside his chair, then set the box in front of him on the table. "I'd like to speak to you," she said in a low-pitched voice, as though she were a schoolteacher about to reprimand a wayward pupil.

Angela grabbed her towel and rose. "I'm going in to change," she announced, though it seemed doubtful anyone heard.

Adam took in the militant sparkle in Jess's eyes, the jutting firmness of her breasts beneath her T-shirt. Errant wisps of red hair peeked from beneath the Confederate Army cap tilted back on her head. Oh, she was angry, all right, but damned if he didn't feel a familiar ache of longing stir to life just looking at her.

"Something wrong?" he asked.

"You know perfectly well what's wrong." In an attitude of irritated impatience, she shook her head and waved one hand over the box. "I can't accept this."

"Jess, men have been giving clothes to women for centuries."

She rejected that logic with a sharp shake of her head. "We're talking about one of the sexiest nightgowns I've ever seen, not a flannel bathrobe. Take it back, Adam. Or I'll give it to charity."

He laughed at that threat. "The fellows who pick up for the Salvation Army ought to get a kick out of that."

He sensed that his response infuriated her even more, and some of his patience evaporated. He'd never had a woman reject a gift before. Didn't she understand the pleasure he got from buying her things? If he could have managed it, he'd have wrapped up the moon and turned it into a Christmas present; he was that far gone. Couldn't she see that?

He leaned forward to take her hand, feeling ridiculously pleased when she made no move to snatch it from his grasp. "Stop fussing, Jess. I saw it in a shop window in town and knew it was meant for you."

"Well, it's not."

"How do you know? Have you tried it on?"

"I don't have to. I know."

"The store clerk said it should be a perfect fit," he said in a low, husky voice. His fingers moved suggestively along her bare arm. "But if you want a second opinion, you can come up to the house later and model it for me."

She drew her shoulders up and pierced him with a determined look. "Adam, I mean it. I don't want it. It's impractical to spend that kind of money on such a small amount of silk and satin." When he made a scoffing sound at that, she added, "And it's much too intimate a gift."

"But we *have* been intimate," he refuted logically. "And I want us to be again. I suppose a scarf might have been more appropriate for where we are in our relationship, but it sure isn't where I *want* to be." He cocked his head at her. Beneath the determination in her eyes lay another emotion, but when he tried to examine it, she turned her gaze away. "Jess, what's *really* bothering you?"

She pursed her lips as though debating her words. After

a long moment she said, "Wearing a glamorous nightie won't make me someone else."

"I hope not," he replied with another laugh, which he quickly stifled when he realized she didn't see the humor he found in her argument.

"I'm just me, Adam."

He pulled her against his body, shifting his weight to trap her between his legs. She gasped sharply and arched away from him, but when he reached out to play with the trailing wisps of hair along her neck, she went still. "What you are is a beautiful woman who deserves beautiful things. Wear it for me," he whispered close to her ear. "Please."

"Wearing it won't get me any closer to your bed."

"Maybe not, but I've got a great imagination. In my mind, I can see you wearing it already."

"Your mind is the only place you're going to see it."

"For now."

She gave him an unhappy look. "Adam," she breathed, his name nearly inaudible as it fell from her lips. She shook her head. "Why do you have to make things so hard for me?"

His mouth curved upward. He steered one of her hands to the front of his jeans. "You make things hard for me," he countered with a playful growl.

She pretended to be shocked by his demonstration, but a moment later Jess laughed and touched him so possessively his breath seared away. It was one of the things he loved about her, this perfect blend of exciting contradictions. Shy and overly cautious one moment, wild and impetuous the next. He never knew what to expect, and he experienced a sudden wild thought of how much he might welcome years of discovering the myriad layers of her personality.

His body radiating heat, he touched his lips to hers. "Angela will be at a friend's house tonight." The words rumbled against her mouth, the suggestion all too clear.

"No. Doc and I play cards or watch old movies on Fridays. It's our night to do the 'father-daughter' thing."

"So I'll send Bill down to do the 'guy' thing. Those two can talk horses all night."

"Do you ever give up?" Jess chided between kisses.

"No," he said as his lips found the sweetness of her cheek, then the wistful corner of her mouth. "I can't help it. These stolen moments are playing hell with my libido."

"I thought we agreed—"

"Stupidest bargain I ever made. Let's renegotiate the terms." He dropped a light kiss on her lips. His eyes lifted to hers, a serious, sensual tether that told her he no longer teased.

"No. Nothing's changed, Adam."

As though resigned, he stared up at the clear blue sky for a long time before speaking. "Our time together is too precious to me to spend it arguing." His voice was warm and thick. When she tried to speak, he placed a finger over her lips. "I'll back off. Just do me one favor."

"What kind of favor?" she asked suspiciously.

"Come to Palm Beach next month." Forestalling her objection, he quickly added, "I'm not asking for myself. Angela's nervous as hell about being around so many horses."

"But she's doing so much better. She even put Misty Lady to a gallop yesterday."

"She's just anxious to please us both."

Jess shook her head. "I won't fit in there. That kind of lifestyle—the kind you like—doesn't suit me."

Adam frowned. "How do you know? You can't possibly know enough about it to make up your mind fairly yet. And isn't that part of what we're supposed to be doing now—exploring our relationship?''

He had a valid point. Feeling desperate she added, ''I'm just not comfortable around your friends, Adam.''

''They could be your friends, too, if you'd let them.''

She wanted to remind him these were some of the same people who hadn't lifted a finger to help Rising Star or the Connors seven years ago, but she didn't. She didn't want to argue with him. Searching for an alternative, she said, ''Take Tim with you. He'll look after Angela.''

He frowned. ''Why would you think of him?''

''Adam, have you considered the possibility that your sister's in love?''

The frown became thunderous. ''She's too young to be in love.''

''She doesn't think so.''

''I'll talk to her. Tim isn't someone she should be encouraging.''

''Why not? He's a nice kid.''

He shook his head, rejecting her words almost before she finished speaking them. ''She shouldn't get involved with any of the men employed on the farm.''

Jess straightened. ''But it's all right for you to get involved with one of the women?'' she countered.

''You're not an employee.''

''There's not much difference.''

He gave her a look that said her line of thinking was way off base. ''You know how stable romances are, Jess. These fellows move from farm to farm. Most of them don't have any long-range goals. They scratch by from season to season, exercising horses to pick up a few bucks.''

"You know Tim's not like that. He's got plans. He'd like to be a trainer."

"He's still not—" He stopped, as though realizing what he was about to say wouldn't sit well.

But the implication was clear. Jess felt suddenly sick inside with the harsh realization that all her worries concerning their relationship weren't groundless, after all. No matter how much Adam might deny them.

"I'm sure he's a good kid. But whatever plans the boy has," Adam amended gruffly, "I've got bigger ones for Angela. And they don't include a sweaty little romance between two teenagers with raging hormones."

Jess took a steadying breath and looked him deep in the eyes. "You really don't think Tim's good enough for your sister, do you?"

He frowned a little at the sound of pain in that accusation. "No. No one's good enough for Angela. But that's my problem, not yours. I'd appreciate it if you'd try not to give them any encouragement."

She slid away from him, leaving the white box containing the lingerie on the table. "I have to go. Doc will be back from the track soon, and I should be there."

She heard him heave a disgruntled sigh as she moved away. She knew he wouldn't understand or agree with her fears. He wouldn't see the similarities, the comparisons that could be drawn between their relationship and one he considered unacceptable for his sister.

"Why are you always fretting over Doc?" he called after her.

The question brought her to a halt. She should tell him, she thought. Tell him that she worried about her father now more than ever.

Two weeks ago, Doc had gone to bed drunk after a particularly rough day at the training track. Four days ago,

Bill Page had brought him back to the cottage after a night out to celebrate Midnight Star's quarter-turn times. The two men had been loud and happy, and it was easy enough to chalk it up to the excitement of knowing they trained a potential winner.

But Bill had been in control. Doc had not. And to her knowledge, he had not kept the second appointment she'd made for him at the counseling center.

She turned back, knowing that she couldn't find the words to explain. Not words that he'd find acceptable, anyway. "You don't understand."

"Maybe I don't." Adam said, and in the crisp afternoon light she glimpsed the sudden curiosity in his eyes. "Enlighten me."

Fear crowded in. What would he say if she told him the truth? What would he do? She couldn't bear the thought of Doc returning to the carnival. Except for those few lapses, he'd made such progress. And he loved the horses. He'd never do anything to put them in danger. She'd have to redouble her efforts to convince him to go back to the center. If Doc got into some sort of regular treatment program, there would be no need to worry Adam unnecessarily.

"I'm no more protective of my father than you are of Angela," she said at last.

Before he could question her further, Jess turned and walked away.

an appendage—the forbidden fruit of his starward flight
would be waiting to bite.

To avoid Adam he went shopping with Adam for their
new cottage for the Palm Beach trip. She redecorated her
study at home. She tolerated Zola, who came every day to
visit Jess and to "read" him as well. But she allowed
Zola to spend hours charting his moods, specifically

CHAPTER ELEVEN

LESS THAN A WEEK LATER Zola came for a visit. Jess was
delighted to see her for more than one reason.

Lately Doc had seemed preoccupied and restless. Twice
she had driven him to the adult counseling office in town,
but she couldn't tell if it was helping or not. After their
initial conversation about it, Doc had refused to discuss
what transpired in his one-hour sessions.

She knew now that Zola was in love with him. Having
the fortune-teller around the cottage should help take his
mind off whatever troubled him, and frankly she was glad
to have another pair of eyes keeping a close watch.

She was also aware that a houseguest might ensure that
she'd be too busy to be alone with Adam.

Adam, damn him, was like a man with a mission. Relentless. Persuasive. And every time she thought she had
the upper hand—that she could walk away from him with
her heart in one piece—he kissed her. And blew every
determined, sensible resolution of hers right to smither-
eens. She was, just as she had known all along she would
be, still most wretchedly in love.

She was hanging on, thank goodness, though barely.
Somehow, in spite of the smooth caress of his lips, the
yearning that threatened to buckle her knees, reason always called her back from the brink of passion.

Adam *desired* her. A generous, caring man, he took
enormous pleasure in making her happy. But the one gift

she wanted most—the commitment of his love—he might never be willing to give.

To avoid him, she went shopping with Angela for some new clothes for the Palm Beach trip. She redoubled her study efforts. She and Zola even captured every one of Doc's pigs and trimmed their hooves. Finally, she allowed Zola to spend hours charting her horoscope, specifically instructing the fortune-teller to forgo any mention of a love life. Over the speculative lift of her eyebrows, the older woman complied.

Having worked so hard to create obstacles and distractions, it came as a shock to return from the library the last night of Zola's visit and walk into a cottage filled with people. Well, certain people. Doc was there, of course. And Zola. Bill Page. And...Adam.

They were all seated around the dining-room table, ready to settle into a night of poker from the looks of it, and every one of them turned when she came in. Every one of them except Adam.

Her mouth went so dry she doubted she could have managed enough saliva for a good swallow. She stood in the doorway, suspended, her arms full of books.

"Pony-girl!" her father greeted. "We've been waiting for you. Pull up a chair. We need a fifth."

She dumped the library books on the living-room coffee table, wondering how quickly she could find an excuse to leave. "Sorry, I really ought to be studying."

Oh, lame one, Russell. You can do better than that, can't you?

Evidently, no one at the table thought it was a very good reason, either. Doc made a deprecating sound, Bill looked surprised, and, although Adam remained quiet, he seemed overly interested in the poker chips that sat in front of him on the table, as though he didn't trust himself not to look at her without laughing outright.

Zola had no such qualms. "Studying for what?" she asked. "You're not in school yet, are you?"

"No, but—"

"Then come. I insist you give me a chance to win back the money you've taken from me this week."

"Zoe, the twelve dollars I won from you playing canasta is hardly going to put you in the poorhouse, is it?"

Adam riffled his chips, capturing her attention. Without looking up at her, he said, "Give her a chance to recoup, Jess. You don't want to be considered a poor host, do you?"

Jess looked at the fortune-teller. "If it's a problem, I'll write you a check."

Zola waved her hand in the air to dismiss that solution. Her bangle bracelets clanked back and forth. "Where is the challenge in that? You know the cards, they talk to me, but I must learn to listen better."

Doc asked Zola innocently, "I thought your specialty was the crystal ball?"

The older woman frowned at him. "My spiritual strength comes from many sources." To Jess she said, "Come, come. You see? I'm dealing you in already."

Jess gave Zola a suspicious glance. Something was up. What was this old faker trying to pull? And why was Adam seated at the table? In all the weeks she and Doc and Bill had sat around playing cards, he'd never so much as inquired who won the pot. Who had invited him?

The desire to know brought her closer to the table. "What are you doing here, Adam? I would think you'd have more important things to do than play cards with us."

"Can't think of anything," he responded mildly. His

eyes never left the table, where Zola was dealing with an efficiency that was almost unnerving.

"This afternoon Angela said she thought you were going to be at some dinner party tonight."

"I've been to about as many overblown, overheated functions as I can stomach lately. You know how it is. Sometimes you just need to kick back, relax a little with friends you're comfortable with. So when Bill told me his plans for the evening, I asked if I could join. You don't mind, do you?"

"No."

He glanced up at her for the first time, and she saw the challenge in his eyes. "Then have a seat."

She pulled out a chair. What else could she do?

For about an hour, they played one hand after another. The pots were small. Jess lost, but she was pleased to see that Adam didn't fare much better. She told herself her lack of concentration was a result of worry over her father. Bill and Adam had brought chips and beer, and it would have seemed odd not to set them out. She had barely drunk half a bottle before everyone else started on their second—even Zola—but Jess's main concern was to find a way to keep Doc from overindulging.

After a while, she relaxed a little. Her father had stopped at two beers and then retrieved a soda from the fridge. Between poker hands the conversation around the table was spirited and varied. Surprisingly, Adam seemed to fit right in. Sitting across from him, Jess still found his eyes too often on her, but she was determined to ignore him. She even won a few hands.

They took a break, and Jess promised to dig up snacks from the refrigerator if the men would just stay out of the kitchen. They obliged by going outside on the front porch, where Doc could smoke his pipe. With Zola's help, Jess pulled items out of the cupboard and refrigerator: cheese balls, a carton of onion dip that still looked okay, raw veggies that she suspected only she and Zola would eat and some chocolate candy pieces she had planned to bake into cookies.

Frowning at the kitchen counter covered in bags and cartons, she asked, "Well, what do you think?"

"A feast!" Zola exclaimed with a flourishing hand.

"Not quite. But it ought to keep the natives from getting restless. And I'd rather have Doc pig out on junk food than—"

The older woman touched her arm. "You need not worry about tonight, Jess. Your father is in control. It is when he is alone that he slips too far into dark memories."

"Then how can I help him? I can't be with him twenty-four hours a day."

"No, you cannot. He needs professional help."

"There's a counseling center in town. He's gone a couple of times, but I don't sense any real commitment from him, and I'm not sure they're even aware of his drinking yet."

"He must make the decision to tell them on his own. But perhaps I can help. I will speak to him when he takes me to the bus station tomorrow."

Wiping her fingers on a hand towel, she gave Zola a quick hug. "Thanks, Zoe. I need all the help I can get." She sighed, feeling a little better. Then she cut the woman a sharp glance. "What about you and Papa?" she asked abruptly. "Any chance of getting him to admit he loves you?"

The fortune-teller laughed. "No. You young people. Always so impatient." Zola smiled at Jess affectionately. "But you, you are under love's spell, are you not?"

Shaken, Jess denied quickly, "No. What would make you think that?"

"Give me your palm," the woman ordered, placing her own hand out to receive it.

"Why?"

"Let me see it."

Jess did as she asked, sensing that it would be futile to refuse. She lifted her eyes to the ceiling, determined not to give credence to whatever silly nonsense the older woman spouted.

"Aha!" Zola crowed after a few moments. "There *is* a man in your future. A tall, dark—"

"And handsome man?" Jess finished for her skeptically. "Zola, it's me, Jess. Remember? I've already seen the show. Done it, in fact. At least have the decency to change the script. How about a Swedish lumberjack?"

Zola's eyes narrowed as she gave Jess a piercing look. She had pulled her long hair tightly back from her forehead, and in the harsh kitchen light the effect and angle of her head made her seem almost intimidatingly exotic. Mabel McAllister from Schenectady, New York, had never been further from Zola's present persona.

"You worry that your love is not returned," the woman said softly.

"I worry about *you*."

Zola touched one long finger to Jess's palm. "This line, the heart. Look how long it is. Perhaps this Adam Connor fellow?"

Stunned, Jess peered quickly down into her hand. She scowled. "That's not Adam. That's Vadar. And I got it when he knocked me down the other day."

"You date a man who beats you!"

"Vadar's a horse. And it's not my heart line, either.

It's the bridle burn I got when the wretched beast tried to nudge me out of his stall.''

"Perhaps," Zola conceded. "But the heart line is underneath, and I still sense its strength." Her voice thickened, becoming more accented and mysterious as she squinted into space. "Beating...beating..."

"Ah. Like Poe's *Telltale Heart* under the floorboards?''

The older woman seemed unperturbed by such criticism. She smiled and placed her hand over Jess's palm. "You make jokes to cover your fears and pain. But you should listen to what your heart is trying to tell you."

A sudden thought struck, and Jess snatched her hand out from under Zola's. "Did Adam put you up to this?"

"No. I am a fortune-teller with many talents. I see these things.''

"Swear it."

Dramatically Zola lifted her fist in the air. "I swear it on the grave of the great Czigany.''

"Who?"

"The queen mother of all gypsies.''

"Oh. I guess that's good enough." Determined to put an end to this uncomfortable conversation, Jess starting opening and closing the cupboards over the sink. "Now stop goofing around and help me find a pitcher. A few more beers and you'll be holding a séance in here, so from now on you're drinking lemonade.''

THE GAME BROKE UP around midnight. Zola came out the biggest winner with sixty-one dollars. She said goodbye to the men, kissed Doc on the cheek and slipped sleepily out of the room. The men stretched and collected their money from the table. In another minute Bill and Adam were at the door, saying good-night as well.

Just when Jess thought she was safe, Adam said, "Jess,

I'd like to speak with you. Could you walk with us a few minutes?''

''Can't it wait until morning?'' she asked, hoping for an easy way out.

No such luck. Her father said from the table, ''Go ahead, lass. I'll start picking up here.''

Reluctantly she nodded and followed Adam and Bill outside. The night breeze cooled her skin and sifted playfully through her hair as she made her way with them across the silent grounds. The gravel beneath her slippered feet crunched softly, still warm from the heat of the day. Really, she thought, there wasn't much danger with Bill Page between them. It was a perfectly controllable situation...

Until Bill decided to check on one of the horses. He sauntered away with a quick good-night. Leaving her alone with Adam. In the dark.

Good grief, she thought. Was everyone and everything conspiring against her tonight?

She watched Bill as he was swallowed by the darkness. Turning, she nearly jumped out of her skin. Adam had moved to stand at her elbow. He extended a hand in the direction of the garden, where a pond and a secluded arrangement of benches formed an inviting spot among rosebushes. ''It's a nice evening. Shall we sit down for a few minutes?''

They had come an equal distance between the main house and the cottage, and right now, in Jess's mind, the lights in the cottage windows burned like a lighthouse beacon to a floundering ship. It was probably the chilly evening air that raised goose bumps along her arms. Adam must have seen her shiver, because he stripped off the leather jacket he wore and dropped it over her shoulders.

''Better?'' he asked.

She nodded, too suffocated by her own heartbeats to speak. The jacket smelled like him. Leather and horses. The warm, clean male scent she thought she could smell even in her bed late at night.

His arms were still around her. "I know what you're thinking, and I promise to behave," he said with a smile.

In the moonlight his features had lost their taut control. The lines of cynicism had faded from around his mouth. He appeared no more than a teasing, charming lover, with a lock of dark hair tumbled against his forehead, and the traces of a smile lifting the corners of his full lips.

"I'm not sure that's good enough," she told him.

His smile widened. "Scout's honor."

"Forget the scouts. What about Czigany?"

"Who?"

"Never mind."

The white wrought-iron furniture stood out starkly under the moon. The scent of roses wafted on the night air, their perfume—a heady pleasure—filled Jess's nostrils as she inhaled deeply and sat down. Adam settled next to her. Neither one of them said anything for several seconds.

"I had a good time tonight," Adam said at last. "Did you?"

"I suppose. If you consider losing money fun."

"I'll give you a chance to win it back. We could play tomorrow night. Just the two of us."

"I'm out of money."

"Haven't you ever heard of strip poker?"

She turned her head to look at him then, and even in the poor light she caught his sexy grin, full of promise and teasing amusement. She shook her head.

"I didn't think so," he said with a regretful sigh. "Thought it was worth a try, though."

"A pretty pathetic one. You said you wanted to talk?"

"Yes. Well..." He straightened and cleared his throat. "Yesterday I ran into a breeder from Lexington. We got to talking, and I told him your father was working for me. He was surprised. He seemed to think that Doc had quit the training business for good. He didn't have any details, but he indicated the break with Carraway Hills was a sudden decision."

Jess heard the rush of her heartbeat in her ears booming so loudly that she wondered that he didn't hear it, too. Whatever she had been expecting from him, it hadn't been this. "He wasn't fired, if that's what you're asking."

"If that's what I was asking, I could find out with one well-placed phone call in the morning."

Adam turned her to face him. His hands gripped her arms, gently, but with determination. When he spoke, his voice was softer, deeper. "What's wrong with your father, Jess? Why are you so protective of him?"

Her pulse became erratic. When she spoke, she was amazed at how natural the words sounded. "He's my father. He's not a young man anymore. I can't help being overprotective." She summoned her pitiful resources, filling the uncomfortable silence with a weak protest. "I'm no worse than you are with Angela."

She heard Adam's sigh, part disappointment, part exasperation. "Don't try to sidetrack me. I know there's something you're not telling me, and I know it has to do with his reasons for leaving Lexington."

"Why don't you just ask *him?*" She glared at him.

"I can," he replied mildly. "If that's what you want. Look, Jess. I'm not trying to hurt you or Doc. From the moment the two of you came here, I could have pressed to get the truth from the people who worked with your father. I haven't. Because they don't love him the way you do. Whatever it is, I'm willing to hear it from someone who cares about him.''

The tender note in his voice made her throat clog with unshed tears, but she felt compelled to defend her father. ''Your opinion of Doc should be terrific! He's put Rising Star back in contention.''

''Listen to me,'' he said gently. ''No one appreciates your father's worth more than I. But I think I deserve to know about any potential problem. I've got a lot of exposure here.''

''Doc would never do anything to hurt you or Rising Star.''

''Then there's no harm in filling in a few of the gaps. Why did Doc sell everything he owned and leave Carraway?''

Adam studied her features so intently that tightness built within her chest. As though he sensed her discomfort, he smiled encouragingly.

She abandoned all hope of evasion. ''Lexington held too many memories. Mother's ghost was everywhere, and he blames himself for what happened.''

A moment passed, then another. At last, in a quiet tone, he said, ''How did your mother die?''

She shook her head, the old, unburied pain of her mother's death making it difficult to form words. Adam's fingers reached out to stroke her arms. With that slow, comforting movement the tension in Jess's body stretched and began to unravel. ''She and Doc regularly went to the auctions. Mother saw a palomino she wanted, a real beauty, but hardly more than green-broken. My father told her he couldn't afford much time to work off the stallion's rough edges, but she insisted.''

''If your mother was as stubborn as you are, it would

be no surprise to hear that your father couldn't refuse her.''

Her gray eyes sought his. ''He never could refuse her anything,'' she whispered through dry lips. ''Never. But he should have.'' She drew a ragged breath. ''Just that once, he should have.''

Adam pulled her closer, cradling her in tenderness. ''Jess…Jess, it's all right,'' he consoled. ''Take it slow.''

''Doc worked the stallion for a few weeks, but Mother was impatient and convinced him she preferred a mount with a little spirit. Against his better judgment, my father turned the palomino over to her. Less than a week later, the animal threw her off. She broke her neck and died on the way to the hospital.''

Lost in memories, Jess remained pressed against Adam's shoulder. His fingers sifted through the unruly tendrils of hair that surrounded her face.

''So Doc blames himself,'' he stated at last.

''I met him at the hospital and the look in his eyes—'' She shivered and shook her head against remembrance. ''He went straight home, took out his old army pistol and shot the stallion in his stall.''

She felt his breathing catch.

Her words came short and sharp, as though she'd been running. ''You have to understand, my father worshiped my mother. It never occurred to him he'd ever have to live without her. Losing her devastated him.''

His hands drifted down her spine. Even through the back of his leather jacket, she felt the warm tenderness of his caress. ''Not long ago, I wouldn't have understood something like that,'' he murmured into her hair. ''But I do now.''

Tell him the rest, her conscience encouraged. *He'll understand.*

Not with everything he owns at stake, her mind refuted.

Adam could be kind and generous, but in business, particularly in his single-minded effort to return Rising Star to prominence, he couldn't afford to be anything but practical. As much as he liked and respected Doc, pampering a trainer with a drinking problem would be a serious mistake. Chafed by uncertainty, Jess's courage crumbled.

When he spoke, his voice was tender. "Doc will get better. You'll see, Jess. And you didn't have to keep all this inside. You could have told me." In gentle admonition, he added, "What else haven't you told me?" Even in the shadow-smudged moonlight his eyes seemed capable of uncovering all her secrets.

"Nothing." That quick denial sounded too much like guilt. She slipped deeper into Adam's embrace, wrapping her arms around his waist to avoid his eyes. "For you, my life is an open book."

He laughed at that. "With a couple of pages missing, perhaps."

He didn't believe her.

Every nerve jumped, but with a flash of eager relief, Jess realized Adam seemed to have lost interest in questioning her further. His mouth suddenly swooped down to capture her lips. "Jessie…" Her name was a soft caress, like the last lilting notes of a love song played in silvery isolation. "Oh, damn…if you don't go back to the cottage right now, I'm going to forget all about promises."

She pulled away and gazed at him with a startled upward glance. She saw enough in his face to know that what he said was true. If she didn't leave now, they were both lost.

Slipping out of his jacket and returning it to him, she

rose and hurried down the path toward the cottage. Leaving him without a word. Leaving her heart to find its own way back.

CHAPTER TWELVE

A WEEK LATER, her father urged Adam to enter Midnight Star in a regional stakes race. The purse was insignificant, but Doc was confident that the stallion would do well and benefit from the experience. Although reluctant at first to chance injury in such a minor contest, Adam eventually agreed.

The horse won by an astonishing twelve lengths.

The farm celebrated with a poolside party. Every member of the staff was invited, along with many local breeders. The back of the house glowed under party lanterns that settled a mellow beauty over each shrub and flower and sent golden light skipping across the water in the pool. The evening air, crisp with the snap of autumn, carried the strands of music, provided by a small band, to every corner of Rising Star property.

A smile frozen in place, Jess idly twirled the champagne glass that had been thrust into her hands by some well-meaning guest. She had discovered that the far side of the pool cabana was the best place for her. From that quiet, dimly lit corner she could survey the entire crowd without having to participate.

She heard her father's hearty laugh and turned her head in his direction. Doc was engrossed in conversation with one of Adam's neighbors, a farm manager loudly lamenting his luck with trainers and flattering Doc by asking his advice.

A pent-up breath escaped Jess's lips. The tension she'd felt rippling inside her all evening was just now beginning to subside. Her worries appeared to have been groundless. The celebration was nearly half-over, and Doc had remained in total control. This evening he'd had nothing stronger than a soft drink. She watched him constantly, but the vivid pictures her wayward imagination had drawn never materialized.

As though he divined her thoughts, Doc turned his head and caught her glance. He shot her a wink and a smile so reminiscent of the loving, secret glances he'd often given her mother that she felt her heart constrict with emotion.

He was so dear to her. She wanted his life to be the same as it had been before her mother's death. This first real win for Rising Star could be the beginning. Shouldn't she take encouragement from his behavior tonight? Maybe this recent success had shown him how little he needed to depend on the small, temporary comfort offered by a bottle.

Or maybe Adam was right, and she just fretted too much.

She wished she believed she was simply being overprotective. That she could safely leave him at Rising Star and enroll in veterinary school. Loyalty to her father was stealing time away from her own future.

Jess shifted her weight. Her newly mended ankle throbbed in protest against the heels she wore, and she felt chilled. She wished she could return to the cottage. Never much of a partygoer, she wouldn't even have come if Adam hadn't insisted.

As they had too often tonight, her eyes strayed to the far end of the pool, where Adam stood surrounded by well-wishers.

He looked happy and relaxed, accepting congratulatory

slaps on the back from his peers and good-naturedly promising them a run for their money at the racetrack. His words and laughter carried across the pool, the rich timbre of his voice sending little tremors of pleasure up her spine even from a distance.

She wanted to be near him, but she had not found the courage to approach him. Surrounded by the people he had known all his life, he seemed locked behind the invisible barrier of a past she could not share. With the exception of Rising Star staff, these people were strangers to her. If she went to him, would he treat her as he had her father, whisking her into an endless round of introductions?

But *how* would he introduce her? A friend? His trainer's daughter? His latest sexual conquest? She wasn't eager to find out.

Instead, she told herself that concern over her father's drinking would be all too apparent in her face tonight. She couldn't let her eyes connect with Adam's. Among all the mingling guests it was easy enough to stay hidden in the crowd.

Of course, this was only a small taste of Adam's world. Soon she'd be in Palm Beach, among more strangers who were important to him. People with money and connections and bloodlines that probably went back to the Mayflower. Good grief, what did she know about polo? Maybe she should see if the library carried anything on the subject.

"*Here* you are!" Angela intruded on her thoughts. "I've been looking for you everywhere."

Jess turned a startled glance toward Adam's sister. She'd been so absorbed in watching him that she hadn't even noticed the teenager's approach. Angela, looking very pretty in a powder blue dress that matched her eyes, smiled at her. A champagne glass dangled precariously from two fingers and the sparkle in the girl's eyes told Jess this wasn't her first drink.

Angela gestured toward the scene before her. "Why aren't you out there socializing instead of hiding back here? You should be dancing. I think several of the men want to ask you."

"Obviously they've never seen me dance."

"Waiting for Adam to ask you?"

"No."

"He's been looking for you, too, you know."

For weeks Angela had been probing for information regarding Jess's relationship with Adam. Jess had given nothing away, but the teenager made it clear she thought a match between them would be only slightly less romantic than Romeo and Juliet.

Remembering that sixteen-year-old girls tended to think in dramatic terms, Jess smiled indulgently. "I can see he's combing the area for me."

Adam was deep in conversation with a gray-haired man who kept shaking Adam's arm to add emphasis to his words.

"I know my brother. He wants to be with you."

Jess lifted her eyebrows as Angela downed the last of her champagne. "How many of those have you had?"

"Not many. And Adam said I could, just for tonight."

Jess grinned. "I'll bet he doesn't know how *much* you've had."

"No. And don't you tell him."

"You're going to have a dreadful headache in the morning."

"Maybe so," the teenager said with a sly smile. "But it's *tonight* that counts."

Jess gave her a puzzled look. Something in Angela's

eyes suggested secrets bursting to be shared. "What does that mean?"

The girl turned her head, tossing a look toward the knot of men near the French doors at the back of the house. Most of them were stable hands at Rising Star, and Jess recognized Tim's shaggy blond hair shining in the light from the lanterns.

"Let's just say," Angela began in a mysterious tone, "that Adam's not the only one who knows how to go after what he wants."

"Angela..."

As though she'd said far more than she intended, the girl sighed heavily and found interest in another topic. "Oh, look, Iwanna's just arrived. Leave it to her to make a late entrance."

Jess couldn't help it. Against her will, she glanced back to the French doors. Tianna, looking cool and regal in an aqua gown that flowed like a satin river around her long legs, was just floating to Adam's side. She twined her arm in his. He didn't disengage her hold, and when he looked down at her, his smile was warm and welcoming.

Determinedly, Jess brought her attention back to Angela. The girl's gaze had fastened on Tim once more. Dreamy, wistful. Thoroughly besotted. Something was brewing here. "Angela, how are you and Tim getting along?"

"I hardly see him," she complained. "Between all the jobs Bill and your father give him to do, he's working himself into an early grave. I don't know why suddenly he's the only one who can—" She broke off. "We're fine," she quickly added, abruptly switching her attention back to Tianna. "It won't do you any good, Iwanna," she said softly. "Big brother's only got eyes for Jess now."

"That's not true," Jess admonished, uncomfortable with the idea that anyone nearby might have heard.

"It is. Adam may have thought Iwanna was the woman for him at one time, but he doesn't anymore."

"When did Adam say Tianna was the woman for him?" Jess couldn't resist asking.

"Last summer. He thought she was just what he needed. Looks, power, money." She clutched Jess's arm, leaning close to confide in a conspiratorial tone, "I'm so glad you've brought him to his senses."

"Thanks. I think," Jess responded. Then looking across the pool to where Adam was laughing at something Tianna had just said, Jess remarked, "It doesn't look to me as though I've brought him to anything."

"You have," Angela insisted, then swung away. "Well, I'm off. Destiny awaits."

"Angela—"

She watched Angela make her way around the edge of the pool with a slight unsteadiness due to the champagne she'd consumed, the teenager's limp a little more noticeable. Definitely a monster headache tomorrow, Jess thought.

The girl veered off the pool decking, following the path that led to the stables. Her figure faded into the night. Jess frowned. If Angela had had too much to drink this evening, she shouldn't be left alone. Sooner or later, all that champagne was going to catch up to her. Remembering her own first overindulgence with liquor at a similar age, she couldn't let Angela go through the sobering-up process alone.

Should she tell Adam? Maybe he wouldn't want to be interrupted. His attention was focused entirely on Tianna, who still clung possessively to his arm. Jess had to admit, the woman looked as if she'd staked a claim there. And their striking looks were a perfect complement to each other. They might have been host and hostess, greeting their guests together.

Was Tianna *really* the kind of woman Adam had wanted? And did he still?

Her heart sank in despair at the same time as she chastised such thoughts. No matter how sure she was that Adam would eventually tire of trying to coax her into his bed, no matter how many times she told herself that Adam would never need her as a permanent fixture in his life, there was still a part of her, a tiny, hopelessly foolish part, that just couldn't give up weaving idealized fantasies about the two of them.

She watched as Tianna lifted one hand to Adam's face to capture his jaw. The sight of her lily-white fingers stroking his dark features was more than Jess could bear. She turned her glance away, eager to find distraction.

She would go after Angela herself. Obviously Adam had more important things to interest him. She could handle one slightly inebriated teenager. Maybe she should ask Tim for help. The boy would talk some sense into her.

Her eyes scanned the crowd, looking for the groom. The knot of stable hands was still beside the French doors, deep in discussion, but Tim was no longer with them. He seemed to have disappeared.

Just like Angela.

ADAM TRIED HARD, but it took Tianna's touch on his face to finally force his attention back to what she was saying. He could tell she didn't like it. She wasn't used to indifference from men.

For five minutes she'd been rattling on about some dinner party she'd been to, and for the life of him, he could hardly suppress the unsettling urge to clamp his hand over her perfectly lipsticked mouth. Good Lord, had she always been this self-absorbed?

Why was he so irritable tonight? It must be all the champagne. Too much of it had left him unaccountably cross and headachy. Or maybe it was the aftermath of Star's win. Delayed reaction had set in, making him tired and impatient.

He mustn't take it out on Ti. She'd always been supportive of his career plans. Finding it easier to let her ramble, Adam forced his features into a smiling mask and tried not to look bored.

"So why didn't you?" she asked.

"Why didn't I what, Ti?"

She favored him with an undiluted gaze of pure annoyance. "Why didn't you come to Daddy's party for the Ocala One Hundred? If I do say so myself, I think I outdid myself with the planning."

"I couldn't get away."

"What have you hired all these people for, if not to free yourself from the drudgery of the stable?"

"I don't consider it drudgery."

"Honestly, Adam. Even Lorne knows it's wise to curry the favor of Ocala's elite. You used to love that sort of thing, but lately you seldom bother to make an appearance."

Nearly at the end of his patience, he decided on the truth. "Frankly, Ti, I didn't come because I couldn't bear the thought of going to one more five-hundred-dollar-a-plate banquet and trying to pretend I wasn't eating the same old rubbery chicken that's always served."

In a petulant, teasing tone, she said, "I'm using a new caterer. We served Cornish hen à l'orange."

"You know what I mean."

She dismissed the topic of conversation with a toss of

her head. "Oh, never mind. You're just like Father and Lorne. All you think about are those damned horses."

He smiled and tried to look sufficiently chastened. "And where is Lorne this evening?"

"At his *mama's* in Boston. Poor woman thinks she wants to sell her cottage on Martha's Vineyard because the damp air bothers her arthritis. Lorne says the place is filled to the rafters with antiques. I say she should entrust them to someone who knows how to get the best price. Like me, for instance."

"So you still consider Lorne to be a potential Mr. Right."

"Well, with his bank balance, he's definitely not Mr. Wrong."

"And if he was?"

"Then I'm willing to settle for Mr. Okay," she said with a shrug. "As long as he brings his checkbook on the honeymoon."

Adam shook his head at her. "Ti, you are a money-hungry little witch. You're incorrigible."

She cast him a superior glance. "I distinctly remember conversations we've had where neither one of us thought it was appallingly bad taste to marry for money or power. Make up your mind, darling."

Oh, God, Adam thought. *She's right.* He rocked back on his feet to look down at her, unable to think of any way to acquit himself.

After a moment, Tianna's features cleared, and she waved away the conversation with a light laugh. "Don't look so unsettled, Adam. I forgive you. It's not like you to be rude. Too much champagne has put you out of sorts, I imagine."

He was spared making any further comment as two neighbors joined them to discuss the latest auction of

breeding stock. With half an ear primed toward the conversation, Adam set his features in a manner he hoped
might pass for interest, but inside his brain, thoughts
whirled and collided.

What do I want?

Everything was so hopelessly muddled. Not very long
ago he had clearly marked a path for the future, a path so
carefully orchestrated that it had almost seemed ordained.
But since Jess had come into his life, his world was out
of kilter, off its axis. He couldn't explain why, or even
exactly when it had happened. He wasn't sure how he
felt. He just knew that the aching need inside him was
worse than any physical pain a human being should have
to endure.

Beside him, Tianna, obviously bored, played with a
lock of golden hair, one manicured hand idly twirling a
curl between her fingers. She was flawlessly beautiful, he
thought. Like a priceless work of art.

*I could still have Ti. Or someone like her. All those
mothers who paraded their pretty debutante daughters
past me at the last club dance...*

He studied Ti out of the corner of his eye as she flicked
a strand of hair away from her throat.

An image formed in his mind.

All he could see were his own hands, plunging into a
riot of unruly red curls, its thick, lustrous mass spilling
over his fingers like living fire.

Jess.

Tianna's beauty, and that of her contemporaries,
seemed pale and undesirable, compared to Jess's charms.

Doc's daughter wasn't perfect. She couldn't control her
hair. She bit her fingernails when she thought no one was
looking, and was too outspoken and stubborn for her own
good. But she had a way about her, a warmth that was

almost frightening in its honest simplicity. And those gray eyes—whether as dark as a storm or cool and light as the finest Spanish steel—were expressive, vivid. Jess didn't know how to looked bored or indifferent. When she talked, her features became animated, as though lit from within.

Damned if she wasn't the most vibrantly alive woman he'd ever met! Ridiculously loyal and protective of her father, gentle with the horses and Angela, but passionate, so wildly passionate that one time with him.

And totally unwilling to succumb again.

It infuriated him that Jess Russell was a woman who could reduce his simplest manipulations to a tumbled house of cards. She resisted all his strategies, made him doubt his ability to control anything in his life, made him question his sanity.

When he was with her, he became someone else. Someone who didn't give a damn about social standing or power or Triple Crowns. Someone who shed every ambition and inhibition, finding enjoyment in the most ridiculous things.

He suspected she was part of the reason he felt so disagreeable tonight. Though he had practically begged her to attend this evening, she had yet to come to him. He'd caught glimpses of her in the crowd, but she seemed content to ignore him. That strict, impersonal distance she kept annoyed him.

Was she that immune to his presence?

He'd watched and waited for her arrival like a child awaiting Santa Claus. Surrounded by well-wishers, he'd known the moment she'd stepped through the patio doors, her arm clasped lightly through her father's. He'd wanted to go to her immediately, but he couldn't, of course. He had guests to think about. So, instead, he'd smiled and nodded, and smiled and nodded, and all the while he'd watched her move around the pool, greeting stable hands like old friends as she stuck close to Doc.

He could admit to himself that the closeness between father and daughter was another irritant. Jess fussed and fretted over the trainer as though he couldn't manage without her. Maybe Adam was jealous, but the daughter-father relationship wasn't good for either of them. The old man was perfectly capable of taking care of himself. Jess needed to develop other interests.

Like him, for instance. A little of that loving care coming his way wouldn't have hurt his disposition any.

"Adam, are you listening to me?"

The words penetrated his thoughts, but it was a moment longer before he could slide his glance back to Ti. He spotted Jess, moving along the path that led away from the house. Was she leaving? Didn't she intend to speak to him at all tonight?

"Adam..."

"I'm sorry," he apologized, making a deliberate effort to focus on his guests. Dammit! If Jess chose not to stay, why should he care? "What did you say?"

"I said, Jack Waverly wants a few of us to go over to the coast tomorrow for an afternoon on his boat. Do you want to come?"

He should want to. Jack Waverly was a good host and one of Ocala's wealthiest businessmen. He had connections that stretched all the way to Tallahassee. Yes, Adam thought, he should definitely want to encourage *that* friendship.

He drew breath, ready to form a response, but all he could think of was that Jess had left the gathering, and with her departure, the night had suddenly lost its enchantment.

JESS CHECKED THE HOUSE, but Angela was nowhere to be found. Not in her bedroom, or the study, or even the kitchen where the caterers, laden with trays, still sallied back and forth from the patio.

That left the grounds and the stables, and though she doubted the girl would visit the horses, Jess decided it was worth a look.

She checked each of the nearest barns. By the time she reached Barn Four, where Misty Lady and the rest of the saddle horses were stabled, Jess was beginning to worry. Wandering down the dimly lit aisle, she stopped at Vadar's stall, giving the animal a perfunctory scratch across his velvety nose and wondering where she should look next.

The gelding's ears flicked forward at the sudden sound of laughter, and Jess turned her head toward the far end of the barn. Snatches of conversation drifted out to her from the tack room, where the door stood open. She approached slowly, trying to make sense of the whispered words.

Reaching the doorway, she froze, and immediately color flooded her cheeks. Two guests were locked in a passionate embrace. For one panicked moment, she considered backing away, hoping they hadn't seen her, but in the next second she recognized Angela and Tim.

Neither of them had noticed her yet. Angela was doing her best to deepen the kiss she'd planted against the groom's mouth. Tim, poor boy, was trying to remain upright as the girl pressed against him. His hands were clamped firmly but gently along Angela's forearms, the young muscles straining to hold her off.

"Angela, we can't," the boy protested in a tortured whisper as he tore his mouth away. "Stop that. If anyone catches us, I could lose my job."

She shrugged and offered him a wide smile. "You mean if *Adam* catches us, don't you? So what? Bill Page says any one of the other farms would be glad to have you on their payroll."

"I don't want to work for any of the other farms. I like it here."

"Please, Tim," Angela begged, her arms curving around his neck before he had time to evade her grasp. In a wavering, barely audible voice, she coaxed, "You've been putting me off for weeks, but I know you want to make love to me. And I want you to."

"You're drunk."

"I'm not!" she objected, then frowned when a noisy hiccup threatened to make a liar out of her. "At least not so much that I don't know what I'm saying. I'm so tired of people running my life. I just want to be with you. Now. You want me, too, don't you?"

"I do, Angie," Tim replied, and his words were so weak that Jess suspected capitulation was only moments away. "You know I do. But—"

"Then I don't want to wait any longer."

With that encouragement, Angela stood on tiptoe and pulled his face down to meet hers.

So this was what the teenager had meant earlier by "destiny"! Obviously no longer satisfied with shy, wistful glances and worshiping her hero from afar, Angela had finally decided to take matters into her own hands. With the situation dangerously close to getting out of control, Jess knew it was time to intercede. She cleared her throat loudly and stepped into the room.

"Here you are!" Her words sounded abnormally shrill in the quiet of the barn.

Both Angela and Tim jumped and swung toward her. The groom flushed guiltily, but to his credit, Jess noticed he hugged Angela closer to him, as though protecting her. The girl blinked several times, and it was a long moment before her gaze focused.

When she realized she and Tim were no longer alone, Angela's forehead puckered in a look she usually reserved for people like Tianna Bettencourt. She drew a deep breath, as though preparing to do battle. "What are you doing here, Jess?"

"Looking for you. I thought you might need some help returning to the party."

"I'm fine. Please go back to the house. Tim will take me home."

Jess flicked a look at Tim. The young groom's feeble, hesitant smile quickly ebbed beneath a look of discomfort. Whatever his feelings for Angela, at the moment he clearly wanted rescuing. For both their sakes, Jess said firmly, "I think you'd better come back with me, Angela."

"No."

She wasn't prepared for the girl's outright refusal. When Doc overindulged, he turned pouty, but manageable, like a child who had to be scolded to bed. Angela, on the other hand, had lifted her chin in a determined gesture of defiance. She tried to affect a stance of unbending hostility that fell short only because of the amount of liquor she'd consumed. Jess tried hard not to find it amusing. "Look, I don't think this is where you should be right now."

"I can make my own decisions."

"I'm sure you can. But trust me, in a little while you're going to feel like every horse in this barn ran over you."

Tim leaned close, his fingers trailing over the girl's jawline. "Maybe you ought to go with her, Angie."

As though his gentle encouragement was the ultimate

betrayal, the color flowed hot in Angela's cheeks. Her challenging gaze turned uncertain and she looked away, catching her lower lip between her teeth.

Jess closed the distance between them. She hugged the girl to her, murmuring softly, "Please come back with me. You don't want Tim to see you this way, do you?"

"Did my brother send you after me?" she asked in a small voice, her eyes sparkling with sudden tears.

"Of course not."

"I know you saw us kissing. I'm not ashamed. I love Tim, and he loves me."

"I think that's wonderful."

"Adam doesn't. He's forbidden me to see him. Did you know that?"

"No, but I'm sure he'll come around."

"He won't," the girl repudiated in a shaky voice, becoming more agitated by the moment. "He doesn't think Tim is good enough for me."

Angela began to cry, the tears sliding silently down her flushed cheeks. Beside her, Tim made a restless movement, clearly uncomfortable and uncertain how to help. Jess ducked her head to find the girl's eyes. "That's ridiculous," she said in a no-nonsense tone, though her own conversations with Adam in the past had confirmed the teenager's claim. "I'm sure that's not the case at all."

"We just want to be together. You understand that, don't you, Jess?"

She brushed baby-fine strands of blond hair away from Angela's face. "Of course I do. And I'm sure we can work it out. But this isn't the way to handle the problem, honey." She looked to the groom for agreement. "Tim knows that, don't you, Tim?"

"She's right, Angie. Listen to her. If we mess up now

it will only get me thrown off the farm. I won't be able to see you at all.''

"You and I can work on Adam," Jess promised her. "And in the meantime, maybe I can set up a date for the two of you. Something romantic. Away from the farm.''

"Would you really help us, Jess?" the teenager asked hopefully.

"Not if I have anything to say about it," a male voice intruded from the doorway.

CHAPTER THIRTEEN

THE THREE OCCUPANTS of the tack room turned to find Adam standing there, watching them with arms crossed over his chest. Jess wondered how much of the conversation he'd heard. From the look of anger in his eyes, she suspected he'd witnessed a great deal. Sudden tension thickened the air. Jess took a step toward him, reaching out in hopes of forestalling an unpleasant scene.

"Adam—" was as far as she got.

His quick look of annoyance seemed to accuse her of betraying him. He leveled his full attention on his sister. Emboldened by the champagne, Angela tilted her chin upward again and lurched forward.

"Don't you dare lecture me, Adam Connor," the girl said. "I know my own mind, and I'm in love with Tim."

Her brother dismissed her words with a derisive sound. "Love! You're a sixteen-year-old schoolgirl. Last year you thought you were in love with the valet who parked my car at the country club."

"Well, I'm not a child anymore. I don't have to do what you say."

"As long as I'm your legal guardian you'll do *exactly* as I say." Adam's cold, deliberate voice struck like a slap. "I believe I've heard more than enough from you tonight. I want you to go to your room."

"I won't."

His gaze flickered momentarily to Jess. "See that she

gets there," he directed, then swung his attention to Tim, who stood stiffly in the background.

"No!" Angela cried. She dragged at her brother's arm, as though determined to keep his anger centered on herself. "If you're going to fire Tim, or beat him up—"

Adam's gaze darkened in a blaze of reaction, and it snapped to his sister as though she'd taken leave of her senses. His nostrils flared, and Jess watched the maddened rhythm of a vein throb at his temple. Her own heart began to bang painfully against her ribs. "For God's sake, Angel—"

The last thing Jess wanted was to be caught in a battle of wills between brother and sister, but she couldn't let temper carry either of them past the point of no return. Desperate to play peacekeeper, she stepped quickly between them, uncertain what she should say but knowing she had to say *something*. "She's had too much to drink, Adam. She doesn't know what she's saying."

"Yes, I do."

"Mr. Connor, I can explain," Tim began.

"Angela, your brother is a sensible man," Jess spoke quickly, although she wasn't sure at that moment she believed those words. His approach with his sister had been too brutal, too arrogant. Didn't he realize a situation like this had to be handled delicately? She sensed he had no idea how to deal with this suddenly rebellious sibling who had always been sweet-tempered and shy. She felt her own irritation with him rise and had to work at keeping it from showing in her voice. "He wouldn't do anything to Tim without hearing him out, would you, Adam?"

In all the weeks spent at Rising Star, she'd never seen Adam so furious.

"Take her to her room. I'll speak to her tomorrow. I'll

talk to you later. Right now, I'd like to discuss a few things with my employee.''

Before Angela could say another word, Jess pulled her out of the tack room and down the barn's alleyway. The courage born of alcohol had begun to desert the girl. She was shivering uncontrollably; her protests at leaving Tim alone with Adam were no more than weak, miserable cries of regret. Jess shepherded her quickly across the front yard, hustling her past two departing guests whose car had just been brought around. She ignored their stares of curiosity and kept Angela moving, up the stairs and into the girl's room.

Moments later she sat beside Angela in the bathroom as the teenager lost her supper and most of the champagne. While Angela retched and wept, Jess stroked her flushed face with a washcloth dipped in cold water and murmured soft, soothing words.

Eventually, when Angela's stomach had settled and her sobs had deteriorated to uneven, hiccuping gasps, Jess made her swallow two aspirin, then ushered her to bed. She looked pale and miserable huddled under the pink satin comforter, so defenseless and so far removed from the adult she had proclaimed herself to be only an hour ago.

Wordlessly, Jess pulled a chair up beside the bed, taking one of Angela's chilled hands in her own. The girl's fingers tightened around hers, seeking comfort.

''I screwed up, didn't I?'' she said softly.

''Not so bad.''

''Tim must think I'm such a baby. And I've never seen Adam so angry. I didn't really think he'd do anything bad to Tim. I just wanted to shake him up.''

''Well, I think you accomplished that goal.''

The teenager responded with a tentative half smile and

a glance that said even she had been surprised by how effectively she'd managed to rattle her brother. With a sad sigh, she asked, "Why can't Adam like Tim?"

"What makes you think he doesn't? Just the other day I heard him tell Bill that he thought Tim had a nice, light touch with the yearlings."

"He's just not good enough to date me."

"Has Adam actually ever said that?" It surprised Jess how eagerly she awaited the answer.

"Not in those words. But I know that's how he feels."

"How do you know?"

"David Sheffield," she said, as if that name explained everything.

"Of Sheffield Farms?" The stable had a reputation as one of Ocala's finest, with a second-place winner in last year's Preakness.

"David is the oldest son. Last week, Adam said if I wanted to date, why didn't I pick someone like that, who could do Rising Star some good? I told him David is one of the biggest creeps in school, always hitting on the girls. Adam just laughed, but I know that's what he wants."

Jess shook her head. Adam wanted a lot of things for the farm, but sacrificing Angela's happiness would never be part of his game plan. "He'd never let anyone hurt you. No matter how advantageous it might be for the farm." She smoothed errant strands of fine hair away from Angela's forehead. "You're always going to be his little sister, Angela. Isn't it possible you misunderstood?"

Angela started to cry again. "I just want—" she had to grab for breath before she could go on "—I just want him to start letting me make some of my own decisions. Is that too much to ask?"

Jess murmured soothingly, stroking the tears away from the teenager's cheeks with her fingers, offering comfort in the only way she knew how. She kept her words soft and hopeful, promising Angela she'd help her find a way to overcome Adam's objections. He would come around. He could be made to understand. The whispered reassurances must have helped because eventually the girl drifted into an exhausted sleep.

Moving softly to the door, Jess closed it behind her, wondering if the promises she'd made could really be accomplished.

To her own ears they sounded empty and hopelessly unattainable.

THE BOURBON BURNED a path down his throat, but even before it had time to hit his gut Adam had poured himself another glass from the decanter in the study. He leaned against his desk, listening to the sounds of the house settling in for the night. The last of the guests had left, and the dull clink and clatter of china told him the caterers were rounding up their equipment from the pool area. He heard Mattie's commanding drawl issuing orders and knew the housekeeper would oversee their departure.

Damn, what a sour end to an evening this had turned out to be! Angela in tears, Jess ignoring him all night, Tianna furious at being left to fend for herself at the party. Was every woman he knew angry with him?

He'd left the party to go in search of Jess, annoyed that she'd deserted him without a second glance. Voices had drawn him to the tack room, and he'd been surprised to find her there, sanctioning a romance between Angela and the groom.

And after he'd specifically asked her to let it alone!

Listening to her encourage the relationship, even offering to set up a date, his irritation had skyrocketed.

At least his talk with Tim had been marginally satisfying. In his best big-brother voice, he'd told the kid he wasn't about to let his sister get involved in a back-barn romance. To his credit, the boy had seemed insulted by the accusation, but he had the good sense to agree that Angela was still too young and immature to be entertaining any foolish notions about love. When Adam demanded Tim stay away from her, anger glittered in the groom's eyes, but he had agreed.

And I didn't have to lay a finger on him, Adam thought with bitter amusement, remembering Angela's outlandish remark in the tack room. Her words had shocked him. He didn't go around beating up his employees to make them toe the mark. What had gotten into his sister lately? And how was he going to make her see that everything he did was for her own good?

Maybe Jess could help.

He frowned as he took another long sip from his glass. No. She was proving to be the wrong kind of influence for his sister, encouraging the girl to be defiant and contrary.

As though his thoughts had conjured her, he heard footfalls along the staircase and knew it was Jess emerging from Angela's room at last. Before she could reach the front door, he moved in a noiseless stride across the study, halting in the open doorway.

"Is she asleep?" he asked.

She turned, obviously startled to find she was not alone in the darkened foyer. He watched her eyes flicker toward the front door, her impatience to be gone evident in every small movement. Had the disordered course of the evening been less of a disaster, he might have let her go. He *should* have let her go. But the jangled irritation that had been building within him for hours had been fueled by the bourbon in his system, and Adam found he was eager to release it.

"Is she asleep?" he asked again.

"Yes."

"I'd like to discuss what happened tonight."

"If you don't mind, I'm rather tired—"

"It will only take a few minutes."

With straight-backed arrogance, he turned and reentered the study, as though her acquiescence was expected. She swallowed the momentary desire to ignore him and leave the house, her own anger making her ready for confrontation.

Inside the study a single lamp burned on the desk. Adam motioned to her with the near-empty tumbler. "Would you like a drink?"

"No, thank you."

In the shadowy light she watched the corner of his mouth tighten and thought she could almost hear the snap of his breath. He refilled his glass, splashing the amber liquid over the side. His movements were uncharacteristically jerky and careless. She stood, unmoving, her arms wrapped tightly across her chest.

Waiting.

"Is she all right?" he asked finally, his voice so soft she had to strain to hear the words.

"If you mean physically, she'll be fine. She threw up the champagne. I gave her some aspirin and put her to bed." After a moment, she added, "She cried herself to sleep."

She didn't attempt to keep the censure from her voice, and she didn't doubt that he heard it, but he chose not to react. Silently, ignoring her presence, he walked around the room, touching various objects as though he'd never seen them before. Beneath his fine silk shirt—he'd shed the tuxedo jacket—she watched his shoulder muscles bunch with tension.

He lifted his gaze to her at last. "You think I handled it badly?"

"Does it matter what I think?"

"Come on, Jess. You're not in the habit of holding back your opinion—" his lips twisted into a grim smile that carried no humor "—and I can see the anger in your eyes."

That tone. Condescending. Sarcastic. If she had felt irritated with him before on Angela's behalf, her feelings quickly shifted into livid indignation. She took a step toward him, her hands balled into fists in the soft folds of her skirt. "You humiliated Angela in front of the boy she loves. How could you do that, Adam?"

"She's not in love—"

"It doesn't matter whether you think it's the real thing or not. It feels like love to Angela, and you treated her like a child."

"I'd rather have her embarrassed than pregnant. I heard enough of the conversation to know where that little interlude was leading. And listening to you encourage them didn't make me feel as though I had any choice. I had to step in and nip it in the bud."

"I didn't encourage anything!" Jess protested. "How dare you accuse me of that?"

"Offering to set them up on a date? When I specifically asked you not to encourage them?"

"I was trying to diffuse a situation that could very easily have gotten out of control," she snapped. "It was almost resolved until you found it necessary to barge in and ride roughshod over everyone."

"Well, it's resolved now," he said, letting his gaze travel out the study window to the backyard. Without looking at her, he added, "I've talked to Tim. He'll stay away from Angela. He's not foolish enough to risk losing his job."

She wasn't truly surprised by that news. She knew Adam was handling the problem in the only way he knew how, commanding and conceited enough to think his word was absolute law at Rising Star. Maybe it was. But the memory of her recent conversation with Angela teased her mind, bringing back her own niggling insecurity and the protective fondness she felt for the girl.

Eventually it became impossible to keep those thoughts to herself. She asked quietly, "Would you have objected if Angela had been out in that tack room with David Sheffield?"

He turned from the window, frowning at her as though the question had taken more than a moment to penetrate his consciousness. "Sheffield? What's he got to do with it?"

"The Sheffields are rich and powerful. Angela seems to think you wouldn't mind if she encouraged *that kind* of attention."

"That's ridiculous," he said sharply. He tossed the empty glass back on the desk where it wobbled a moment before settling. His hand raked through his hair in annoyance. "What's gotten into that girl?"

"You didn't say it?" The question came soft, the power of her words stolen by a hasty sense of relief.

"Of course I said it—as a joke. I said if she ever got married, she could do her big brother a favor by making it someone who would do Rising Star some good." Frustration edged his voice, but above the grim slash of his lips, his eyes were worried. "I wasn't serious, and I never expected her to take it that way."

"Well, she *did* take you seriously. She's certain that's

the basis for your objection to Tim. No money, no power, nothing to offer the farm.'' She didn't add that in his neat, orderly plans for the future, those were the things he had professed to hold most dear.

''That part's true enough,'' he muttered. On the desk lay a letter opener, its hilt fashioned into the Rising Star emblem. Adam picked it up. The lamplight arrowed off its silver blade as he turned it over and over in his hands. With a sigh that seemed to release the remainder of his anger, he said, ''Look, Jess, as far as I'm concerned, no one's ever going to be good enough for her. And she's much too young to be dating anyone seriously.''

''Face facts, Adam. She's growing up.''

''Maybe in years, but not in maturity. She's been sheltered all her life. I know I'm partly to blame for that.''

''You've put golden handcuffs on her. Now you've got to give her some freedom, some control over her life. If you don't, it will only get worse. She'll fight you every step of the way.''

''I can't do that.'' He shook his head. ''I can't let her be hurt—''

He broke off, moving his attention back to the letter opener, but not before she glimpsed the depth of feeling in his eyes, not before she saw the uncloaked anguish in his features. Silence came, and Jess knew in that moment what drove Adam to behave as he did with Angela, the guilt and regret that hammered at his soul even after all these years.

Slowly she crossed the room and placed her hand along his arm. Beneath her fingers, muscles bunched reflexively. In a quiet, careful, voice she said, ''What happened to Angela was an accident, Adam. How long will you try to atone for the fact that she limps?''

He looked at her, his features schooled, his face scoured

clean of every line of pain and remorse that had betrayed him. "That's not what I'm doing."

"Isn't it? Because you made one mistake as a child, you're trying to keep her from ever being hurt again. You can't do it. Sooner or later, she'll rebel. Resentment will drive her away from you."

"That's not going to happen."

"Why? Because you say it won't? You can control a lot of things, Adam, but this isn't one of them. Sixteen-year-old girls can be awfully hardheaded."

"So can *twenty-six*-year-old women."

Sensing a weakening of his resolve, Jess pressed softly, "Please. Just a little freedom. She won't disappoint you."

His expression shifted into a tender smile, causing attractive creases to bracket his mouth. "I know you mean well, but you're asking me to change the habits of a lifetime."

"Would you at least *think* about what I've said?"

His gaze turned quizzical. "Do you champion every cause so ardently?"

"Only the ones I truly believe in."

His hand stretched out, and she felt the stroke of his fingers along her cheek. He frowned, yet when he spoke, his voice was softly abstract. "Do you know, when I called you in here, I wanted to be angry with you? I *was* angry with you. Now I find myself wanting to kiss you instead."

As always, his touch produced a melting warmth within her, making her thoughts want to free-float in a silken haze of pleasure. "Why should you be angry with me?" she asked, relieved to find that her vocal cords had not deserted her.

"You ignored me all evening."

"You didn't look like you were hurting for company."

His fingers continued to drift, finding the turn of her neck and tracing delicate patterns down the line of her throat. "Not the company I really wanted."

"Tianna Bettencourt would be furious to hear you say such a thing."

"That sounds like jealousy." He smiled, angling forward to plant a gentle kiss above the sloping neckline of her gown. "I like that in a woman."

Could she really carry on this conversation much longer? Her thoughts were no longer rational. All reasoning seemed to have fled, along with her breath.

She swallowed hard. "Delusions of your own importance..." Momentarily, the words slipped away as Adam's mouth traveled a ravishing, leisurely journey across the tops of her breasts. "In addition to overbearing arrogance. I would...expect that from you."

"Why *did* you avoid me all evening?"

"Tonight was your moment. You didn't need me there."

His head lifted. The expression in his eyes was solemn, sincere. "I *wanted* you there."

"Adam, try to understand. The position you've put me in here makes me uncomfortable."

"There are lots of positions I want to put you in," he replied with a smile. "None of them standing up."

"I'm serious."

She had placed her hand against his chest, intending to hold him off. Instead, Adam curled her fingers in his, touching her knuckles lightly with his lips like an old-world courtier. "I'd never intentionally hurt or embarrass you, Jess. Those people tonight were my friends and associates. I want you to share that part of my life."

How easy he made it sound! But she had lived all her life on the fringes of the horse racing world and knew the difficulties that could arise. Why couldn't Adam understand her reluctance?

"I'll make a bargain with you," he said. "I'll try to give Angela more freedom, if you'll agree to give my friends a chance to get to know you."

"Adam…" She tried to extricate her hand and found her fingers clutched even tighter.

"What do you say? Will you let fear hold you back from getting what you want for Angela?"

How could she refuse such an offer? With his mouth once more bringing heated arousal to her senses and his hands intent upon their own mischief, it was a wonder she could think at all. Besides, she had little to lose. She'd have to get through the upcoming polo match, but after that surely there wouldn't be many other occasions where she and Adam's friends would have reason to interact.

Certain he had made a fool's bargain, Jess turned her hand in his, trying to form a handshake. "It's a deal," she said with a superior smile.

He glanced down at their entwined fingers, and merriment danced in his eyes. "Uh-uh. My agreement, my way to close the deal."

With that, he pulled her against him, sealing their bargain with a kiss.

CHAPTER FOURTEEN

THE RIDERS THUNDERED down the field, past Jess's seat on the sidelines. A few onlookers leaned forward to catch the action, but most seemed absorbed in conversations that had little to do with the polo tournament. An appreciative murmur rose as Adam whacked the ball toward the goalposts. Remembering the boisterous applause always given Doc's pigs as they surged toward the finish line, Jess hid a grimace. The observers here at the Palm Beach polo fields didn't seem to get excited over anything. She wondered why they'd bothered to come.

Why had *she* come, Jess asked herself for the hundredth time. She should never have let them talk her into it. She was miserable here, trying her best to have a good time for Adam's sake, struggling to find common ground with these people and failing completely. Since arriving yesterday morning, throughout the welcoming brunch at Geoffrey Wilson's opulent estate and last night's champagne cocktail party, Jess had made a spirited attempt to participate. But the truth was, she was bored by endless discussions of social obligations and boardroom tactics, political maneuvering and divorce agreements. Jess tried to convince herself that, given time, she could learn to enjoy this lifestyle. But in her heart, she knew she never would.

She felt restless, out of place, and eager to return to Rising Star—a thorough mix of misery, made worse by the obvious pleasure Adam seemed to take in being with these people. He was gregarious, charming and totally at ease. Everything she was not.

She tilted her sun hat, letting the wide brim shield her eyes. Her lashes lowered as she tried to will away the headache that pounded at her temples. Directly behind her, two young socialites engaged in a brisk discussion about the latest designer to open a shop on Worth Avenue. Jess struggled to shut out the sound of their annoying laughter, and wished, more than anything else, that she could just get up and go home.

"Adam won't find it very flattering if you fall asleep while he's out on the playing field," a voice came at her elbow.

She opened her eyes to find that Tianna Bettencourt had slipped into the chair beside her. Two glasses of champagne from the refreshment tent were cradled in her hands. She offered one to Jess, who took it gratefully.

Tianna looked radiant, with sunlight trapped in her long blond hair and a dress of the palest pink swirling around her body, hugging all the right curves. At last night's party she'd been pleasant, and though Jess wasn't foolish enough to imagine a friendship was in the making, she couldn't think of any reason to ignore one of the few people who'd taken the time to talk to her.

"You're not having a good time, are you?" Tianna asked. Her knowing smile said she'd already guessed the answer.

"I'm not much of a polo fan," Jess admitted. "All the sharp turns and deliberate bumping take a lot out of a horse. Some of those players out there play too aggressively."

"It wouldn't be much of a game if there weren't a little risk involved." She fastened her gaze on the field. "And

Adam loves it. If you're going to snare him, you'd better love it, too.''

Jess stared at her in surprise. "I'm not out to *snare* anyone.''

Tianna laughed and took a sip from her glass. "Of course you are. Nothing wrong with going after the man you want.'' Her eyes flashed brilliant blue in the sunlight. "And Adam presents quite a challenge—for *any* woman.''

Tianna's puzzling mix of cordiality and mocking remarks left Jess unsure how to respond. She was relieved when the blonde turned to the two women in back of her, entering into their conversation with the ease of an old friend and leaving Jess to settle back into frustrated anonymity.

She listened as Tianna maneuvered the discussion toward more personal memories, reminding the women of events and places they had all enjoyed together. Adam's name came up more than once. It struck Jess that this was Tianna's subtle way of pointing out how little he had in common with a horse trainer's daughter.

Jess could have told her that particular lesson wasn't necessary. As much as she wanted to dismiss the importance of shared experiences with Adam, a past they could build on, she couldn't. It was plain for anyone to see that she and Adam were as different as two people could be.

Annoyed beyond endurance, Jess drained the last of her champagne, then rose. She offered the three women a vague smile of farewell, which they ignored with the same lack of manners they had shown earlier.

Weaving through the crowd, she made a careful effort to smile at people who glanced her way. Few did. A round of mild applause signaled the end of the fourth chukker. Adam's team led by one point.

While she stood beside a table laden with fresh shrimp and raw oysters, Jess watched Adam walk his mount to the sidelines. He smiled down at Tianna, who hadn't missed the opportunity to come up and lay her hand against his breeches-covered thigh.

Did Adam enjoy her fawning attention? It certainly looked that way.

ADAM SHIFTED in the saddle and wished Tianna would go away.

He didn't want to spend the few precious minutes he had before the next chukker listening to her prattle on about what a good player he was. He'd managed to hold up his end of the game all right, and he didn't need Tianna's effusive approval of his ability. What had *Jess* thought of that last goal point he'd made?

"Ti, have you seen Jess?" he cut across the woman's nonstop compliments.

"I think she's wandered over to the clubhouse. Redheads can't get a lot of sun, you know. And I'm afraid the game bored her." With an amused glance, she added, "Did you know Jess thinks you're all rather cruel to your horses, bumping into each other the way you do?"

Bored? Cruel? Adam stroked the neck of the polo pony he'd borrowed from Geoffrey Wilson. Some of his enthusiasm for the day vanished. A strong sense of frustration settled around his heart.

He'd placed a lot of hope in this weekend. He wanted Jess to have a good time, to find a friend or two among the people who were so much a part of his life. He'd even entertained a half-formed dream that she'd come to him before they returned home tomorrow, excited, happy, having made the startling discovery that she loved this lifestyle.

But she hadn't. After last night's party, he'd escorted Jess to the third-floor suite Wilson had given her. She looked exhausted. When he asked if she was enjoying herself, her answers were evasive. More disconcerting than words, Jess's eyes held a look of alarm. That left him confused and uneasy. Of all the reactions he'd expected, fear wasn't one of them.

He didn't know why it had suddenly become so important that she find a niche for herself among his friends and associates. Never before had he sought to push a woman into becoming part of his world. If anything, before he'd met Jess he'd taken great pains to keep his relationships quiet and low-key.

Now, to his surprise, he discovered he actually welcomed the interest of his friends, the whispered asides of other players on the field. Who was the good-looking redhead who had come with him? they asked, and he was eager to tell them.

Why? He could have understood it if he'd been contemplating marriage with Jess. But he wasn't. As the woman was so fond of reminding him, they had a hard enough time managing their current relationship.

He struggled under a mixture of feelings: concern, resentment, disappointment and damaged pride. With a curt goodbye to Ti, he set his heels to his mount and rode along the sidelines.

TO JESS'S CONSTERNATION, even Angela seemed to have found a place among Adam's wealthy friends. She caught sight of the teenager near the tally board, talking animatedly with a group of young people. As much as the girl had protested coming, she didn't look as if she needed rescuing or missed Tim very much.

Adam had still not relented concerning the groom, but

after badgering him incessantly, Angela and Jess had convinced him that there could be no harm in the four of them taking in dinner and a movie. The outing had gone well, and by the end of the evening, big brother had actually conceded to Jess that the boy had a lot of potential.

That night had not come without a price, of course. The bargain she'd made was the only reason she was here this weekend.

The next chukker began. She caught sight of Adam's black gelding racing after the ball and was almost relieved there'd been no time to talk with him.

At the far end of the playing field, strings of relief ponies were tethered amid a haphazard gathering of tack, horse trailers and lawn chairs. Here the employees of the different stables watched and waited, a cheerful mix of people who seemed to take a great deal more pride and interest in the tournament than the elite crowd closest to the action. It wasn't surprising that Jess found herself drawn in that direction.

She wandered along the line of horses. Most were Thoroughbreds that hadn't done well at the racetrack, but there were Arabians, quarter horses and even a few Morgans.

She lost track of time, talking to the handlers, watching the intricate way they tied tails and manes out of the way. She met a veterinarian who was dealing with a recalcitrant pinto, and introducing herself, Jess offered her help. Delighted for the opportunity to gather practical experience, she followed as he inspected the ponies, filing into memory every word he said. The afternoon wore on, and though she heard occasional bursts of applause from the playing field, she had no interest in returning and doubted if anyone would note her absence.

When Adam found her, she was holding on to a gelding's halter for dear life while the doctor bandaged its bowed tendon. The animal's eyes rolled in fear. It blew noisily, then dipped its head to push against Jess's chest. Heedless of the damage to her white blouse, she crooned softly into the horse's ear, and glanced up to see Adam approaching.

He looked bone-weary, his breeches smudged with dirt, his boots caked with Florida dust. As he came toward her, he ripped his chin strap away and removed the polo helmet. His hair lay close against his head, sleek with sweat.

He gave her a smile, but there was a distinctly danger- ous glint in his eyes. Jess knew he was angry but pre- tended not to notice his annoyance. She greeted him with her own hopeful smile. Barely able to find her voice, she introduced the doctor, then avoided Adam's eyes as she returned her attention to the horse. "Is your game over?" she asked.

"Half an hour ago. I've been looking for you ever since."

She didn't have to raise her eyes to know Adam's mouth had tightened. His calm, deliberate words told her his temper stood at a precarious level.

She took a quick breath. "Did you win?"

"Five to three. We're in the play-offs tomorrow."

"I'm sorry I missed it. I was—"

"Bored?" Adam finished for her in a low voice. "I understand completely. *This* has got to be much more in- teresting."

The unpleasant flippancy brought her own temper to the fore. She lifted her eyes, treating him to a level stare and cool tone that she hoped matched his. "As a matter of fact, it is. At least the horses don't spend all day in- dulging in petty gossip and comparing divorce lawyers."

He stepped forward to lace one hand through the geld- ing's halter. The horse jerked in surprise, but Adam ignored it. Turning toward the vet, he said, "Finish up here, Doc. You're about to lose your assistant."

His words infuriated her, and her mouth pulled into a mulish slant. Whether angrier with his high-handed attitude or her own feelings of guilt over deserting him, she couldn't have said. She only knew that she'd had more than enough pretending for one day.

She shook her head sharply. "I can't leave. I promised to help—"

"There's a celebration at the clubhouse," he said in a low tone. "There are people I want you to meet."

"The only place I'm going is back to Geoffrey's."

He shook his head. As though impatient with her disheveled appearance, he reached out to brush wisps of straw from the sleeve of her blouse. She pushed his hand away.

They stared at each other. Adam's eyes narrowed as he reassessed her features. She took a certain satisfaction in seeing him taken aback, but found his silence more ominous than words. Her experience with his anger was too limited to tell what he would do in the face of absolute rebellion.

Finally, he said, "I'll be at the clubhouse. You can clean up and meet me in the lounge in fifteen minutes."

Without a backward glance, he turned and walked away.

Oh no you don't, Buster! Who do you think you are? Drawing in a deep breath for courage, Jess fixed her sights on Adam and went after him.

It surprised Adam when Jess caught his arm. In his world, he was used to unquestioned authority, but he'd forgotten just how *out* of his world he'd ventured lately. He could tell the men at Rising Star what to do and expect no argument. He could direct Bill Page in circles if he

chose to. He could even order Angela around with a modi-
cum of success. But Jess Russell? He stood a better
chance of getting the sun to rise in the west tomorrow.

She stood before him now, her cheeks suffused with
color and her mouth so drawn with tension that the beauty
of it had all but disappeared.

"And if I don't join you at the clubhouse?" Jess demanded. "What are you going to do? Sling me over your
shoulder like a caveman and carry me there?"

"You're being deliberately difficult."

"I don't think so," she countered. "But what do you
think you're doing, Adam?"

Adam wished he had a clue. Nothing about this weekend was turning out the way he'd expected. The way he'd
hoped. He knew he was being unreasonable, demanding.
But dammit! He wanted Jess to be with him, meet the
people who were an important part of his life.

"You have no right to embarrass me in front of other
people," she said.

"We can discuss this later if you like," he replied.
"Right now there's a roomful of people wanting to pro-
pose a toast to me, and I'm not there to receive it. Fifteen
minutes."

She watched him go, then returned to the doctor's side.
She gave him a weak smile, which he returned with a
sympathetic look. Her anger reasserted itself. Adam had
no right to order her around like that.

She finished assisting the vet. He offered her his card
and the promise of professional help if she ever needed
it. Giving herself no time to consider the consequences
Jess marched past the clubhouse, stopped at a pay phone
and called a cab to take her back to Geoffrey Wilson's
mansion.

I SHOULD HAVE KNOWN, Adam decided.

One of the hard, fast rules his father had taught him about being in charge—don't threaten or issue ultimatums to people unless you were prepared to back them up with action.

Jess had escaped the moment his back was turned, leaving him to wait in the clubhouse lounge for half an hour. Every person in the room knew he'd been stood up, and though he'd tried to make light of the situation, he felt like a damn fool.

He'd have been angry, except he realized he should have seen it coming. He'd been out of bounds this afternoon. *Way* out of bounds. The harsh words had been the result of frustration and disappointment. He'd been tired after the game, and low on patience, but none of that had been her fault. He knew she'd tried to fit in this weekend. Maybe tried too hard.

He refused to accept the fact that Jess might be right. Their different lifestyles, their expectations for the future—there were a dozen reasons to discourage them from trying to establish any kind of relationship, and only a short time ago he would have been the first one to point them out.

He went up the marbled front steps of Geoffrey's mansion, past rooms filled with antiques, along corridors hung with paintings that made the place feel more like a museum than a home. He could imagine Jess's reaction to all this wealth.

Just outside her bedroom door, he paused, unsure how to proceed. He had considered numerous ways of confronting her, but none seemed right somehow. He'd never been so uncertain around a woman, but then, he acknowledged to himself with a wry smile, he'd never wanted a woman as badly as he wanted Jess.

He knocked lightly. "May I come in?"

At her muffled response, he entered. Jess rose to a sitting position on the bed. She'd been reading a book. Probably another veterinary manual. Her hair was a wet, silky cap against her head. Fresh from a shower, she looked pink and dewy in a white terry-cloth robe that hung a little too large on her. She sat primly on the edge of the bed, her hands folded over the closed book.

There was no apology in the look she gave him; he hadn't expected any. Her gaze moved over him as he lowered himself beside her. She seemed so calm and composed. He swallowed convulsively, aware of his nervousness.

Finally, with absurd awkwardness, he said, "I missed you at the clubhouse."

"Then you should have made it an invitation, not an order."

No fury. No fire in those gray eyes. His heart jammed in his throat. He could have dealt with anger. But this cold, blank indifference filled him with dread. "I know," he acknowledged. "That was a mistake, and I apologize."

She said nothing, only gazed at him. She was still damp from her shower, and crystal beads of water lay against her skin, giving her a delicate, vulnerable look. One shimmering drop fell from a strand of hair, and nearly mesmerized him. Adam watched it trickle a path downward until it disappeared between the swell of her breasts.

She made a small sound, perhaps one he wasn't meant to hear, and turned away. He watched her throat work and her mouth tuck into lines of regret as she shook her head. "What's going to happen to us, Adam?"

"Wonderful things, Jess," he replied softly. "If we let them." He tried to make his words determinedly optimistic.

"There's no place for me in your life. Not here. Not at Rising Star." She turned back to meet his eyes. "I can't be happy in the kind of life you lead."

He found fascination in her expressive gray gaze. So beautiful. So soft. Nothing seemed to exist beyond the need to hold her. "And *I* don't think I can be happy in a life without you."

Her lips lifted in a wistful half smile. "Adam, haven't you figured it out yet? I can't be what you want me to be. We're so different."

"Not in ways that really matter."

"I don't want money and power and all the things these people set such store by. I want respectability, a family. A career that leaves me with a feeling of accomplishment at the end of the day."

"Do you think I don't want the same things? I do."

She glanced at him sharply, and he realized how those words must have sounded to her. Did she think he was offering marriage? No, why should she?

Clearing his throat, he added, "Look, Jess, *eventually* I'm going to want the kind of life you're talking about. But right now, all my energies are devoted to rebuilding Rising Star's reputation. Money and power happen to be a part of that goal, and I don't think there's anything wrong with that."

"Adam, don't you see—"

"Jess, I *do* see," he interrupted by placing his hand against her lips. Her eyes widened and her breath came warm and soft against his fingers, an inadvertent caress. Even this small contact sent an exquisite leap to his nerve endings.

He wanted to kiss her.

He wanted to make love to her.

He resisted the temptation to push her, knowing that

would be one more mistake. She needed the reassurance only his words could give. "I see two people who share the same basic goals in life but have separate ideas about how to reach them. That's the only difference between us."

He removed his hand to catch her fingers and bring them to his chest. His other hand found hers, placing it over her own heart, anchoring it there. "Do you feel that?" he asked, pressing her hand hard against the throb of his heartbeat. "There aren't any differences here, sweetheart. Here we're just the same. Can you feel my heart, Jess? It's racing just like yours."

Deep inside, a part of him reached out, trying to make her feel what he felt, trying to make her see how incomplete his life would be without her. A little desperate, he said, "I'd wager everything I own that with time and patience we could make our heartbeats match. Perfectly."

She wanted to believe Adam's words. She wanted so desperately to believe.

He lifted the back of his hand to her cheek. Jess leaned into the contact, sensing it was a mistake, for his touch brought confusion as well as pleasure. She cursed herself for being a fool, knowing his words changed nothing. She looked into his eyes, bright now with desire. As bright as she knew her own must be.

Fool. You can never fit into his world. Never. And even if you could, he's not asking you to be there forever.

"Please, Jess," Adam added softly. "Give us the time to find our way."

Speechless with need, she slowly nodded.

A glimmer of pleasure lit his dark eyes, but unexpectedly, when he reached for her, it was to pull the two edges of her robe closer together. "It's all right. I'm not taking this any further. I think I've overstepped as much as I dare in one day. Now let's see if I can do better." He lifted her hand and placed a kiss on the back of it. "Miss Russell, if you have no other plans, would you join me for dinner tonight?"

CHAPTER FIFTEEN

AFTER THE WEEKEND in Palm Beach, they continued to see one another, but Adam surprised Jess by concentrating less on getting her back in his bed, and more on courting her romantically. He was patient, considerate and methodical. He didn't pretend he wasn't eager to make love to her again, but he never pushed his advantage beyond teasing suggestions and long, deep kisses. On the few occasions when things might have gotten out of hand, *he* was the one to draw back.

He was so practical and calm that Jess began to think she was losing her sanity. More and more she found herself longing for their moments together, the little snatches of time that never seemed to be enough.

Determined to put all gloomy thoughts of Adam out of her mind, Jess moved to the small writing desk that sat in the corner of the cottage's living room. There was time to finish the letter she'd been writing to Zola before Doc came home for supper.

There was good news to share. Two more Thoroughbreds had won small purses. The barns hummed with excited energy. Adam had doled out bonuses and hosted an employee picnic. He had insisted Doc accompany him to a breeders' association dinner, and afterward, her father had come home beaming under the effusive praise he'd received.

Papa seemed—here her pen hesitated a moment—fine.

Jess couldn't admit the truth. Zola had kept her promise and spoken to Doc. Unfortunately, nothing seemed to have changed. Jess knew that her father had stopped going to the counseling center. He'd sworn the grueling training schedule made keeping the appointment impossible, and she had tried hard to believe that was the truth.

She let her letter drift into a lighthearted account of her father's threats to have Carmen butchered into bacon if the sow didn't stop harassing the other pigs. From there she slipped into a description of her birthday, which had been the day before yesterday. Her lips curved into a smile as she picked up the leather gloves that sat on top of the box of stationery. Such a wonderful day.

Angela had baked a chocolate cake and given her a lovely antique bonnet to add to Jess's collection of hats. Her father had presented her with a hard-to-find medical journal, so lovingly inscribed inside that it made her weep. And Adam, protesting that birthdays were a waste of time for anyone but children, had nevertheless withdrawn from behind his back a box that held a beautiful pair of hand-made riding gloves.

Later, gift in hand, she had found him in the barn in order to thank him once again, and he had shown her how soft and supple the leather could feel against her skin. In ways that had nothing to do with riding. Even now, Jess blushed, remembering the hot, quick fire that had spread outward from the very center of her body when Adam had trailed the gloves slowly against her cheek. Her throat. The tops of her breasts...

Communicating through gesture, they both had sensed the moment when effortless delight became urgent, when desire became necessity. Resistance to those feelings became dulled, like a faded garment that seemed to be no longer worth wearing. Only when Tim had emerged from one of the stalls had they broken apart and tried to find some thread of conversation they could latch on to.

Oh, yes. This birthday had been very special.

Jess's musing was interrupted as her father came hurriedly through the front door. She glanced up in surprise. It was still hours before the farm settled in for the night. His face was flushed, his expression thunderous, and when he headed for the kitchen, she caught the glimpse of a liquor bottle clutched in his hand.

Apprehension knotted her stomach. Because he knew she worried, Doc seldom drank in front of her.

She waited and watched as he broke the seal and splashed whiskey into a shot glass, downed the contents, then poured another. He set the glass on the kitchen counter, bracing his hands wide along the edge. Head down, he stared at the amber-colored liquid as though the glass had the power to move of its own accord.

Rising slowly, she approached her father, realizing she'd expected something like this. For days she'd sensed the tension in Doc, an underlying edginess that begged release.

She thought she knew the reason.

Beth Russell's birthday was only four days after Jess's own. They'd often celebrated the dates together, just the three of them. Her father wasn't likely to have forgotten that.

Cautiously she approached him. "What's wrong, Papa?"

Her father looked startled, and Jess wondered if he'd even been aware of her presence. "I fired Brian Gallagher today."

Gallagher was a cocky, slovenly exercise rider who often pushed his mounts too hard. In Jess's mind, his departure would be no loss. Doc had fired workers before, so she knew there was more to his mood than that.

"Why?" she asked. "What happened?"

"He blew out Suwannee this morning. Took her out against the direct orders I'd left on the day sheets. Connor will have to scratch her from the race this weekend, and it'll take months to get the animal back to form."

Jess laid her hand on top of his, feeling the taut ridge of his knuckles against her palm. "Those things happen. You know that."

He withdrew his hand to scoop up the glass. When he'd emptied the contents in one gulp, Doc slammed it back on the counter, so hard she wondered that it didn't shatter. He shook his head sharply. "My fault, lass."

She watched him fill the glass again. She wanted to stop him, but she couldn't think of anything that wouldn't make the situation worse. "You're being too hard on yourself. You can't assume responsibility for everything that goes wrong."

He laughed, but the sound carried no amusement. "I should have fired him a month ago, but I gave him a second chance. I can't afford misjudgments right now, lass. In horses *or* men. Connor's lost a potential winner."

"Adam's never thought Suwannee would prove out. He knows it's too early in the season to expect perfection. Why should you?"

"It's that kind of mistake that's cost me everything—" His words ended abruptly and he looked away.

Closing his eyes, he rubbed the bridge of his nose with two fingers. "I'm tired," he said in such a weary, wavering voice that Jess looked at him in alarm. "I'm fighting the flu, I think."

Whether that was the truth or not, she recognized her father was physically and emotionally drained. She saw suddenly how old he looked, how his posture sagged with fatigue. Her hand closed around his arm. A proud man, he made a motion to straighten away from her support, but Jess was ready for it, and hung on.

"I'll call Bill Page and tell him you're sick," she said in a firm voice. "You need to rest. You've pushed yourself too hard these past few weeks."

He gave her a tight, unhappy look as she steered him toward his bedroom, but the very fact that he didn't resist her maneuvering meant he recognized the truth in her words. Beneath her hands his flesh felt warm. Too warm.

Jess gave him two aspirin, tucked him into bed as though he were a child and called the farm manager's office to tell Bill her father wouldn't be back to the barns until tomorrow.

Three hours later when the telephone rang, Doc was sound asleep, having dozed off after eating a bowl of chicken-noodle soup and a slice of dry toast. His temperature had dropped a little, but Jess forced two more aspirin on him anyway. Knowing he needed the rest, she snatched the receiver before the second ring.

"I'd like to think you were sitting there just waiting for me to call," Adam said.

"Of course I was."

"Liar," he teased. "Why are you whispering?"

"Doc's asleep, and I don't want to wake him." Anticipating his next question, she added, "He's down with the flu."

"Bill told me he shortened his day. Everything all right?"

Was there more curiosity in Adam's voice than the situation warranted? Her breath drew tight and she fought the temptation to fill the silence with rambling excuses.

His concern was natural, she chided her overactive imagination. No reason to read things into those few words.

"He'll be fine," she said in a level tone. "Knowing Doc, he'll be his old self by morning." Afraid it would seem odd to Adam if she made no mention of Gallagher's firing, she added, "I suppose you've heard what happened to Suwannee."

"Bill told me when he picked me up at the airport," he said, referring to the fact that he'd been out of town overnight. "I hate to lose Suwannee this season." Then, a moment later, he said, "Can you come up to my office? I'd like to talk to you."

Her heart sank to her toes. She pressed her lips together, unsure how to respond. Her first thought was that he was going to fire Doc. Her father's drinking had been discovered. Dry panic seized her throat and she had to swallow hard to get around it. "I'll be right up."

A late-afternoon breeze sifted through the trees with a gentle tug, encouraging the first autumn leaves from their branches. It fanned Jess's cheeks as she walked to the main house, but she hardly noticed it. She might have enjoyed the crisp snap of fall against her skin, if she hadn't been so worried about the reason behind Adam's summons.

By the time she knocked on the study door, Jess had fortified her courage with the reminder of how much Doc had helped Rising Star. Adam knew her father's value. Surely he wouldn't do anything rash without considering the cost to his training team.

He sat behind the wide desk, sifting absently through a stack of mail, dressed in an expensive-looking business suit that contrasted admirably with the disheveled darkness of his hair. He didn't look up right away, so Jess had time to admire the view.

Finally, Adam tossed the mail onto the desk. He looked at her but didn't speak, and a brief spurt of panic returned. Somehow she managed to find her voice. "You sent for me?"

She cringed at the puppetlike subservience in her words. Adam cocked his head to give her a quizzical frown. "You're awfully formal today."

She tried to relax her stance, and hated her inability to look anything but nervous.

He came around the desk, shedding his jacket as he moved, then loosening the top button of his shirt. Jerking away his tie, he hitched one hip against the edge of the desk. In a quiet voice, he commanded, "Come here, Jess."

Bow-strung tight with tension, she moved toward him. When only inches separated them, he smiled and looped the silk tie around the back of her neck. With a light urging of the two ends, he tugged her closer. "God, I missed you," he said, and then his mouth found hers.

Cool and dry against the surprised parting of her lips, his touch felt like velvet. His tongue grazed her teeth, and she welcomed him with eager relief. She felt his lips tug upward at the corners and knew he was delighted with her response.

They broke apart, and huskily he murmured, "Guess you missed me, too." His fingers tipped her chin upward. He studied her face, frowning slightly. "What's the matter?"

She shrugged away his concern. "Nothing."

"You look like a kid hauled up before the principal. Has something happened while I was gone?"

"Nothing more than you already know. When you called me to come up here, I thought it was something serious."

She knew her response sounded nervous and curt, but her emotions were so jumbled she couldn't sort through them fast enough to mount an appropriate answer. Fortunately, Adam didn't seem to notice.

"Our relationship *is* serious," he replied, stroking her cheek with affection.

A smile played on his lips. It occurred to her that he was in an exultant mood, so pleased about something that even the news regarding Suwannee couldn't dull his disposition.

"Adam," Jess said suddenly, "what have you got up your sleeve?"

"Up is the right direction. But it's not my sleeve." He brought her against his body, imprisoning her in such a way that she was immediately aware of his arousal. "Try a little lower," he said with a wicked laugh.

He nuzzled the tousled thickness of her hair. His open palm stole under the loose blouse she wore, sliding along her flesh to caress and fondle. Before she could lose herself in his touch, Jess pulled his hand away. "Stop that," she commanded with mock severity. "Suppose Angela or Mattie walk in?"

"They won't."

"You don't know that."

"Yes, I do. Mattie's gone to see her kids in Chicago, and Angela's staying with friends this weekend. We're alone. Just the two of us." One eyebrow lifted suggestively. "Does that give you any ideas?"

"Like what?"

"Like how conveniently wide this desk is."

She pretended to be shocked. "Adam, it's broad daylight!"

"I'll close the curtains."

She shook her head.

"Why?"

"This is your father's study."

"I doubt if he'll mind."

"Well, I will." This time there was a note of seriousness in her tone. This room held so much of Adam's past, as well as his hopes for the future. The idea of making love here made her distinctly uncomfortable.

"Damn," he muttered. With a pouting, resigned glance, he fell back against the edge of the desk. "All right. Then take a walk with me. There's something I want to show you." His hand captured her wrist.

He pulled her outside, letting go of her hand only when she fell into step beside him. In the stable yard the grooms were closing up the barns for the night, wiping down equipment and giving final rubdowns to several of the Thoroughbreds. He waved to Bill Page as they passed the farm manager inspecting a late-afternoon shipment of grain.

They crossed the freshly raked lane that led to Barn Four. Behind the green-tin roof, the sun began to sink into the horizon, a vivid wash of lavender and orange.

"I'd like you to go to the Breeders' Ball with me," Adam said quietly. "It's in two weeks."

She opened her mouth to refuse, then stopped herself. His tone had been casual, an offhand invitation. But in contrast to his words, she sensed an underlying tension. The annual event might be important to him, but he was unwilling to let her know just how much her acceptance meant.

She bit down on every objection that swirled suddenly in her mind. "I'd love to."

His lips lifted imperceptibly as he nodded. She knew she'd done the right thing. Later she could worry about what to wear, how to get through another gathering of Adam's friends.

"Angela's getting better, don't you think?" he remarked as he pulled open the barn door.

"She's riding nearly every day. If not with me, then..." Jess hesitated, not sure she should admit that Tim often accompanied Angela now. "By herself," she finished lamely.

Adam tossed her a look that said he hadn't been fooled by her evasiveness, but he didn't seem inclined to press the issue. As they strolled down the alleyway, Misty Lady nickered a welcome. Adam gave the mare's nose a quick rub as they passed. With an air of studied nonchalance, he remarked, "How's Vadar?"

"Stubborn as ever. He nearly scraped me off under a tree limb last week."

As though aware he was being discussed, the animal in question snorted loudly from the confines of his stall.

"Perhaps you ought to consider another mount."

"I can handle him."

"I know you can. But maybe it's time for a change."

Jess glanced at him. If he didn't want her riding Vadar anymore, she wished he'd just say so. It wasn't like him to be so indirect. "Adam, what are you getting at?"

He walked to the stall beside Vadar's, which had always been empty and closed. Unhooking the latch, he swung back the top half of the door, then stood aside. He turned to face her and, with a small smile, said quietly, "Happy Birthday, Jess."

At first she didn't know what to think. Her gaze shifted from him as she realized a horse stood in the stall. For a moment she thought Adam had simply purchased another pleasure mount. Then her eyes focused on the animal's sleek red coat, the dappling of white across its withers.

The horse swung its head in her direction and nickered softly.

Shock left Jess momentarily speechless. Then, with a whoop of delight, she fumbled at the latch and rushed forward. It couldn't be true after all these years! But it was! "Pie! I don't believe it!"

She threw her arms around the mare's neck. The animal submitted to this with placid disinterest.

Adam watched Jess, and it came as it always did, that fine-edged feeling of contentment and joy he experienced in seeing her pleasure. Her head tilted back; her hair streamed behind her, silken flame against the whiteness of her blouse. She looked small and fragile pressed up against the big roan. Desire sifted through him.

She glanced over her shoulder. Even in the shadows her eyes sparkled with happiness. "Where did you find her? How?"

"I tracked her down through racing association records. I'd hoped to have her here in time for your birthday, but the previous owner wanted to play games. She's still a little doped from the trip, I'm afraid, but I think she's fairly fit. I'll have the vet come out tomorrow to give her a thorough exam."

"I ran her when I was sixteen, so she can't be more than…" She did quick addition on her fingertips. "Fourteen." She pressed her cheek against the mare's velvety-white face. "Do you remember me, Pie?"

Lucky beast, Adam thought. *I wouldn't mind a little loving like that.*

As if in perfect agreement, Pie's head bobbed several times. With a delighted laugh, Jess said, "I think she *does* know me. She was always very smart."

"But not very fast, I gather. According to the records,

after your father had to sell her, she never placed better than fourth in a race.''

Jess waved that information away as unimportant. After a few more minutes during which she lavished attention on the horse, she came back to Adam. "How can I ever thank you?''

His heart threatened to shudder to a standstill. He cursed the promise that kept him from pressing this sudden advantage. He didn't want to go slow with their relationship. He didn't want to give them time. He just...wanted.

He forced his voice into teasing lightness. "I can think of a few ways.''

She expected that response and grinned. "I knew you could.'' And then, with an odd kind of intensity in her eyes and a thrilling sweetness in her voice, she added, "I love you for remembering how much Pie meant to me.''

He knew she didn't mean those words quite *that* way, and after a split second's disappointment, he discovered an irrational desire to see just how much she *did* mean them. Enough to consider a future beyond veterinary school and Triple Crowns? Enough to consider a future with *him?*

Like a man suddenly coming awake, he realized then that he wasn't thinking in terms of a one-night stand or a love affair or even a long-term relationship that ended amiably when they both got tired of each other. He was thinking wedding bells and babies and coming home to the one person in the world that your heart leaped to see.

God help him, he was head over heels in love! He—Adam Connor—the man with the foolproof, ironclad game plan for life, had been upended by this petite, stubborn redhead who loved horses and hats and...*him?*

Damn! He couldn't be sure. Desire, that was one thing.

But love? Just how successful had he been in convincing her she couldn't live without him?

She was looking at him with a smile that seemed like a caress, and he would have asked her then. *Marry me,* he would have said, because in that moment he felt her soul reaching out, coming within his grasp. It drifted over him like warm sunshine, stealing inside to touch him everywhere. Its warmth chased away all his darkest worries and frustrations.

He started to speak, and she must have sensed it, must have seen the question on his lips, because she moved away, her attention suddenly returning to the horse.

The damn horse.

"I promise she won't be any extra bother," Jess said.

He wanted to believe it wasn't his imagination that heard the underlying shakiness in her softly spoken words.

"Pie's home is Rising Star now," Adam said carefully. "There will always be a place for her here."

Jess went utterly still. Silent. Her back was to him, and he thought if he could see her face right now, he'd know the truth. And as much as he wanted that knowledge, he realized he was holding his breath, that a part of him was afraid to test the depth of her feelings.

He moved forward with slow, measured steps. When he spread his hands across the slim straightness of her shoulders, she didn't flinch or try to move away, but he felt tension slide into every muscle and bone.

He lowered his head until his lips came close to her ear. "There's no reason for either of you ever to leave here, Jess."

He punctuated that statement by pushing her hair to one side and planting kisses along the slender curve of her neck.

"Adam..." The word drifted soft from her lips.

"How can you torment me like this?" he murmured, his voice no more than a husky whisper. "Ah, Jess, how can you be so cruel? Don't you know..."

His lips found the hollow of her throat, a warm, inviting pool of life. He touched his tongue to her pounding pulse and felt her breath diminish.

The bolt of the barn door slid back. The realization that they were about to have company pierced Adam's awareness. With a muttered oath, he pulled away, putting respectable distance between them. Scattering the magic.

The wooden door creaked open and Bill Page came in. His eyes skipped between them. With a brief acknowledging nod, he began the nightly ritual of inspection. If he thought their presence together in the barn was at all unusual, the man was smart enough to keep his opinions to himself.

Leaning against the wall, Adam watched as Jess stroked Pie's nose in thoughtful silence. She didn't glance his way, but he noticed the slight tremble in her fingers as she brought her hand to the horse's head. Struggling to get a grip on his own unsteady emotions, he was pleased to witness the feigned calm Jess tried to project.

She could protest as much as she wanted, but her body hadn't lied. The passion had been shared. Her need ran as swift as his.

But what about her heart?

CHAPTER SIXTEEN

ADAM'S HAND at Jess's waist nudged her forward into the ballroom of the Ocala Breeders' Club, an elegant, cavernous room whose occupants glittered in a rainbow of silks and satins. The air was redolent with exotic perfume. At every wrist and throat, the flash of expensive jewelry made the participants' social status blatantly obvious.

There was money here. Lots of it.

Adam leaned close. "Stop looking like you've just sat down in the dentist's chair. None of these women can hold a candle to you tonight." He frowned as he surveyed the crowd. "It's the men I'm worried about. I'll probably spend the entire evening chasing Romeos away."

She threw him a look that said he shouldn't tease her, before realizing he was utterly serious. Ridiculous. She didn't think for one moment she could hold her own with these people.

Her aqua satin dress, the only remotely fancy gown she owned, wasn't nearly daring enough, in spite of the fact she'd cut and resewn the back so that it fell nearly to her waist. And thank goodness the tousled look was in. It made the haphazard tumble of curls down her back seem almost planned.

She spotted Tianna Bettencourt near an hors d'oeuvre table, chatting with a good-looking blond man who seemed to hang on her every word. Nothing unplanned about *her* looks. In pristine white, with the sparkle of diamonds at her throat, she appeared as delectable as an adornment on a wedding cake.

Catching the direction of her glance, Adam grinned. "You've got nothing to worry about from that corner."

She made an unladylike sound of disbelief. "Ha! She's probably already had towels monogrammed with your initials."

On the pretense of brushing aside a wisp of red curl, his fingers brushed along her cheek. "Jealousy becomes you, little gypsy."

"I most certainly am not jealous of that woman."

"No?" he questioned with a sigh of disappointment. "I had such hope."

Their gazes met and meshed. The overhead chandeliers set bouncing highlights in his dark hair, and the cut of his tuxedo accentuated the width of his shoulders, the leanness of his hips. Adam could have any woman here, she thought.

As though sensing her uncertainty, he said, "I'm crazy about you. Just remember, together we can do anything."

With that last bit of encouragement, he pulled her farther into the room, beginning a round of introductions to friends and competitors.

An hour later, Jess began to relax. The initial panic that had clutched her stomach muscles loosened its hold. To her surprise and delight, she found herself actually enjoying the evening. There was none of the snobbery and spitefulness reminiscent of what she referred to as the "Palm Beach fiasco."

The guests were serious breeders who shared the common goal of improving Florida's standing in the world of horse racing. When Adam introduced her as Doc Russell's daughter, more than one of them made a point of telling her how much they respected her father. Since she was as knowledgeable about Thoroughbreds as most of the breeders, Jess found herself involved in many conversations where her opinion was sought and given serious consideration.

In spite of their elegant gowns, the wives of the breeders seemed down-to-earth and friendly. Most had helped their husbands every step of the way. Their conversations veered toward amusing anecdotes about lean times and the proud retelling of their children's accomplishments. They indulged in gossipy small talk, but it lacked the venomous jealousy and pettiness Jess expected.

Even Tianna, after a brief, cool hello, left Jess alone. Adam, realizing she no longer felt the need for his hovering presence, loosened his protective grip on her arm and disappeared long enough to find them both refreshments.

A few moments later, he slipped her fingers around a glass of chilled champagne. Together they watched the crowd.

"Admit it," Adam remarked beneath the rim of his glass. "You're having a good time."

"I admit it. Your friends aren't what I expected."

He smiled. Tonight had been everything he'd wished for. He'd watched Jess the past two hours, delighted by how comfortable she looked. She laughed at his friends' jokes and listened to their rambling stories, never betraying boredom or disinterest.

She was radiant tonight. The simplicity of her gown only enhanced her beauty. The lack of extravagant jewelry gave her a natural, delicate purity.

He yearned to reach out, pull her from the crowd and find a secluded room in the club where she could be his alone. The longing to hold her spread, until he felt pummeled by uncontrollable emotions.

A transient thought crossed his mind. He could force her hand tonight. He could announce their engagement, proclaim to everyone present that this was the woman he intended to marry. It was a wild, improbable idea, but, buoyed by her success with his friends, Jess might agree.

He discarded the notion an instant later. He'd long since abandoned the idea of getting her to do anything she wasn't ready to do. Tonight's triumphs paved the way, but hadn't he learned real victory came with patience?

"You've charmed them, Jess," he said, swallowing his eagerness with the last of his champagne. "Even Tianna's father told me you were a delightful change from the women I've dated in the past. He nearly choked on his finger sandwich when he remembered that list included his daughter."

"He didn't say that!"

"He did. I think I'm off the hook as a prospective son-in-law." He nodded toward the far side of the room, where the blond man still danced in attendance at Tianna's elbow. "Lorne Vandivert, Green Meadows Farms. Lots of money. Rumor has it he's looking to expand, but all he's done lately is follow Tianna. She's after bigger fish than me now."

"Well, I'm glad she's thrown you back in the pond. I don't want anyone catching you but me," Jess said with a light laugh, a laugh that died instantly.

As a blunder, she suspected it ranked among her worst. She bit her lip and frowned down into her glass, as though the champagne had somehow tricked her. Had she really said that? The words sounded so daring. What must Adam think?

For a fragile moment, neither of them spoke. The sheen of amusement had vanished from Adam's eyes; he regarded her with an unfathomable gaze. In the bright confusion of the ballroom, Jess felt nothing but the swift, steady thudding of her own heart, heard nothing but the quick catch of his breath, followed by a soft exhalation.

Then his features softened with tenderness. "Careful, Jess," he remarked in a low voice. "I might be more than willing to take you at your word."

"Adam, I—"

"Oh, hell," he cut across her faltering voice. "Here comes the true test of endurance. Harold and Margaret Lassiter, Springview Farms. Prepare yourself to listen to all kinds of complaints and to hear more than you ever wanted to about their three ungrateful children. Let them talk for a few minutes, then I'll cut them off."

Adam's assessment was correct. The couple had no sooner been introduced before they launched into a litany of criticism about the quality of food on the buffet table, the lack of good help at the club and the ineptitude of the small orchestra that provided dance music. Jess gave them her full attention, avoiding the look in Adam's eyes that revealed his impatience to be alone with her once more.

A few minutes passed and Harold Lassiter pounced on a new topic—the latest training methods used at their stable. When he drew breath, another man standing on the fringes of the conversation took the opportunity to interrupt. He introduced himself as David Cathcart, president of the breeder's association. "Excuse me, Harold, do you mind if I borrow Adam a moment? He's one of our speakers tonight, and I want to discuss a few changes we've made."

Harold waved them away. "Of course not. You two go on. Margaret and I will look after Miss Russell." When both men hesitated, he added, "Don't worry, Adam. We'll take good care of her."

"I'll catch up with you later," Jess reassured Adam.

"I'd like to hear more about Harold's problems with his new trainer."

Given tonight's success, she could afford to be generous with her time. Besides, Doc would love to know what the competition was up to. And she wasn't at all certain she was brave enough to return to the level of intimacy that had developed between her and Adam before the Lassiters had descended upon them.

Adam gave her a look that said she deserved a medal. Together he and Cathcart wound their way toward the raised platform at the far end of the room. She felt momentarily bereft at the loss of his company, but Harold Lassiter quickly captured her attention again.

Minutes later, she found herself wondering how two such chronic complainers could remain in a business where they were so obviously unhappy. The Lassiters' voices grated on her nerves, and behind her eyes she felt the warning throb of a headache.

When a waiter tapped her on the shoulder, Jess turned toward him with all the enthusiasm of a drowning woman reaching for a life preserver. "There's a telephone call for you at the front desk," the young man informed her.

Thanking providence, she excused herself and followed in the waiter's wake. Halfway to the reception area, uneasiness began to scrape along her nerves. It seemed unlikely anyone but Doc would call her here. And certainly not without a good reason.

A very good reason.

Filled with foreboding, she picked up the receiver in the telephone alcove.

ADAM SEARCHED the ballroom, unable to locate the Lassiters or Jess. He hoped they hadn't whisked her into some tucked-away corner. He'd spent ten minutes with Cathcart, and in less than that time he was scheduled to speak on the improved standing of Florida breeders in the horse racing community, as well as make a few comments on his own recent successes. He wanted Jess to be there, knowing she'd be pleased by the public praise he intended to give her father.

But when he couldn't locate her, he ended up speaking without Jess in attendance. Irritated and a little disappointed, he stepped down from the stage, and the crowd surged forward, offering handshakes of congratulations and words of praise. His eyes scanned the sea of faces before him.

Where was she? Why hadn't she been here? Fear kindled within him as the dark realm of memory sent reminders of Palm Beach into his brain.

His mind balked. No, this wasn't anything like that. Tonight had been different. Jess had been enjoying herself. Even the Lassiters' complaints hadn't been able to dampen her enthusiasm.

Something was wrong.

He pushed through the crowd and went in search of answers.

IMPATIENT WITH the cabbie's slow pace, Jess leaned forward. "Please hurry," she encouraged him.

She pressed back in her seat, biting her lip against anxiety that made her want to snap at the man. Her hands twisted in her lap, and she forced them to stop. Outside, Ocala night traffic rushed silently past her window. She tried to focus her attention on the sweep of white headlights that occasionally illuminated the darkened interior of the cab.

Everything would be all right, she told herself. Surely there was still time. It couldn't be too late.

The call from Rising Star had left her momentarily numb. She hadn't expected to find Tim on the line, the groom calling on direct orders from Bill Page. Nearly incoherent with agitation, the young man told her that Doc, drunk and out of his head, was causing a commotion in one of the barns. Bill was doing his best to calm him down, but the situation was worsening. If she returned to the farm, perhaps she could convince her father to go back to their cottage.

Jess had agreed immediately. After scribbling a short note to Adam telling him she'd return within the hour, she had hailed a cab. She knew he would be furious, but she would rather have his anger directed toward her than Doc. This way she hoped that somehow this incident could be diffused with no real harm done.

The cab pulled into the front driveway of Rising Star.

Her hope of salvaging the situation died the moment she got out of the vehicle and smelled the smoke.

WHEN THE RECEPTIONIST gave him the note Jess had left, Adam's mind barely registered the words. He stood rooted to the spot.

He couldn't believe she'd actually left the ball. Was she sick? Upset? They'd come so far in their relationship. Why hadn't she sought him out? Didn't she know he would have taken her home?

Common sense told him that he, not Jess, would be the one contacted if there was trouble at Rising Star, but the flare of fear that hit his gut was too real to be ignored. He called the house. Angela, who had promised she'd be in her room all evening studying, didn't pick up the phone. Nor was there any answer at Doc's cottage or Bill Page's apartment.

A few moments after he hung up the receiver, gravel

spun from beneath the Mercedes' tires as Adam wheeled out of the club parking lot.

JESS KNELT in front of her father. Her hands moved consolingly along his shoulders. "It's all right now, Papa. It's over. Calm down."

Doc lifted pain-filled eyes to look at her. Soaked to the skin, he shuddered and sucked in a shaky breath. "Oh, God, lass," he whispered. "What have I done?" His glance darted around the interior of the barn, taking in the damage. "What have I done?"

Gooseflesh crept over Jess's skin, but her own damp clothing wasn't the cause of it. She didn't have to take another look to know the severity of the situation.

The sprinklers had tripped on at almost the same moment she had entered one of the barns to find her father struggling in Tim and Bill's grip. Tragedy had been averted, but the knowledge of what this could mean to Doc's future filled her with dread.

The damp, burned smell of wood hung in the air, a horrible reminder of how close Rising Star had come to disaster tonight. In every corner of the barn, water from the depleted overhead sprinklers trickled into pools with hollow, plinking sounds. Outside, she could hear the night watchman issuing curt orders to the stable hands. Directly behind her, Midnight Star, the only animal to be injured, pranced and snorted nervously as Bill Page tried to press a sterile bandage over the bleeding cut on the Thoroughbred's shoulder.

The stallion squealed in protest as the farm manager swabbed the cut with antiseptic. Hanging on to the halter, Tim crooned into the horse's ear. Behind the groom, Angela, who had come to the barn after the alarm had sounded, began to cry softly.

Doc's horror-stricken eyes widened, then he dropped his head into his hands, as though to shut out the sights and sounds of the night. "The 'breds. Midnight—"

"He's all right, Papa. It's just a scrape. Tell him, Bill."

She turned her head, pleading with her eyes for the manager to confirm her words. Bill's features tightened with hostility. The damage Doc had caused tonight was inexcusable. After a long moment, he said uneasily, "Midnight will be fine, Doc. Damn fool tried to plow through his stall when the sprinklers went off."

The effect of the alcohol had begun to wear off. Doc shook his head. "It's over, pony-girl. I've killed all my chances."

His words deteriorated into a harsh sob that echoed in the near-empty barn. Huddled on a bale of wet, ruined hay, Doc looked so wretched, so completely broken, that Jess's eyes filled with tears. Behind her, the other occupants watched silently.

Jess hated that they should see her father reduced to this state. Moving quickly, she hugged him to her. "Papa, please," she urged softly. "Let's go back to the cottage. Tomorrow we'll see what needs to be done."

"I'll have to call the club to notify Adam," Bill said.

"That won't be necessary," a quiet voice cut through the tension in the barn.

They turned to find the owner of Rising Star standing at the barn's open front door. He moved out of the shadows with slow deliberation, his eyes flicking back and forth across the littered corridor. Among the jumble of sodden hay and charred boards, he looked oddly out of place.

Angela moved into his path. "Adam—"

"Please go back to the house, Angel," he interrupted calmly. "This isn't the place for you."

He moved into the circle of light, approaching Midnight Star to inspect the injury. Adam's mouth and jaw were set in hard lines of barely checked rage; his features might have been chiseled from granite. He didn't spare Jess or Doc a single glance but instead turned toward Bill. "Is there any muscle damage?"

Bill shook his head. "It's nothing more than a scratch, boss."

He nodded and glanced at Tim. "Throw a blanket, then put him on the hot walker until he calms down. We'll keep the exercise light tomorrow. Just enough to work out any stiffness." He stroked the stallion's neck, and muscles rippled along the Thoroughbred's hide. "I want the others settled down as quickly as possible, but they're not to be put back in here until we get rid of the smell. Understood?"

Tim nodded and rushed to do Adam's bidding.

"What happened, Bill?"

The farm manager looked uncomfortable and cast Doc a regretful look. His attention shifted momentarily to Jess, then back to Adam. "A spark from Doc's pipe set the hay on fire. Tim and I were here when it happened, so it was easy enough to trip the sprinklers before much harm was done."

Smoking was strictly forbidden in the barns. Adam swiveled, leveling such a cold look on Doc that Jess was tempted to take a protective step in front of her father. Doc reeked of alcohol, and she knew his condition was more than apparent. She watched Adam's eyebrow arch the moment suspicion became comprehension.

Doc's head remained buried in his hands. He didn't see the loathing in his employer's face, but Jess did, and fear exploded within her.

"I want you out of here by morning," he said quietly. "Bill, write out a check for the rest of what's owed him."

Absolute silence fell. Doc sat unblinking, unfocused, his shoulders bowed in defeat. Jess had to lock her knees to keep them from buckling as Adam's words sliced into her subconscious.

No! She couldn't allow this to happen. Her father had brought so much to Rising Star. He deserved a second chance. She'd make sure he received the help he needed to stop drinking. She'd watchdog him herself if need be. A dozen possibilities raced through her mind. Willing to subjugate her pride, Jess lifted her gaze to Adam, ready to beg for his understanding.

And that was when she saw it.

His eyes bore into hers, and in the thunderous anger she glimpsed in their dark depths lay full-blown contempt and revulsion. No longer directed solely at her father.

"You knew all along, didn't you?" Adam asked, his voice sharp and cutting.

Jess bit her lip as the accusation hit home. Her vision blurred. Realization swept through her as quickly as the warmth fled her skin. That fragile bond between her and Adam, so promising a few short hours ago, had snapped. His trust in her was gone.

Fighting limp exhaustion in every bone and muscle, she shook her head, unwilling to let it end this way. She could acknowledge Adam's feelings of betrayal, but that didn't mean love had been destroyed. Surely it was still there.

He was already turning away, putting distance between them as though he couldn't bear to remain in her presence. She hurried after him, picking up handfuls of her wet, ruined gown when it threatened to trip her. She called his name, but he ignored her. He was on the pathway back to the house before she made him stop, before her hand dragging on his arm made him accept that there could be no simple parting.

In the moonlight Adam's eyes looked cold and lifeless. His features had turned to hard planes and angles.

She drew a deep breath. "Adam, please. Let me explain."

With slow distaste, he plucked her hand from his arm. "There have been plenty of chances to explain," he said icily. "Your father's an alcoholic, isn't he, Jess? *That's* why he left Carraway."

"No. I told you the truth about that."

"But not about his drinking."

"I didn't think I'd have to."

"Did you think the problem would just go away?"

"I thought Doc would have his drinking under control before it became necessary to tell you. He promised me he'd get help."

"You should have come to me."

"I couldn't."

"Because you didn't trust me." As though aware the words he'd planned in anger had come out in ragged hurt instead, Adam jerked his eyes away, settling his gaze along the line of barns. In a clipped tone, he added, "You treated me like a lovesick fool and let me put everything I've built at risk."

Unable to keep the tremble from her voice, she said, "I know. I was wrong. I'm sorry." The words seemed hopelessly inadequate.

"Sorry!" he lashed out, his eyes swiveling back to her. "What if everything had been destroyed tonight?"

"It wasn't. It was an accident, and no serious damage has been done. Can't you understand—"

"I'll tell you what I understand. I understand that you're willing to run interference for your father no matter what happens. How long do you intend to go on making excuses for him? How much damage would the fire have had to do to make you force him to face up to life and take responsibility for his own actions?"

She shook her head. "It's not that way."

"It *is* that way. And until you realize it, you're never going to have a life of your own, Jess."

"My father needs me."

"I needed you," he refuted quietly, and with such bitterness that her heart twisted in anguish.

"Adam, I know you're upset. I don't blame you. But, please," she pleaded with the last bit of hope left in her heart. "Don't fire him."

"Don't ask that of me. Even Doc wouldn't expect it."

"He needs this job."

"Then he should have taken better care to keep it."

It was hopeless. The flat, unyielding finality in his voice told her they'd reached an impasse. She lowered her head, chewing at her slackened bottom lip until she tasted the metallic bite of blood. There was nothing left. Nothing more to be said but a few words that would leave her with hollow, empty pride.

When she spoke, those words came in a rush. "If you fire Doc, I'll have to go with him, Adam." Tears prickled the back of her eyes, starring her vision. "I'll have to."

Silence reigned for a long moment. And then, though his features were lost to her, his voice came low and weary and filled with its own brand of misery. "I don't expect you to stay."

CHAPTER SEVENTEEN

ADAM ESCORTED the detective down the front steps. When they reached the unmarked police car, he turned and offered his hand. "I appreciate your coming to give me the news personally."

The detective's smile transformed his face, softening stern, sagging features that had probably seen too much unpleasantness. "I used to work on one of the farms as a kid, and I know how important it is to maintain a reputation. I'll be in touch, Mr. Connor. Good luck at Burlington."

Adam thanked him again, then watched as the car wound its way down the long driveway. He turned to go back into the house just as Angela came around the corner, her cheeks flushed with color from an afternoon ride. They mounted the front steps together.

"How was your ride?" he asked.

"Great." After a moment's hesitation, she added, "Tim talked me into putting Lady over a low hedge today."

He smiled absently at her words, wondering if she had expected an argument. She didn't have to worry. With Jess gone, he had reluctantly allowed Tim to assume the role of Angela's riding companion. It had been much easier to acquiesce to his sister's request than to continue to fight her relationship with the groom. Angela had already been hurt enough by Jess's departure more than a month ago, and frankly, he knew now he'd been wrong about the boy. He'd watched them together, and Tim was good to his sister, patient and affectionate, but sensible enough not to be led by the girl's more romantic tendencies.

"Who was that man?" his sister asked.

"A detective from the Ocala Police Department. Come into the study. We need to talk."

He led Angela to the leather couch and took her hands in his. She gave him a pale, wary glance. For all her efforts to be an adult, she still looked like such a kid, he thought.

"Is it bad news?"

He smiled at her with affection, using his fingers to massage some of the tension out of her grip. "Angel, they've caught the man who set fire to the stables the night Dad died. You probably won't remember him, but it was Will Hazelton, the head groom for Barn Five. Dad cut him from the staff a month before the fire."

"But how…and why are they just catching him now?"

"He's been a veterinarian's assistant in Birmingham, but when he was let go recently, he set fire to the clinic. He was caught, and now he's confessed to several arsons. Rising Star was one of them. Eventually he'll be extradited back here."

There was a short silence while Angela absorbed the news. Then her head whipped around to find her brother's eyes, her expression gleeful. "Do you realize what this means! All those people who thought Daddy set the fire—"

"Will finally know the real truth," he finished. "Dad's name will be cleared."

"Oh, Adam, this is so wonderful! Next to winning the Triple Crown, it's what you've always hoped for." She jumped up from the couch, too excited to sit still. "No one at school can ever say anything again. I can't wait to tell Tim! Oh, I knew all along Daddy wouldn't do something like that.''

Adam watched her, enjoying his sister's exuberance and wondering why he felt no urge to join her in celebration. Seven years of gossip and innuendo laid to rest. It didn't seem possible. The relief was indescribable, yet inside, he felt numb.

A few moments later, Angela turned to face him, her hair swinging over her shoulder like a wind-tossed flag. She gave him a puzzled look. ''What's the matter? You don't seem happy.'' When he didn't respond right away, she added, ''You miss Jess, don't you?''

They had not discussed the Russells' departure, and Adam had no intention of doing so. ''It's complicated, Angel. You wouldn't understand.''

''I bet I would.''

''Let's not talk about it. The truth is, I guess I'm a little shocked that after all these years of trying to restore Dad's good name, it can really be over.''

That wasn't too far off the mark. The detective's visit *had* left him feeling as though he'd just been broadsided. But it was more than that, and deep down inside, he knew it.

Angela favored him with a surprisingly grown-up, speculative look. ''I know you probably think I'm only your silly baby sister, Adam, but sometimes I think I'm a lot smarter than you. At least when I'm miserable, I have sense enough to try to fix things.''

''And exactly how would you do that?''

''I'd go after Jess, of course.''

''It's too late for that,'' he finally admitted. Touched by her concern for him, Adam tapped her affectionately on the nose. ''I think I blew it, sis.''

"Maybe not. And anyway, since when did you ever give up so easily?"

JESS HUNG OVER the corral fence, watching Doc flake hay to a small herd of pleasure mounts. His job as barn manager at the Gainesville riding stable called for more physical labor than she liked to see him doing, but the support counselors at the alcohol-abuse center had helped to secure this position and promised to monitor his progress. He was happy to have the job, and truthfully, with each of her weekly visits he looked healthier.

Since leaving Rising Star, her father had been determined to stop drinking. The near disaster had shaken him badly, finally forcing him to face his problem. For the first time since Beth Russell's death, Doc had talked openly about his feelings of guilt, his lack of self-worth and his gradual abuse of alcohol. The advisers at the center had counseled them both, slowly convincing Jess her father would never recover as long as she continued to protect him.

The memory of those early sessions still brought a sad, ironic twist of regret to Jess's lips. Adam had been right about her overprotectiveness. How foolish she'd been not to see it. Now it was too late.

Just as well, she reminded herself. They'd been an unsuitable match from the start. So different, and neither one of them willing to accept that fact.

She hardly ever thought of him now. Almost never.

Except when the sports news came on television and she heard about another win for one of the Rising Star Thoroughbreds. Or when she smelled new hay and remembered that first twilight kiss he'd stolen from her in the barn. Or late at night, when she tossed and turned in bed, and imagined she could feel his hands on her tingling flesh...

Oh, no. Almost never.

"You should call him, lass," her father's voice came to her.

She looked up to find Doc standing at the railing in front of her. She'd been daydreaming again. Somehow she'd have to learn to lock away those memories someplace safe where they couldn't torment her anymore.

She didn't pretend not to know who Doc meant. "No. I couldn't," she replied, shaking her head.

"Why not?"

"Adam was so angry that night."

"He had cause to be."

"I know. But I don't think he could ever forgive me."

"You'll never know unless you ask him."

"No. It's over."

Her arm lay stretched across the top railing and Doc squeezed it gently. "Seems to me I'm not the only one who needs to learn how to take control of life, pony-girl."

One of the horses came to push against him, begging a scratch. Jess reached out, running her fingers along the animal's neck. He was a roan, a little lighter than Pie, but with the same sweet eyes.

"Reminds me of that worthless nag Adam bought you for your birthday," her father observed.

Jess nodded. Her throat clogged with unshed tears as she thought of Adam's gift, still stabled at Rising Star. The morning after the fire, when she and Doc had quickly gathered their belongings, Adam had already left the farm. She couldn't take Pie. What would she and Doc have done with a horse, when they weren't even sure where they'd be going? It had been difficult enough to trot the pigs into the back of the pickup.

After a pause, Doc said, "That gift carried a lot of thought and love, lass. I wouldn't think a man like that is unforgiving by nature."

In her loneliness and dreams she wanted to believe that, but the memory of his face that last night haunted her still. There'd been no forgiveness in his features. Her father didn't understand how deeply Adam had been hurt, how much hope and trust he'd placed in her.

Unable to discuss Adam with her father, Jess pulled back from the railing. The sudden movement startled the roan, and it shambled over to join the others.

"I spoke to Zola last night," Jess said in an effort to change the subject. "The carnival's going to be in the area next week. I thought I'd check to see how the girls were doing."

"It was good of her to buy them from me."

She lifted her eyes and looked straight at him. "You know, Papa, she's a very special woman. Someday she's going to meet a man who realizes that."

"Maybe she already has, lass." He plucked a splinter of wood from the railing and investigated it as if it held the secret of the ages. "I'm thinking she'd make a fine wife. Not right now—I've too many problems to make any woman a proper husband. But one day. I have feelings for her, and I think she has the same for me. Would that please or upset you to have her for a stepmother?"

"Are you kidding?" Jess asked in delight. "She'll make a great addition to the family." Growing more enthused by the moment, she clutched Doc's forearm in both hands. "Why don't you take the day off and come with me? Zoe would love to see you."

"I can't," Doc said. "This is where I need to be right now. At this point in my life, I have to take every day as it comes, lass."

"I know."

"The job's going well. My boss is happy."

"Looks like a lot of hard work."

"It's honest labor, and there's nothing wrong with that." He spared a momentary glance toward the small herd munching hay. "And I'm lucky to be around the horses again."

"I want to see you training. It's where you belong, Papa."

"Not until I get my own life under control. Connor was right to give me the boot, and you know it."

"I wish things could have turned out differently," she said, aware that her tone conveyed far more than those simple words.

He chucked her under the chin, so that her gaze rose to meet his. "Pony-girl, take some advice from a foolish old man who's learned the hard way. Wishing won't change a thing. Only you can do that."

ADAM SAT AT HIS DESK in the study, his fingers idly tracing the etched scroll across the face of the silver loving cup. First place at Hartford Downs, another win for Midnight Star. The Thoroughbred's times had been excellent. By Christmas he'd be unstoppable.

The Derby...the Belmont...the Preakness...

They weren't just fantasies anymore. With the new year, his dream of running a Triple Crown contender could be a reality.

He stared blindly at the shiny trophy. And felt... *nothing.*

With a sound of disgust he pushed away from the desk and began to prowl the room with agitated strides. Success ought to feel better than this. Hell, it ought to feel *great.* His father's name finally cleared, the wins—what in hell did he have to be unhappy about? It seemed appallingly stupid of him not to find real joy in the very things he'd always told himself he wanted so badly.

But instead of elation, there was an emptiness inside him now, as though everything good and worthwhile in his life had been flung into an abyss. Each day passed with stale, flat sameness, and it had become increasingly difficult to find any pleasure, any purpose in activities that had once meant everything to him.

He knew the cause and cursed his inability to crush the longing that plagued his waking hours, that left him tossing in frustration every night. He had made the right decision.

The *only* decision, dammit!

But when every excuse had been exhausted, every argument turned over in his mind again and again, the problem remained the same.

He could not banish Jess Russell from his thoughts.

Lightning strobed into the room to bounce off the silver cup, then leave the study in late-afternoon shadows once more. A drumroll of thunder rumbled accompaniment. With a sigh of discontent, Adam strode out of the study to head for the barns.

In the yard, the stable hands hustled to close the barns before the dismal skies produced a winter downpour. Thick with the smell of rain, the gusting breeze lifted stray leaves into dancing patterns, then pirouetted them across his path. He pulled open the door to Barn Four. Along the line of stalls, the lamps glowed as though night had already descended.

He moved forward, inspecting the pleasure mounts, offering a scratch to an outstretched neck, a pat to a twitching nose. He had not ridden in more than a month, not since Jess and her father had left Rising Star, yet he found himself visiting this barn often, always heading for Pie's stall.

Pie in the Sky swung her head over the stall, anxious to be indulged. Reaching out with both hands, Adam scratched the roan's ears. The horse responded with a sound of contentment and pushed harder against his chest.

"What's the matter, girl?" Adam asked softly. "Doesn't anyone pay attention to you anymore?" As if in response to the question, Pie shook her head and Adam laughed. "Did you really understand me? Maybe you're as smart as Jess said."

The memory of Jess smiling up at him sprang to mind, so vivid that even now he could smell the perfume she had worn the day he'd given her the horse. He could see the glow of excitement and desire in her eyes, like the shine of diamonds.

The smile died on his lips. Jess had said a lot of things. But it was what she *hadn't* said that he remembered most.

He let his hands drop. Pie lipped his sleeve to object, then subsided with a lusty snort of disappointment.

"Do you miss her, too?" he asked, but the animal didn't seem to have an answer.

Where was she? he wondered. Angela had been right. He'd never given up so easily before in the face of adversity. But then again, he'd never felt so betrayed, either. Still, he had promised a weeping Angela that he would find out how the Russells were doing. Though it was for his own sake that he'd begun a search for Jess's whereabouts.

Even as he made telephone calls and asked questions, he told himself he only wanted to be sure Jess and Doc had managed to settle someplace. Nothing more than that. But each negative response left him feeling far more despondent than such slight interest should have warranted.

In the next stall, Vadar calmly pulled hay from the rick. Adam watched the gelding a few moments, remembering times when the animal had nearly broken down his stall at the sound of an approaching storm. In spite of the fact he'd told her not to take such foolish chances, Jess had continued to "race the thunder" with Vadar. Now the horse's fear seemed a thing of the past, banished by Jess's tenacity and Doc Russell's unorthodox training methods.

The old man had left his mark on more than the Thoroughbreds, Adam reflected. Just as Jess had affected more than his heart.

And he had shut them both out.

JESS STOOD OUTSIDE the entrance of the fortune-teller's tent. She watched Zola head down the midway toward the flat, grassy track where Russell's Racing Pigs performed six times daily. This stop outside Gainesville had proven profitable for the carnival, and her visit with Zola had been snatched between palm readings and pig races, and a dozen other small chores the older woman handled.

She turned reluctantly and entered the tent. *I shouldn't have agreed to mind the store.* Maybe she shouldn't even have come. This place held so many memories, and memories tapped into emotions that weren't to be trusted.

She moved to the small table in the center of the room. Its scarred surface was covered with the same fringed scarf she remembered from so many months ago, the same dusty crystal ball that had utterly failed Jess in her attempts to predict an accurate future.

The future. What did it hold for her now? What *might* it have held, if only...

With deliberate force she slammed the book she'd been carrying onto the table. Her father was right. Wishing accomplished nothing.

School—that was her future. She'd finally enrolled for full-time classes in the spring. Instead of fretting over the past, she had to concentrate on the present. Doc was in treatment; there was no longer any reason to delay veterinary college. None at all.

She sat down and opened the book, flipping to a chapter she planned to read until Zola returned. In the distance she heard the P.A. system announce the next running of the pigs.

A few prospective customers peeked through the tent's opening, eager for a reading. She quickly encouraged them to come back in the afternoon when Madame Zola would return from meditation. Although her friend had laughingly made the suggestion as she left, Jess wasn't foolish enough to try her hand at fortune-telling again.

"Still trying to predict the future?" a soft male voice interrupted her concentration.

Her head jerked upward in shock, distrusting the evidence of her own ears.

But he was there, standing in the sunlit opening of the tent with the same power and grace that had pestered her dreams and made sleep an impossibility. He moved into the tent, coming up behind the empty chair across from her. She wanted to rise, but the strength for such action eluded her.

"Haven't you leaned your lesson by now?" Adam asked.

Struggling to appear poised and credible, she replied carefully, "I've learned a lot of things."

"Do you mind if I sit down? I'd be interested in a reading."

"Zola won't be back until two."

"I'll wait."

Her mind tried to fabricate an acceptable response and came up empty. "I was just leaving."

She didn't know why he had come here, but little pin-pricks of knowledge played a warning in her brain. Her frail composure was dangerously close to snapping.

Somehow she got to her feet in a quick, awkward movement, but when she made an effort to slip past him, Adam's hand closed around hers. Nerves under her skin fluttered. She hated that reaction. As always, his slightest touch could enthrall her. Such a foolish, pointless response.

"Jess, please don't go. I just want to talk to you."

His hand dropped away. She lifted her gaze, glimpsing in his eyes a tender wariness that surprised her. It was the first time she had looked at him since he'd entered the tent, *really* looked at him, and now she could see that this was not the man she remembered at all. He looked tired. There were deep lines of strain around his mouth and across his forehead. But it was the undercurrent of sorrow, the haunted uncertainty about him that Jess found the most unsettling.

After a moment of silence, she returned to her chair. He moved into the seat across from her. As though uncertain how to proceed, he reached out to lift the book that lay open on the table.

He read the title. "*Zoological Advances in the Twentieth Century.* So you're all the way through the alphabet now?"

"Yes."

"What's next?"

"School. I've enrolled at the veterinary college in town."

"Ah, yes. Of course," he said with a brief nod.

Another long moment ticked away.

"How's Angela?"

"Good. Tim makes sure she doesn't backslide with her riding lessons."

That response surprised her a little. She'd never thought he would agree to Tim's continuing involvement with Angela once she had gone. "Then you've decided it's all right—"

"You were right about Tim all along. He's very levelheaded. Good for Angela."

The soft note of acknowledgment made her throat clench with emotion. Right about Tim. But wrong, so wrong about other things.

She didn't know what to say, and desperate to fill the silence, she asked, "How's Pie?"

"She misses you," he replied.

I miss you, too, he thought. Irritated with his inability to create any semblance of normal conversation, Adam let his gaze wander. He was managing this poorly. All the pretty phrases he'd rehearsed had deserted him. He couldn't remember them. Seeing the closed, tight look in Jess's features, he had the terrifying, hopeless suspicion they'd do little good anyway.

"How did you find me?" Jess's soft inquiry cut into his thoughts.

"Doc called me."

Jess's heart sank. She lowered her face, mapping the paisley pattern in the scarf with one finger. Doc. She couldn't bear the thought that Adam had come here out of pity, or some idea that he owed her father something. "He shouldn't have done that." Her tone was brusque, curt.

"I'm glad he did. I've been looking for you."

Her head came up at that. *Why?* she wondered, and found she didn't have the courage to ask.

He cleared his throat. "I thought he sounded well."

"He's getting his problem...his drinking, under control." Jess bit her lip, aware that, if nothing else, she owed Adam the truth. She went on quickly, "We've both been through a lot of counseling. You were right. I was doing him more harm than good by sheltering him."

"It was well intentioned. Aren't daughters notoriously overprotective?"

Tell her, he chided himself. *Stop sounding like a principal lecturing a student, and just get it out.*

"I've asked your father to come back to Rising Star."

She blinked in astonishment. "What?"

"We need him. We've laid some ground rules, but I'm willing to work around his counseling program to get the kind of training help I need."

"You're doing well enough. First place in the Hartford."

It gave him a ridiculous sense of pleasure and hope to know that she continued to follow the stable's success. Maybe there was a chance, after all.

"Winning races isn't everything," he replied quietly.

He looked away again, knowing with sudden, gut-wrenching agony that no words he ever spoke would have more truth to them. Sitting here, being with Jess again, he didn't give a damn about breeding a winner or taking the Triple Crown. He needed this woman beside him. If the memory of their brief time together was all he had, it would never be enough to carry him through the rest of his days.

He turned to face her. Confusion wavered in her eyes suddenly, and he knew his thoughts and feelings were written in his features.

In a voice that carried forced lightness, Jess remarked,

"Winning isn't important? That doesn't sound like the Adam Connor *I* know."

He met her eyes unflinchingly. "Maybe I'm not that Adam Connor." He drew a quick, uneven breath. "Jess, I've never regretted anything more in my life than I regret that last night. I was angry you'd left the club, and scared when I got to Rising Star and saw what had happened. All I could think about was the last time, how devastating that fire had been. I overreacted."

Jess shook her head. "You didn't. I should have been honest with you from the first, knowing that the stable means everything in the world to you."

"That's the really funny part. It doesn't."

"What?"

"It doesn't mean everything in the world to me. *You* do."

"Adam—"

"Do you want to hear something really incredible? I finally figured it out. All those years I was planning what was right for me, who could do me the most good. I got carried away chasing some dream I thought I wanted, and all the time it was right in front of me. You, Jess."

"But Adam—"

"I know I screwed up. But I can't do anything about that now. I just want to fix it." He reached out to capture her hands in his. "That future was there for us, Jess. We both saw it at the club that night. I want it back."

"Adam—"

"You can still go to school," he said swiftly, desperate to counter any objection. "Gainesville's an easy commute from Ocala. And when you're finished, you can start your practice right at Rising Star. We need a full-time vet."

"Adam—"

"I want to marry you, but I'm willing to give you whatever time it takes. Teach me to race the thunder, Jess. I can't do it without you. I need you. I love you.''

"Adam, will you please be quiet!''

He released her hands and fell back in his chair, sickness cramping his stomach muscles. *Oh, God. Oh, God.* He'd made such a mess of it, blurting out everything he felt. He drew a shuddering breath. Feeling empty and drained, he stared with numbing disbelief at the wobbly, sad excuse for a table in front of him, knowing he'd ruined all his chances of making everything right.

"Adam, would you give me your hand, please?'' Jess asked in a quiet, matter-of-fact voice.

He complied, hardly aware of the moment she took his hand in hers and turned the palm upward.

"You were wrong,'' she said.

He couldn't have agreed more. He opened his mouth to speak, uncertain what he planned to say.

"You were wrong about me,'' she continued. "I'm a much better fortune-teller than you know. I *can* predict the future. I can even divine the past. Shall I tell you what I see?'' Her finger traced the lines of his palm, a gentle, teasing touch that made him stare at her.

"I see a kind, loving man who tried every way he knew how to make a place in his life for the woman he cared about. And when that didn't work, he did his best to fit into hers. But she was scared and insecure and afraid that what she'd found wouldn't last, that it couldn't be the real thing. She had a lot to learn.'' She paused to take a deep breath. "But she did. She came to the realization that sometimes you just have to take a chance. This man's been more than patient, and he probably deserves better. But the woman loves him very much, and she doesn't want to lose him—''

Jess broke off, realizing her voice was close to quaking

out of control. Her vision threatened to blur with tears, but the play of emotions in his features washed away her doubts and made her heart soar with excitement. Their love was a risk, but without it there would be nothing for either of them.

In a voice so thick with emotion she could hardly get the words out, she said softly, "I love you, Adam."

Seconds shaded into one another.

And then, his mouth lifted in a slow smile.

"What about the future?" he asked in a low, husky voice. "The guy wants kids. And years and years of happiness working side by side with the woman he loves. Growing old together."

Wordlessly Jess rose from the table, moving into the shelter of Adam's outstretched arms. She kissed him. "I see all of that, and so much more."

He drew back, his eyes never leaving her face. "I don't know," he said in a gentle reproof. "I heard you weren't very good at predicting. And my love line's been kind of screwed up lately. Are you sure?"

He extended his palm. She placed a kiss in its center and smiled up at him. "I'm very sure. It's a long, long love line. Only one woman, I'm afraid, but she's crazy about you."

"Tell me more, little gypsy."

They looked at one another with wide, delighted eyes, like children on the brink of a stolen pleasure. In the gentle shadows of the fortune-teller's tent, with her lips and hands and heart, Jess began to dole out a future for them both.

It was filled with love and laughter, and somewhere in the middle of it, Adam swept her up into his arms, and she lost herself in the telling.

EVER HAD ONE OF THOSE DAYS?

TO DO:

☑ at the supermarket buying two dozen muffins that your son just remembered to tell you he needed for the school treat, you realize you left your wallet at home

☑ at work just as you're going into the big meeting, you discover your son took your presentation to school, and you have his hand-drawn superhero comic book

☑ your mother-in-law calls to say she's coming for a month-long visit

☑ finally at the end of a long and exasperating day, you escape from it all with an entertaining, humorous and always romantic Love & Laughter book!

ENJOY
LOVE & LAUGHTER
EVERY DAY!

For a preview, turn the page....

Here's a sneak peek at
Carrie Alexander's THE AMOROUS HEIRESS
Available September 1997...

"YOU'RE A VERY popular lady," Jed Kelley observed as Augustina closed the door on her suitors.

She waved a hand. "Just two of a dozen." Technically true since her grandmother had put her on the open market. "You're not afraid of a little competition, are you?"

"Competition?" He looked puzzled. "I thought the position was mine."

Augustina shook her head, smiling coyly. "You didn't think Grandmother was the final arbiter of the decision, did you? I say a trial period is in order." No matter that Jed Kelley had miraculously passed Grandmother's muster, Augustina felt the need for a little propriety. But, on the other hand, she could be married before the summer was out and be free as a bird, with the added bonus of a husband it wouldn't be all that difficult to learn to love.

She got up the courage to reach for his hand, and then just like that, she—Miss Gussy Gutless Fairchild—was holding Jed Kelley's hand. He looked down at their linked hands. "Of course, you don't really know what sort of work I can do, do you?"

A funny way to put it, she thought absently, cradling his callused hand between both of her own. "We can get to know each other, and then, if that works out..." she murmured. *Wow.* If she'd known what this arranged marriage thing was all about, she'd have been a supporter of Grandmother's campaign from the start!

"Are you a palm reader?" Jed asked gruffly. His voice was as raspy as sandpaper and it was rubbing her all the right ways, but the question flustered her. She dropped his hand.

"I'm sorry."

"No problem," he said, "as long as I'm hired."

"Hired!" she scoffed. "What a way of putting it!"

Jed folded his arms across his chest. "So we're back to the trial period."

"Yes." Augustina frowned and her gaze dropped to his work boots. Okay, so he wasn't as well off as the majority of her suitors, but really, did he think she was going to *pay* him to marry her?

"Fine, then." He flipped her a wave and, speechless, she watched him leave. She was trembling all over like a malaria victim in a snowstorm, shot with hot charges and cold shivers until her brain was numb. This couldn't be true. Fantasy men didn't happen to nice girls like her.

"Augustina?"

Her grandmother's voice intruded on Gussy's privacy. "Ahh. There you are. I see you met the new gardener?"

HARLEQUIN WOMEN KNOW ROMANCE WHEN THEY SEE IT.

And they'll see it on **ROMANCE CLASSICS**, the new 24-hour TV channel devoted to romantic movies and original programs like the special **Romantically Speaking-Harlequin® Goes Prime Time**.

Romantically Speaking-Harlequin® Goes Prime Time introduces you to many of your favorite romance authors in a program developed exclusively for Harlequin® readers.

Watch for **Romantically Speaking-Harlequin® Goes Prime Time** beginning in the summer of 1997.

If you're not receiving ROMANCE CLASSICS, call your local cable operator or satellite provider and ask for it today!

ROMANCE CLASSICS

Escape to the network of your dreams.

Reach new heights of passion and
adventure this August in

ROCKY MOUNTAIN MEN

Don't miss this exciting new collection featuring
three stories of Rocky Mountain men and the
women who dared to tame them.

CODE OF SILENCE
by Linda Randall Wisdom

SILVER LADY
by Lynn Erickson

TOUCH THE SKY
by Debbi Bedford

Available this August wherever
Harlequin and Silhouette books are sold.

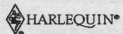HARLEQUIN® Silhouette®

THE FRAUDULENT FIANCÉE

(#751)

by Muriel Jensen

*Amnesia. A marriage of convenience.
A secret baby.*

Find out what it's all about in August 1997.

Available wherever Harlequin books are sold.

Don't miss these Harlequin favorites by some of our most popular authors! And now you can receive a discount by ordering two or more titles!

HT#25700	HOLDING OUT FOR A HERO		
	by Vicki Lewis Thompson	$3.50 U.S. ☐/$3.99 CAN.☐
HT#25699	WICKED WAYS		
	by Kate Hoffmann	$3.50 U.S. ☐/$3.99 CAN.☐
HP#11845	RELATIVE SINS		
	by Anne Mather	$3.50 U.S. ☐/$3.99 CAN.☐
HP#11849	A KISS TO REMEMBER		
	by Miranda Lee	$3.50 U.S. ☐/$3.99 CAN.☐
HR#03359	FAITH, HOPE AND MARRIAGE		
	by Emma Goldrick	$2.99 U.S. ☐/$3.50 CAN.☐
HR#03433	TEMPORARY HUSBAND		
	by Day Leclaire	$3.25 U.S. ☐/$3.75 CAN.☐
HS#70679	QUEEN OF THE DIXIE DRIVE-IN		
	by Peg Sutherland	$3.99 U.S. ☐/$4.50 CAN.☐
HS#70712	SUGAR BABY		
	by Karen Young	$3.99 U.S. ☐/$4.50 CAN.☐
HI#22319	BREATHLESS		
	by Carly Bishop	$3.50 U.S. ☐/$3.99 CAN.☐
HI#22335	BEAUTY VS. THE BEAST		
	by M.J. Rodgers	$3.50 U.S. ☐/$3.99 CAN.☐
AR#16577	BRIDE OF THE BADLANDS		
	by Jule McBride	$3.50 U.S. ☐/$3.99 CAN.☐
AR#16656	RED-HOT RANCHMAN		
	by Victoria Pade	$3.75 U.S. ☐/$4.25 CAN.☐
HH#28868	THE SAXON		
	by Margaret Moore	$4.50 U.S. ☐/$4.99 CAN.☐
HH#28893	UNICORN VENGEANCE		
	by Claire Delacroix	$4.50 U.S. ☐/$4.99 CAN.☐

(limited quantities available on certain titles)

	TOTAL AMOUNT	$ _____
DEDUCT:	**10% DISCOUNT FOR 2+ BOOKS**	$ _____
	POSTAGE & HANDLING	$ _____
	($1.00 for one book, 50¢ for each additional)	
	APPLICABLE TAXES*	$ _____
	TOTAL PAYABLE	$ _____
	(check or money order—please do not send cash)	

To order, complete this form, along with a check or money order for the total above, payable to Harlequin Books, to: **In the U.S.:** 3010 Walden Avenue, P.O. Box 9047, Buffalo, NY 14269-9047; **In Canada:** P.O. Box 613, Fort Erie, Ontario, L2A 5X3.

Name: _____

Address: _____ City: _____

State/Prov.: _____ Zip/Postal Code: _____

*New York residents remit applicable sales taxes.
Canadian residents remit applicable GST and provincial taxes.

Look us up on-line at: http://www.romance.net

HBKJS97

HARLEQUIN SUPERROMANCE®

EMERGENCY!

If you love medical drama and romance on the wards,
then our new medical series by bestselling author
Bobby Hutchinson will bring you to fever pitch....

August 1997—THE BABY DOCTOR (#753)

by Bobby Hutchinson

Dr. Morgan Jacobsen is a skilled obstetrician.
Unfortunately, outside of work she's a klutz. Her
new partner at The Women's Center, Dr. Luke Gilbert,
brings out the worst in her, but Morgan brings out
the best in *him*—and his daughter—until their
children become friends. Then there's more
trouble than even Morgan can handle....

**Look for *The Baby Doctor* in August wherever
Harlequin books are sold.**